THESE TREACHEROUS TIDES

ONCE STOLEN

D.N. BRYN

ONCE STOLEN

Printed in the United States of America
First Printing, 2021

Print (paperback) ISBN 978-1-7362966-0-8
Print (hardcover) ISBN 978-1-7362966-2-2
Ebook ISBN 978-1-7362966-1-5

For information about purchasing and permissions, contact D.N. Bryn at dnbryn@gmail.com

www.DNBryn.com

Edited by Chih Wang with CYW Editing.
Cover design by Laya Rose.

This work is fictitious and any resemblance to real life persons or places is purely coincidental. Should you discover the existence of snake-like mermaids in a mist-laden swamp, please also treat them as fictitious. They prefer to live in peace.

To my mom, to me, and to every other person whose sensory perception doesn't quite match the reality of most.

Different is just that. Different

ONE

---◡◠◡---

ALL THE SHADES OF GREED

Banishment isn't a curse if it means escaping all of you.

THE THRUMMING POWER OF the ignits calls to me. Five small variants of the round stones lie in the gambler's pot, their slight glow barely visible beneath the cartel boat's canopy. From the shade of the nearby mangroves, I grip the blue ignit on my wire necklace of precious stones. Blue for thunder, like two of those in the pot. But the gamblers have a yellow and a pair of small reds as well.

The ignit beneath my fingers pulses into my scales, primed to soothe whatever skull-shattering nonsense my body decides to throw at me today. But one lonely stone can be easily lost, easily taken. With one stone, the pain still stalks just behind me, waiting to strike. Besides, I *want* the gamblers' ignits.

Tightening my serpentine tail around the roots of the half-submerged tree, I lift my head a little farther out of the water. I flick out my tongue. The boat humans smell of oil and gunpowder, of arrogance and cowardice and anger, and a touch of fear.

Three of them sit on the boat's main deck, huddled around a table. The vibrations of their voices tingle across the patterned ridges along my scaly scalp. I feel the tug the nearest gives to their beard as they anxiously put down their cards, the slight splash of the lizard dipping into the river downstream, and the landing of the parrot in the tree branches far above.

But the fishers don't know I crouch so still that the murky water blends with the brown and black patterns along my half-snake body. The boat humans won't notice me like this—won't try to kill me. But if I stay here, those ignits will never thrum in my hands or hang from my wire mesh necklace.

My banishers said this desire would latch inside me like claws through flesh, like my spiny retractable teeth digging into a freshly caught capybara, like a viper's toxin eating me from the inside out. And it has. Oh, it fucking has.

It's just so hard to care now that it's caught me.

The tallest human slams their cards down and strolls to the boat's railing. Their dark skin gleams with a layer of sweat as they wave to a little vessel across the river. The fan at the back of this smaller boat thrums to life, powered by an ignit buried somewhere in its engine. It pulls alongside the larger boat.

"You already out?" the driver asks with a series of hand motions stolen from the swamp natives. I assume the boat humans use them to talk over the vicious whirr of the fans and roar of their motors, though most also sign whenever they use spoken language, which I have no ability to hear.

"Lay off," the disgruntled human signs. They climb onto the smaller boat and speed down the river.

My gaze jumps to the remaining gamblers. Even with one human gone, these two still look like a challenge. The bearded player sports muscles as thick as my own, and their slighter opponent crouches in the shadows like a jaguar, hidden beneath a wispy cowl and shawl.

I guess we're all gambling today.

Unfurling my tail from the roots, I take a deep breath and slip into the water. I undulate as I swim, though my humanlike torso moves with far less precision than my flexible tail, its bulk twice as powerful and three times as long as two legs combined. The fish withdraw around me, the flex of their muscles tingling along my head ridges. I keep to the dimly lit river bottom.

As I pass over a scattering of stones in the clay-heavy soil, I skim the silt with my fingers. A round grey rock that could almost be a clingstone or maybe a perfectly worn hematite tempts me, but the blotch of red on its back proves it to be just a normal river pebble. I leave it be, the vision of those glorious ignits still burning in my mind.

The image of a fang embellishes the front of the boat's flat hull, and a large cabin sits at its back, a stairway leading up to its cargo-filled rooftop deck. Two fans swoop out from either side, their blades currently dormant. I surface beneath one. With the cabin shielding me from the human's view, I climb the fan blades like a ladder, twisting my tail into their ridges to brace myself. Unlike the massive central fan at the back of the boat, these will only bruise me if turned on. Bruises fade. The scars I received learning that lesson won't.

I near the cabin's roof, but the rumbling vibration of a shout halts me. I peek around the corner. At the gambling table, the bearded human's face shifts, their mouth and brows moving. These expressions mean little to me, but eagerness wafts from the human as potent as the sweet burst of an overripe mango on the jungle floor.

I pull myself onto the cabin's rooftop deck and slide between the crates, just out of sight. A burst of new scents hits me—leather and wine and the sun. I spot the owner through the cracks between two crates: Rubem, the newly established head of the Fang Ignit Cartel, who slipped in like a rat in the wake of the last leader's sudden death. When the crew talk about him, they keep their signs small and their mistrust big.

He crouches near the back of the boat, his mass of dark braids tied in a high bun. Three claw-like rings sprout from his right earlobe. A pistol glimmers at his belt, the sheen of the dark copper hilt matching his skin. Its embedded emeralds contrast the shock of scarlet hemming his loose brown clothing.

I try not to look at his hands, at the fishnet gloves I know I'll find there, but when he flicks a vial of glowing green liquid between them, my gaze goes to his fingers anyway. My scales itch, a creeping pain that only diminishes when I focus on my ignit's gentle pulsing.

Despite the vial's impeding presence, Rubem signs with a contained sharpness, the motions fluid but precise. "You know where they are, you were her *daughter*. But you clearly aren't using the damn things. Let them not go to waste."

The person he speaks with looks delicate, the soft curves of her tan face placing her somewhere well beyond childhood but not quite worthy of anyone's respect yet. About my age, then. Her brown curls spill down her back, and grey and green fabrics hang off her in layers, a scarf wrapped like an anaconda around her neck. A chain on her ankle rattles when she hugs her legs closer. "I don't care." Her hands tremble as she makes the motions, her lips remaining closed. "The cartel can't have them."

"You realize that whatever you choose, I *will* find them." He makes his claw-handed grabbing motion for the word *will* far stronger than the rest. "There are stakes here more important than you realize."

But the prisoner only stares toward the front of the boat, tapping a steady rhythm against her leg. She jerks at the vibration of a laugh from downstairs.

Rubem flinches as well, glancing over his shoulder. When he looks back at the prisoner, his expression makes her curl tighter into herself. "If—when—*she* finds out you're here, she'll flay you alive and string your guts from the canopy to get ahold of your mother's hoard. So, I would be quiet for a while if I were you." He pockets his glowing flask with a sharp snap, bursting to his feet. "And we'll have a longer conversation about this later. Giving up that hoard is for the best, you'll see."

Threats, kidnappings, torture—all usual cartel methods. But this sounds different. Bigger.

I duck as Rubem marches by my hiding place and descends the stairs, his footsteps remarkably silent for such fury. His shouting vibrates off my head ridges a moment later. It fades as he and the shadowy gambler walk into the cabin beneath me. The bearded human continues to watch their cards—and the ignits. I rub the ignit on my necklace and clench my jaw, unhinging and rehinging it.

Motion behind me flickers along my head ridges. I turn to find the prisoner poking her head around the crates. Her eyes widen, long black lashes drawing back to reveal hauntingly blue irises. A shiver runs through me. I coil the extensive loops of my tail, preparing to lunge at her.

She lifts her hands. "Stop, please—I don't know if you understand this, but please—help me."

I can't smell her emotions, can't tell whether she's truly panicking or only trying to lure me in, but her words still make me pause. I have absolutely, positively no desire to talk to this scentless boat human. But being banished to a place where most people want to kill and eat you does weird things to a person. Things like making them hesitate.

"Please," the prisoner repeats. "I just need your ignit and a transitioner from that box on your left."

Clever boat human. If she puts the blue ignit into the lock in her ankle cuff and activates it with the transitioner, the energy it produces might rattle the mechanism free. With a glance at her too-blue eyes, I pop the stone from its necklace holder and dangle it between my fingers.

Her hand jerks toward it.

Before she can steal it, I shove it in my mouth, wedging it between two sets of my teeth.

Her face pinches and her chest gives a little hitch. "Don't be such a shit." She moves her hands faster now, more aggressive. "You're the only one who can help me."

I stare at her. "Help you, you say?" My signs come out huge, and a single slither of my tail carries me into her space. "Like your people have helped the swamp's natives since they so graciously claimed all our big rivers and started killing anything that doesn't look like them? No thanks, boat *shit*," I snap, turning her own word back on her.

The prisoner's shaking extends to her shoulders, but her lips bunch. "I'm just a dancer. I'd never hurt anyone."

"Just a dancer. Then why does Rubem want you?" I sign the cartel leader's name like a mix of ruby and enemy.

She skips right over my question. "When he comes back—when he brings that lady downstairs with him . . ." Her hands stutter. "Please, I'd only need the ignit for a moment."

I grin at her, showing off my rows of hooked teeth. "Yeah? Why should I let you borrow it? There's nothing in it for me."

The tremble bursts from her, turning into a vibration in her throat, low and heavy like a growl. "Because it's the right thing to do!"

Oh, muck, she's one of those people. "The right thing is meaningless. It's right for *you* maybe, but it's inconvenient and useless for *me*."

The prisoner's face shifts, her thick brows lowering. "Are all snake people such rude scaly bottom dwellers?"

"Just this one. I'm special." I widen my smile. "Now, I have ignits to steal. Unless . . ." The conversation between Rubem and the prisoner slots into place. An ignit cartel looking for a hoard of something? Little wonder what it might contain. "Unless the legends are true, and there really is a massive stash of ignits out there somewhere. And you know how to reach it."

She avoids looking at me, her fingers tapping a rhythm into her leg.

Rubem's lifted voice grates across my head ridges, rattling up from the cabin. I glance back at the stones in the gambler's pot. It still sits under the bearded human's watchful gaze. My fingers itch to hold them. If Rubem wants this person so badly, then it might distract them all if something happens to her—

6

something like her dangling over the side of the boat. Should her chain reach that far.

No time like the present to test it.

"So, if you don't have ignits, then I guess Rubem won't care if I toss you overboard?" I lean toward her.

She tucks her legs in closer. "You—you blistering wet rag— you can't do this!"

Grabbing her chain, I yank her ankle toward me, pulling apart her tight knees. I loop the links once around my wrist to keep the chain in place while I sign, "I can. I think I will."

The prisoner strains against my hold, but with her back already against the boxes, she has nowhere to go. She closes her eyes, the too-blue vanishing. "It belonged to my mother." Tiny signs, the simple pat for *belong* nearly eclipsed by the swoop of her fingers beneath her chin for *mother*. "The hoard, I mean."

I let the chain go. "And you'd give it to me instead?"

Her throat bobs. "Help me get away from Rubem. Please."

None of those words are a yes, but I can wring one out of her later. A single look from Rubem turned her into a curling mess. As long as the chain still keeps her from running, I could do the same. And worse. "Fine. I'll get you free of the cartel, and then you give me your ignits." One way or another.

"Thank you—"

I ignore her. Moving as fluidly as possible, I follow her chain to the clamp at the end. It encircles one of the wooden beams holding up the canopy. Stretching out my shoulders, I wrap my body around the beam, once, twice, then a third time. The prisoner waves her hands, but I ignore her. Bracing my arms on the top of the pole and the extra length of my tail on the deck's railing, I snap the wood in two. My muscles twitch as I relax, slowly letting down the top end of the broken beam.

The prisoner's eyes widen. "Hurry, that was *loud!*"

She barely finishes signing before the bearded human clambers up the stairs, machete drawn. I yank the clamp up and off the split end of the beam. It tightens a notch in my hands. Holding to it like a leash, I leap for the railing.

My tail hits the floor with a thud. The prisoner comes tumbling after me and lands on my back, knocking my head into the deck. A slew of nasty vibrations rattle through my skull.

By the time I can see through the throbbing in my brain, I find the bearded human halfway back down the stairs. Only the gambling table stands between us. The gambling table with its glorious ignits. I could have both them and this mysterious hoard. I could.

I take the clamp connecting me to the prisoner and shove it onto my arm to keep her from running off. But as I lunge for the table and its ignit bounty, she hauls on the chain. It tugs at the clamp. I strain against it, reaching for the ignits. The clamp pulls three notches tighter. For one terrible moment, I wonder if it will keep tightening until it severs off the limb, but then it hits the last notch.

I jerk forward, and my fingertips brush the ignits. My mouth twists into such a grin that my jaw almost dislocates. And here they said I wouldn't thrive outside the Murk.

Before I can snatch the stones, Rubem storms out the door to the lower cabins, the other gambler in his wake. The world slows. My muscles go too taut, as though made of wood instead of flesh.

The other gambler is not of the cartel. Her few months of murder since arriving here have marked her as the best damned hunter in the group of poachers and boiuna killers who call themselves the fisher's guild. When her name is signed, it uses the motion for a lily, twisted upward like that for north, or sometimes skewed around the chest as the boat humans do when encountering an omen of evil: Lily of the North, the One Who's Not to Be Fucked With. The face she covered in her cowl is pale but for a million freckles, and a strand of bright orange hair cuts down her harsh cheekbones.

Before I can flinch, Lily lifts her net launcher and yanks the trigger. The net barrels toward me. It opens at the last moment to engulf my torso, just missing my head. Its impact knocks the air from my lungs, dislodging the ignit fixed between my teeth in the process, and slams my body away from the gambling table.

My ignit shoots from my mouth, dragging its calming thrum with it, and the pain in my bones takes root. My scales burn every place the net touches, as though a thousand tiny catfish eat me alive. My lungs seize and my spine shatters. I rip out of the netting, crashing into the far railing. My chest heaves. Human shouts—Rubem's, Lily's, the bearded human's, I don't know—rattle around my head. The prisoner yanks on the clamp around my arm, and ignitless, we plunge into the water.

TWO

———— ⌇ ————

THE CHAIN BETWEEN US

Rocks are better than people.
They have no emotions.
And also, they don't suck.

THE MOMENT WE HIT the water, I yank the prisoner under and swim us through the silt. We break the surface in the heavy shade of the trees, their twisting roots blocking our view of the river where Rubem's and Lily's shouts still vibrate. The prisoner gasps. With shaking arms, she pulls herself against a trunk. Her dark hair clings to her face, and she wipes water from her eyes.

I tug at the clamp encircling my arm. The metal bites my scales just above my wrist, refusing all attempts to tug it off. Worthless piece of junk. I stick my fingers into the slots in its side, but the stupid thing stays tight no matter how I finagle it—stays tight because the shitty boat human pulled it that way.

She pulls on me again, swimming fiercely toward the bank.

"Cut it out!" I try to make the motions, but with one arm jerked in front of me, they come out half-formed, a single drop of a hand that looks more like a flail without the rest.

Instead of stopping, she waves me toward her, her too-blue

eyes obnoxiously wide. Her gaze burns.

I grab the links between us and haul them backward in retaliation.

Her chained ankle comes up, her torso slipping under the surface. She struggles back to her feet. "I'm just trying to—" She slips deeper into the water as she signs. Pausing, she steps onto a root. "Trying to save us! Rubem will be here any minute."

"I didn't need your saving." My frustration crawls beneath my skin like a living thing. I cling to the powerless stones on my necklace to keep from falling prey to it. My excruciating want bundles back into something primal and innate. For this instant, I would trade all my future gambles just to have my one little well-worn ignit back. "I should never have freed you. I should have just gone after those damn ignits and left you for Rubem." Her ignit hoard be damned, if I'm stuck with her for one more minute, I might just chew off my own fucking arm. The moment I think it, though, images of a huge pile of glowing stones assault me, begging for my attention.

"You greedy rock-headed—"

"Yeah, yeah I am!" My hands fly through the signs so quickly my fingers blur. "I'm greedy and pathetic and all those other elegant insults you're so fond of. And I'm okay with that!" An old memory sears my heart, but the scales covering it are too thick for even that bitter knife to penetrate.

Her lips bunch. She looks away, only to recoil at the roar of a boat's fan blasting to life nearby. "We really should go."

"Fine. But if you pull on me—"

"I won't if you don't."

"Fine."

"Fine." She shoves her hair behind her ears and slides through the water, her chin held high as she works her way toward the land.

She swims like a boat human, all jerking arms and spinning legs that were trained for decks instead of rivers, and she fumbles when she climbs on the roots. Each of her motions contrasts pointedly with those of the new cartel leader, the serpentine stillness he exhibited so different from the others he works with. I shiver at all that he reminds me of, at the near vibration-free steps of the Murk warriors.

I duck under a root only for the chain to tug at my arm, forcing me to return to the path she took. I pull my torso over the wood and slip back into the water on the other side. The mangled ridges along my tail gleam grey and black against my natural brown.

The shitty boat human at the end of my chain trudges onto the riverbank. I follow, though I do so with the utmost care, scuffling away as much evidence of us as I can, until not even a fisher could tell we'd left the river here. Through the gaps in the branches behind us, I can just make out one of the Fang Cartel's smaller fan boats poking long poles into the water near the tree line. But the way ahead looks clear, at least of people.

We work our way into the lush jungle, dodging branches and shoving aside ferns. Animals scatter out of our way. The plants rustle. My scales blend perfectly with the rich ground, but lugging my entire weight through the underbrush strains my muscles more than I care to admit.

Layers of drenched scarf stick to the boat human's neck. Mud coats the bottoms of her pants, and the once billowing fabric now clings to her like a leech. An unexpected amount of strength trembles in the toned muscles of her arms and legs, and while her torso curves with less gusto than some humans, she's filled out more than a boiuna's tree-trunk figure. Her shirt cups the layer of chub on her belly. She tucks her arms over her chest. Her signs grow stunted. "It's rude to stare."

The realization makes me want to jerk my gaze away, but I force myself not to out of sheer spite. "Then, I'm rude."

"But you won't look me in the eyes."

"Because you're a nosey muck-face."

I don't tell her that eyes confuse me, dragging me in and shoving me out all at once, or that everyone seems to know the right times to meet each other's gazes or glance away except me. I also don't tell her that I've looked at hers more than anyone else's in the last year, or that they're haunting and terrible and almost, almost lovely—so much like sky-blue ignits. Would be lovely, anyway, if they weren't *hers*.

Her: the person with a hoard of the precious glowing stones. I try to focus on that instead of my growing desire to rip off my own hand to stop the rattle of the chain between us. Ignits, all the ignits I could want. And I only have to force their location out of her. Ignits, ignits, ignits.

She kicks with her chained ankle, sending an obnoxious vibration through the links. "Since we're stuck together, at least tell me your name. I have to know what to call you if I want to properly choose my insults."

I roll my eyes so hard my pupils undulate, turning my vision blotchy for a moment.

Her throat vibrates. "Fine. I'll go first. I'm—" She pounds a rhythm in the air: *buh-bum, buh-bum, buh-bum*. I almost decide to call her *drums* when she continues. "It sounds like the beginning of *taunt* and the funny *ice* stuff they transport here from the northern isles: Thais." She makes the drumming motion again.

Boat humans are so dumb. "Boiuna can't hear sounds like that, you sludge-brain. And we have scent names, we just convert them to words for you ridiculous species without noses."

"What do you call this, then?" She shoves a finger at her nose.

"Facial ornamentation."

A little vibration leaves her throat, a huff or a laugh or a growl, maybe. "You still haven't given me your name."

I could refuse, simply out of spite, but then she might just keep badgering me, and I need to conserve my energy for coercing the hoard's location out of her. "It's Bittersweet Earth, male, he."

"You must smell like the taste of unsweetened chocolate! You're a cacao bean."

"I am not!"

"Cacao," she repeats, lips curling.

I want to strangle her.

"Do I need to give you a gender and pronoun too?" Her shoulders bounce, and her face wrinkles a bit. "Because *she*'s fine, I guess, but I'm not really a girl. Or a woman. I'm just me." She makes a new expression, and I wish she smelt stronger so I could tell what the fuck that look is supposed to mean.

Our conversation gives way to the rustle of birds through the leaf canopy and the slog of us pushing back the under-brush as we try to keep our chain from catching on roots. Tired patches of sunlight seep through the thick branches. Their languid touch makes me yearn to loop a few times around a tree and nap. My fingers linger more and more on my necklace stones, tracing their dull stagnant sides. Too stagnant; beautiful corpses, but dead rocks all the same. I'll have to steal a new ignit as soon as possible.

A single ignit I can lose, though, just as easily as my last slipped from between my teeth. I glance at Thais. This far from the river, I bet I can masterfully torture a hoard location out of her without anyone hearing her scream. But as long as her jabbering continues, I should take advantage of it. Thais could have been lying to me back on the boat.

"It's awfully convenient, having so many ignits just sitting around." I give her my best impression of a smile.

She returns it with something that could only be a frown. "Not convenient for *me*. Without them, I'd be performing in the main square of the village just upstream from Rubem's boats, and not drenched, stomping through the jungle, chained to a sulfurous chocolate bean."

Sulfurous. "I told you, I smell like bittersweet earth."

"Cacao."

"Boat shit," I shoot back, scowling.

"Pathetic boneless reptile."

"Not a reptile, a *mer*." I'm also not boneless. Or pathetic.

Probably.

"A mer-*snake*. Sounds like a reptile to me."

I roll my jaw around. Useless boat human. "So, your mother really created one—a hoard of ignits just like the rumors?"

"They're mine now, technically," Thais replies. "You know, she was a lot like you."

"A greedy bottom-dwelling idiot?" I expect her to correct me.

Thais merely nods.

But if she equates greed and idiocy to her mother, and her mother collected ignits, then something doesn't add up. "Why didn't you give your mother's hoard to the cartel if you're not using them and you don't even want them?"

Her throat vibrates with something almost like laughter, but too rough and tense. "I might have no use for the hoard, but those selfish cartel bastards drive up the price of the stones until they're nearly unattainable, and the ones they sell go to weapons and machines that tear through the jungle like a tempest. Besides, anyone who wants ignits that much doesn't deserve to have them. They're only going to use them for evil."

The selfish and the self-righteous, chained together by pure stupid fate. But her reply confirms two things: that Thais truly does have a hoard, somewhere, sparkling with ignits, and that she never planned on handing it over to scum like me. No surprises there.

I bare my teeth and lift my torso higher. The scarier and meaner I am, the sooner this will be over. "I guess my brand of evil will have to do, then."

Thais stares at me. "What are you—"

I grab her shoulders and shove her against the nearest tree. Her throat vibrates, eyes wide and brow tight. She tries to slide from my grasp, but I wrap my tail around her legs, holding her in place. "I freed you from the cartel, so you're going to lead me to your hoard."

Despite all my threatening, the shaking mess that huddled before Rubem remains a distant memory. "Or what? You'll eat me?"

I wish her muck-filled human nose could smell my stubbornness. "I can be just as ruthless as a cartel leader—more so, maybe. You think you're strong, suddenly? You were quaking before him."

Her raised chin barely wavers. "Rubem scares me because I'll never give in to him. And I suspect the cartel and that northern woman he runs with won't believe that until they've broken every one of my bones."

"That's going to be a lot of bones for me to break in their place." I lean toward her, closing so much distance that my hands nearly brush hers as I sign. "I guess we'd better get started."

A little shudder runs through her this time, but she steadies. "Then do it already."

This close, I finally catch her scent: like the air after a heavy rain has cleansed the land, like fresh sharp nothingness, so subtle and empty the wood and the soil almost cover it. The smell matches her eyes. But it doesn't matter what she looks or smells like, she's a boat human, and one I'm going to tear apart, piece by piece, until she gives me her ignits.

Twisting my tail farther up her body, I wrap it around her arm instead, coiling until I feel the crook of her elbow go stiff. She draws in a sharp breath. I peel back my lips, every pointed tooth bared.

But as if the strength has gone out of it, my tail won't tighten, won't make the sharp snap it did with the pole back on the cartel boat. Instead, the muscles shake, a sharp tremble that rises all the way up to my shoulders and pulls at my chest, closing my lungs. I brace against it. I've killed boat humans before.

But they were all trying to kill me.

I barely make out Thais's one-handed signs. "You can't, can you?" She doesn't smell surprised.

Thais may be annoying and self-righteous and demeaning enough to make me wish I could eat her. But words are hardly weapons, even when they sting, and that determination, that fire—it won't come like this. She's right: I can't do it.

The admission leaches out the bulk of my willpower. I wheel away, letting my tail slump off Thais. A single slithering burst takes me to the end of our chain, though, dragging my arm back toward her. Fuck this.

Fuck all of this.

I can't wait around for Thais to suddenly feel like a threat. I have to find a new ignit, soon. And for that, Thais must go. "I want this fucking chain off."

"Something we actually agree about." Her eyes close, and she relaxes against the tree I pressed her to. With the scent of her still prickling in my nose, I notice fresh hints of it in the air. I swear I pick out fear, but it hovers so close to something warm and bright that maybe I imagined it. "My cuff won't come loose," she continues, "but we might be able to pry the one on your arm open."

I filter through the dirt for a rock long and sharp enough to do the trick. A bulky common thing comes loose, dull on two sides, but still the best the jungle seems willing to supply. I hand it over. It pains me to extend my clamped arm for Thais, to give her all the power after I failed to torture her.

She grabs the metal without touching me. Her mouth twists as she wedges the rock into the cracks of one of its notches and wiggles it. The clamp shifts, just a little, but it snaps back into place with enough force to shoot the rock away. The damn thing feels like a proper crossbow bolt when it hits my shoulder.

I pull my arms free of Thais to rub at the spot.

"Are you hurt?" She smells so rain cleaned it sears the inside of my nose.

"Of course not. I'm a boiuna, descendant of the great serpent, Boiacu." It's a name first given to us by terrified humans, but we embraced it for so long that it pushed out whatever we once called ourselves. "We're not so feeble as you fleshy humans."

I only notice there was tension in Thais's expression once she relaxes it. "I was staying in the village just downstream from Rubem's boats. There's a mechanic's shop. I bet they'd have the tools to break both our locks."

I toss my arms into the air, nearly smacking a low-hanging branch in the process. "Perfect! They can serve me to Rubem for dinner."

She straightens her shoulders like she might heave a spear into my chest. "I won't sell you to them, Cacao. Unlike one member of this chain-ship, I'm a decent person. Whatever cruelty you think you're capable of, I don't have to respond in kind."

"Fine, fine," I sign, though I mean *ugh* and *fuck*. "Then we'll sneak in after sunset. Just don't cry when I betray you for less shitty boat filth."

"You know, I don't . . . I don't think you . . ." But Thais's hands falter.

What had she nearly said? I shove the curiosity away and redirect our course to the village, doing my best to ignore her. It becomes easier the longer we move. Parrots tear through the trees above us, shrieking with such power that my ridges tingle. A small snake skitters out of our path, and I glare at it, wishing my weighty mass could move that quickly on land. Eventually, Thais picks up a pair of sticks, drumming them in the air and swishing her feet as she walks, her hips rolling and her bare toes digging into the dirt.

The last of the evening sun catches on a pretty coppery stone that peeks through the clay-red dirt. I pause to pick it up.

Thais clambers to a halt, too, saying something in her vocal language, and finally drops her sticks to sign, "What's that?"

I spit on the little rock, cleaning off the dirt until its rough sides gleam in circles of browned red, and grey. It lacks the glow and thrum of an ignit, but the sight of it still brings me a sliver of peace. I hold it up for Thais to see.

She stares at me. "A rock?"

"No, not just a rock. This is bauxite. Because it's high in iron and aluminum, it's called a lateritic bauxite, which are from porous rock layers buried beneath the soil. It probably came out of one of your boat-human mines up north, fell from a truck rumbling down a nearby road, and ended up here. So, no, not just a rock." I poke my tongue at her, rolling my eyes until my vision twists about.

The soft rumble in her chest startles me. I yank my tongue back in. The smell of her amusement sticks to it, leaving a weirdly sweet taste.

I huff back into motion, rubbing my new stone. Rocks make sense. They don't have expressions I can't read, or ask questions I don't want to answer, and they encourage my greed, every acquisition just as bright and wonderful as the last.

"Rocks..." Thais's hands flutter. She shakes her head, her laughter still thick in the air. "That's why you wanted those ignits so badly." Her brow shoots up as she continues, "You've failed at that before, too, haven't you? Been caught by the cartel for it? Or the fishers? Is that why you panicked so much in the netting?"

"What?" I balk, almost dropping the rock. "No, that's not— there was one time with the fishers, when I first moved to the rivers, but they never netted me. I'm not *that* much of a fool." As I say it, my mangled scales twitch where the boat fan seared into them. Maybe I'm just a different type of fool. But I won't tell *her* that. "The nets have always hurt, and things like them—rough tree bark, rotting things, tortoise shells—ever since I was born. I don't know why. Everyone claims I'm being dramatic." My gut twists, and I wish I could retract the signs. At least I have the pulse of the ignits to quell the pain. Usually.

Thais watches me with an expression so far out of my grasp that I finally have to look away. Rocks. They're better than people.

The leftover light fades to grey as thick fog rolls toward us like a stirred riverbed. I know without a doubt that we're near its source: my birthplace, the Murk. Its enveloping mask encases the world in a deadly stillness. Even the animals go quiet. Our movements become the only vibration but for the distant holler of a monkey. I latch and unlatch my jaw to keep from thinking about the mist too hard, and what else lies within the deep swamps where it originates.

The jungle gives way to a thin line of water-rotted mangroves. A few glowing patches pierce through the deep-grey veil beyond: lights shining from a pair of cartel boats, their orange beams cascading off the fog.

"Under the water," I sign, "before they see us."

Thais slips in first. The river pulls at me when I follow, tugging with a vengeance. Farther downstream, its vibrations tumble through the air, then pound into a flurry of ruckus.

I glare at Thais the same moment her eyes widen.

"Shit," she signs, barely keeping above the surface. "We're too far west. The river splits here. The far side widens to a gently flowing arc toward the town, and this side—"

"Drops the fuck off?" I summarize.

"Exactly."

I grab our chain, trying to heave her back as the current carries her deeper into the river. My motion tugs at the cuff around her ankle, though, dragging her head under the water. I stop short at the fast-approaching buzz of a small boat fan. It heads straight for us.

Just as Thais drags in a breath, I lunge at her, grabbing her by both shoulders. I shove her under the surface, forcing my body down after. She flails and digs her nails into my arm, but her motions quiet as the flat bottom of the boat careens by over our heads. She trembles. In a stream of bubbles, she swims back to the surface, breaking it with a gasp. I come up beside her.

Through the mist, the fan boat slows and turns, its pitch-black form making a ghastly shadow in the fog. A spotlight cuts from its bow, blazing down on Thais and me. No cartel symbols mark the boat's hull, but the bundles of nets and hooks and harpoon guns nestled along the deck give it more weight than Rubem's fangs ever could.

Lily stands at the wheel, the spots on her white skin hidden at this distance and her orange hair gone amber in the dim light. Her brother, his name signed like the word for wolf, carries her net launcher. He preps it, his boat zipping back toward us while the current zips *us* back toward *him.*

He lifts it, and my skin tingles treacherously. I seize Thais, yanking her back down. The river pulls us along like a fruit caught in a flood wave. The boat passes over us once more, and Thais thrashes toward the surface, jerking the clamp around my arm. Pain pounds along my scales and through my shoulder.

When I reach the air, the hammering in my head ridges bombards me with warning signals. It drowns out everything else, even the vibrations of Wolf's and Lily's voices as they shout, Lily jabbing her finger upriver while Wolf slaps the side of his net thrower.

With a shake of her head, Lily turns the boat toward us. Toward the waterfall. Wolf levels his net thrower. I prepare to dodge for all I'm worth, but he only edges forward, his knees pressing to the railing as he aims. And re-aims. The pound of the cascade reverberates just behind us. With a final shout, Lily wheels the fan boat away. Wolf twists to argue, but the boat jolts against the current, and his legs buckle. He spills over the side, into the ravenous flow with us.

I brace myself against the river's drag, but the force of it plummeting over its worn edge tears through my straining muscles, towing Thais and me with it. The water engulfs us like a tomb. I pick apart its crashing vibrations for rocks, and when the current shoots us into the air, I twist us both an arm's length to the left.

We fly. Then we fall. The wind rushes over my scales, its muggy touch nearly cold for once. My stomach launches into my throat. I wrap myself around Thais, and she vibrates in a shrill scream.

We hit the water like a bullet, the force of it spinning me out from around Thais. My head throbs, my bones too light and my muscles too heavy. The clamp tugs at my arm. Thais's hands wrap around my wrist. I cough out bubbles and shake away the daze.

Wolf comes over the falls after us. I just make out the tiny thud of his head against the rock I so gracefully avoided. His limp body follows us for a few tumbles and settles out in the steady drift of the nearly flat river, which meets back up with its much broader other half and glides peacefully toward the orange glow of the village.

I swim for the surface, but Thais tugs me toward Wolf. My protests only earn me a harsher yank. I let her catch Wolf under the shoulders. She drags him with us as we crawl into the shallows. My whole body aches like a boat actually ran me over instead of narrowly missing me, and my stomach lurches from side to side, the remains of my last meal protesting almost as violently as it had when the small deer was alive.

Thais lugs Wolf onto a little muddy beach. A caiman hisses at her from atop a log, but I slap my tail against the water, scaring it off. If anyone gets to eat Thais, it'll be me. I deserve it after this wretched inconvenience.

She tips Wolf on his side, and to my disappointment, he coughs, spewing up water. Between Wolf's pathetic twitches and the way Thais checks his eyes, her lips moving as though soothing him, my blood boils. I snatch our chain, tugging her away from him.

"What are you—Cacao!" She heaves right back.

Instead of fighting, I burst toward her, teeth bared. "He's a fisher, Thais!"

Thais's face pinches like a jaguar preparing to snarl. "That doesn't mean I can just let him die."

"Can't you?"

Wolf coughs again, still on his side. My chest burns. Him, I can hurt. I lunge, sweeping my tail toward his neck, but Thais wrenches the chain, leaning against it with all her weight. The clamp digs through scales, biting into muscle and tweaking my arm painfully as it twists me back toward her.

Her flurry of signs blur, and the chain still looped over one arm writhes with each sharp motion. "Understand this, you bitter pod of rotting cacao: you may be the most self-centered closed-up cruel piece of sewage to ever clog this river system, but I won't let your filth rub off on me. I won't stand by while anyone, human or boiuna or goddamn cartel leader, suffers undeservedly. So, you will let me do what's right and get the fuck out of my way."

Her hands stop moving, and the rattling against my clamp lessens. But the damage is done. My raw flesh oozes beneath the metal, the scorch of something she doesn't need to say burning through my chest.

"Stop that. Look your elder in the eyes when they're speaking to you. Rude, insolent, selfish. You never learn. You're doing this on purpose. Greedy, worthless, cruel. We've had it with you—"

I stare at her dirty cheeks, her stained scarf hanging lopsided over tense shoulders, her stance offensive, like she's preparing to shoot. My mouth curls. "You think you're some fucking hero."

"Yeah. That's exactly what I am." She wipes a clump of mud off her face with the back of her hand, and her eyes bore into me, so full of fire that my scales crawl. But her aggression seems to fade, or maybe I just fail to read her for the millionth time today. When she steps closer to me, the soft tint of worry clouds my nose. "Is that blood? Let me see."

I wiggle away, baring my teeth. "Fuck off." I want to say so much more, or maybe nothing at all, to instead coil up and let my pain bury me alive, but the harsh thrum of Lily's fan boat comes through the fog behind me, and I can do neither. "We have to go. The fishers won't let me live or you go free just because you saved one of them."

"But you're hurt!" Her signs grow, like enough repetition

will carve the accusation straight into my bones.

I refuse to let it. The throbbing lessens the longer she watches me, as though the mere smell of her animosity triggers my body to collect itself and prepare for a fight. "My body is tougher than yours, and heals faster than yours, and feels less than yours." I lift onto my tail, leering down at her. If she wants repetition, she can have it. "So. Fuck. Off."

She watches me, the air sweltering between us, muggy and hot. Her indecipherable expression twitches. When she stays silent, I shove past her, past the barely conscious Wolf, too, toward the light of the town. The orange halos in the grey beckons, cascading out from the shore a little farther down and arcing across the now expansive river, the human village alive and bright in the deep layer of mist attempting to weigh it down.

After a moment, I feel Thais pick up the excess chain and loop it over her shoulder as she follows. We say nothing for the rest of the trek.

THREE

---❦---

FLESH AND SCALES AND OH, MUCK

You know that feeling when someone surprises you
so damn thoroughly
that you just have to ignore it?
Because if you don't,
it'll ravage your world?
Yeah. That.

THE TOWN OF SQUARE houses and wooden pathways sits on stilts above the shallow riverbank, locked drainage gaps revealing the dark expanse of water beneath. We travel under the long eaves of the roofs, painted deep reds and blues on their undersides. Lights dangle in clusters at their edges and drape from poles arching over crossroads. Every lamp glows a pure golden into the blackening fog.

I wonder if they try so hard to shine light and life throughout the tightly packed buildings because they fear the mists of the Murk will eat them if they don't. Dark things come from the Murk; everyone knows it. But dark things live in these villages, too, hanging boiuna pelts from their walls and wearing necklaces made of hoatzi bones. Their brilliant lights can't hide that.

I cling to the shadows like they're ignits, pasting myself into every crack and crevice. The clatter of the humans clogs my ridges too much to form a clear picture of the world beyond my sight, but I've seen glimpses of this region before. The river here runs deep and wide, slipping beneath the village until even the larger boats draw easily into the docks on the far side. There's no bank across the way, only the dense swamp of the Murk, but the water eventually twists southeast, turning through more jungle valleys and opening to an estuary of a hundred rivulets and wide bays that eventually meet the sea. But to the river's north, the Murk stretches on and on, a dangerous mist-laden world the boat humans rightfully fear.

I'm glad to be free of the wretched swamp. I've only kept so close to the Murk because this happens to be the home of such a prosperous cartel. My staying here has nothing to do with its nearness. Nothing at all.

A group of humans turns down the corner toward us, their forms still a blur in the fog. I rear onto my tail, and Thais's gaze snaps to mine. I look down to her flying hands.

"You will *not* attack them!"

Annoyance grates through me, but I only hesitate a moment before climbing onto the nearest roof, leaning down to pull her up after me. "It would be too much work anyway," I reply.

Thais's lips bunch, but she goes still. We wait for the humans to pass beneath us, and I drop her back down, a little harder than necessary. Her feet smack the wood. She watches me as I land beside her.

One of the humans in the departing group stops. They turn so suddenly I've no time to lean into the shadows, much less run. Their eyes lock with mine, and fear shudders its way through me. Their mouth opens.

Thais grabs our chain, and we rush around the corner. She drags me across the path, down a much smaller lane, and stops at what must be the back of a shop. "These are the mechanic's attached living quarters." She hesitates. "I think."

"You better be right." I coil my tail to keep it out of the

walkway. Somewhere in the fog behind us come the over-lapping vibrations of shouts. My scales crawl.

Thais rattles the shop's window, but the latch refuses to budge. I wedge her out of the way. Unwrapping the strongest stone in my necklace, I hurl it at the window. The clank of the rock and the crack of the glass thrum through my ridges, and the stone recoils, knocking me square in the forehead. It drops through a grate and into the river below. Sparks run through my vision as I try to blink away the pain. It only settles into a rough ache.

Thais waves her hands, one elbow holding open the shop's back entrance. Her face twists. "Cacao! It's unlocked."

I slide carefully into the building, sitting on top of my tail as she closes the door behind us. My head still pounds too hard to feel the street, but someone talks at a rapid pace from the story above us, their vibrations coming in so fast they feel like a buzz in the back of my head. I don't move, surveying the room for signs of life.

It holds a number of furnishings: a counter with a pump and sink, a huge thrumming ice chest, a table of deep-red wood, two boxy sofas, and a scattering of baggage, gadgets, and papers. The room is just as filled as any boiuna's den but far more chaotic. A human lies on one of the sofas, their booted feet propped up. A wide-brimmed hat sporting a massive red feather lies over their face, blocking out the light of the ceiling lamp.

Thais darts to the window to pull the curtain over it, but not before jabbing a finger at the crack I left in the glass. "You silt-stunted moron, you might have woken her!"

"Yeah, well. I didn't." I hone my frustration onto the loss of the stone instead of my own stupidity. My head feels like an overripe fruit where the damn thing hit me. My speech to Thais may have been half a lie: boiuna certainly injure less and recover faster than humans, but that hardly negates the pain in the meantime.

Thais moves toward a hallway. She moves a step too far,

and the chain goes taut between us, digging like a knife into my arm. Flicking my tongue, I follow after her. I attempt to move things out of my way as I go, but my tail still shoves into an overstuffed bag of clothes. My attention jerks to the sleeping human. Though they don't budge, I keep watch until we're out of the room. The voices grow stronger as we pass a stairwell.

"What are they saying?" I ask.

"They're talking about mechanic's stuff, I think. One of them has an accent from the siren seas." After a pause, she adds, "We should hurry," and continues to the shop's front room.

Longer than the rest of the house combined, the room is filled with tables and shelves. Pipes, cogs, wires, and screws litter every free space, tools of all shapes and sizes hanging on wall hooks and lying beside half-finished projects. Completed works sit orderly on a counter along the wide front window overlooking a fog-cloaked main street. Each has a groove for an ignit, but to my great sorrow, I spot none of the stones themselves.

Thais yanks the curtains over the window, and I survey a row of tools. How easy it would be to skin a boiuna with some of these terrors. My scales prickle and my gaze darts to Thais. She searches a box of the mechanic's things across from me and pulls out a long thin piece of metal and a rod. She props her ankle awkwardly and finagles them both into her cuff.

"Help," she manages, the motion half-formed as she refuses to let go of the tools entirely.

"Take off my clamp, then I'll help," I retort.

A bang from the street shoots through my nerves like thunder. I grip my necklace. No matter how determined Thais seemed when she claimed she wouldn't let anyone here kill me, I'm still just a greedy worthless piece of trash to her. My heart pounds at every twist of her tools, and the jiggling of the chain shoots pain through my arm scales. If she attacks me like this, can I fight her, or will she be the one who strangles me?

Another tremor bursts from outside, followed by such an onslaught of vibrations that I can't pick out boots from shouts from whatever else might be intermingling.

Two boat humans appear in the hallway, flooding the room with the scents of oil and salt and sweat. The once sleeping woman wears her feathered hat crookedly. Tan blotches stretch across her dark, wrinkled skin, much like my patterned back, her eyes so thin and curved they seem not to be there at all. Most of her hair has gone grey in the way of aging humans, but she seems no weaker for it. Her companion holds a long pipe in a scarred brown hand, their hair cropped around their chin. Their jaw trembles once. They shout something.

The vibration fires through me like an electric shock, terror and anger boiling together. I rear back, coiling over my tail. My hand shoots to my necklace in a dismal attempt to soothe the pounding in the back of my skull. I am a predator—I will eat them before they eat me. I will not die here. Not here, with the Murk so close and so far.

I lunge toward the hallway, but the clamp around my arm snaps tight. A rush of pain shoots through my shoulder. I jerk back, slamming into the table. The metal atop it flies to the ground. I shake, but I manage to focus on the other end of my chain. Thais holds the cuff that is no longer bound to her ankle but clutched between her fingers, pulling me back, her free hand rubbing her chest in a motion for *sorry*.

I bare my teeth, my whole body shaking, but the ache in my chest hurts more than the sting of the metal. I wanted to trust Thais. Even after everything the Murk did to me and every unlovable thing that I am, I wanted to.

The pipe-wielding human rushes at me, their weapon raised. I tell my limbs to move, but they refuse, fan blades held in place; the moment the obstruction gives way, the fan springs back into motion. I flinch like that loosed blade, jerking back from the human so hard I knock into the shelves behind me. A bundle of netting topples out of it, unwinding across the floor. Panic careens along my bones, flinging me away from the net, toward the human once more, and the pipe they swing at my head ridges.

A long metal tool stops it, bursting forth such a tremor that my whole skull seems to quake. Thais holds the end. She knocks the other human's weapon away and shouts a series of useless vibrations. My brain fills the gaps: *Wait, he'll eat you if he's attacked head on,* or maybe *We can't sell his pelt for as much if his skull is caved in.*

The pipe-welding human replies, and the woman with the feathery hat hisses something, her gaze on the front entrance. Thais and the pipe human continue arguing, softer now, their voices almost drowned by the commotion outside.

I have to get out of here. Clamp or not, I won't stay and be eaten.

I scoot back, but my tail slides over the netting, and it feels like a hoard of spiders tear along the undersides of my muscles, spinning webs in my spine. My thumb rubs instinctively across my favorite plain energy-lacking stone, but it's not enough. I need an ignit.

Through my pain-smeared vision, another well-wrinkled human charges into the room, dyed red curls aflame atop near-black skin and faded designs running up one of their arms. In their hands glow a cluster of blue and red ignits. My need turns visceral. I spring at the person, knocking them to the ground. They wail something, but I wrap my tail around them, squeezing them silent as I dig my fingers into their fists. I tear for the stones within.

Get the ignits and leave. Get the ignits and leave. Get ignits and leave.

The brush of my fingertips against the thrumming stones dissipates some of the pain the net caused—just enough for me to sense the rush of a fist just before it slams into the back of my head. The world darkens and sways. Someone shoves me onto my side, but I roll, bringing the human with me. I slam into the hat woman and the pipe bearer. They leap out of the way.

The hat woman grabs my chain as I pass and yanks it. The smell of my own blood hits me so hard I can taste it. It seeps from my arm in ripples each time I tremble. A throbbing fog clouds my thoughts, broken only by Thais's scream.

The hat woman barrels into me and digs her fingers between the patterned ridges running along my scalp. The chaos it casts through my skull overwhelms me, shatters me, cuts me off from my body and my thoughts and my very existence. As I writhe, the redhead vanishes from my grasp.

Then Thais is there, a swirling mass of dirt and rain, sliding her body between the hat woman's and mine. Her lips move with a fury, and she presses her hand beneath the woman's digging one, forcing her grip to withdraw. For a moment, all I can feel is the thrum of Thais's pulse in her fingers, like the beat of an ignit.

As soon as her hand comes away, I thrash out from under both humans. The chain drags after me. Netting wraps around my tail. I plunge into the shadows beneath a long table, curling against the wall behind it. Movement from the main street echoes through the wood. *Run, escape,* part of me thinks, but the rest of my mind sobs too loudly to hear it.

A knock at the front door turns the room utterly still. From my vantage beneath the table, I can't see the door itself, but the hat woman pauses from helping up the redhead, and the pipe lover picks up another metal pole. All their eyes fix on the entrance. I shake, and my blood drips over the clamp, splattering on the floor.

Quick as a snake, Thais snatches a blue ignit out of the stunned redhead's hands and runs to me. I flinch and grip my necklace like it might free me from this disparate black place I'm spiraling toward. But Thais only grabs my fingers, placing the ignit between my palms, and rips the netting away from my tail. She bunches it up, shoving it out of view.

Under the soothing rhythm of the ignit, my spiraling stops.

Stops because of Thais. *Thais.*

But the knocking continues.

A human calls into the shop, and from our nook beyond the door's line of sight, Thais translates their words for me: "Is everything all right in there?"

My heart skips, but the ignit I strum beneath my fingers soothes the ache in my bones. The pipe bearer's gaze bounces from Thais to the other two humans. Feather-hat shrugs and the redhead just stares at me, a crooked tweak in their full lips, their curls a mess around their face.

More shouting from beyond the door. Thais's hands shake as she relays the new message: "Open up in the name of the Fang!"

Oh, muck. My new ignit almost slips from my fingers when I sign. "They found me—they'll take me—"

Thais touches her fingers to mine, a soft quick brush. "We won't let them."

Why? Why is this muddy frustrating insulting boat shit of a human so determined to do good, even if that good means helping someone like me? "You really are a fucking hero."

Something blooms warm in my chest as I sign it, but Thais looks toward the other humans too soon to see my words. She scrambles to hide the revealed parts of my tail with empty boxes and the fallen shelves before scooting back under the table with me.

The pipe bearer opens the door, and Thais continues to translate.

"Hello?" This must be the pipe bearer. "How can I help you?"

Now, the person at the door: "There's a savage boiuna reported loose in the village. What happened here? Were you attacked?"

I feel the new human step over the threshold, and I stop breathing, wishing the shadows would eat me up.

The pipe bearer laughs. It grates a little along my ridges with an awkward stutter that digs like claws into the bruising on my scalp.

"No, no," Thais translates the pipe bearer's words. "I was working on a—" Thais pauses and then goes with, "machine, and it backfired, made a bit of a mess. But we'll watch out for the boiuna." The pipe bearer pauses, then adds, "What are we supposed to do with this snake if we find it?"

"Rubem Veneno prefers it alive, but it might be dragging around a young village dancer. If you have to kill it to get to her, or to protect yourself, then so be it."

My blood runs cold, another drop of it seeping onto the wood.

The pipe bearer speaks again, "Compensation?"

"The Fang Cartel supplies you quite nicely as it is," the cartel human replies. "Be happy that you're doing us a favor, and maybe Rubem will throw a few more ignits into your next shipment."

"Well. Then, I'll be sure to let you know if I stumble across this boiuna. What's it supposed to look like?"

Thais finishes the signs and adds two of her own, pointing at me, then tapping her head: "What do you think?"

I fit the ignit into a spare bit of my necklace wire with one hand, letting its gentle throb calm my growing panic, and sign with the other, "I don't trust the mechanic."

Thais nods. "I don't either. They could be a decent person, but they could also get a nice bundle of ignits if they sold you directly to the fisher's guild. They could just be biding their time. I don't want to risk it."

The cartel human speaks again, but instead of translating for them, Thais reaches her hand up, feeling along the table above us. Two pieces of metal clank together. The hat woman and the redhead glance at us, and while the first looks away, the redhead's eyes seem glued to me. Their mouth opens, but their companion wraps an arm around them, whispering something in their ear.

The humans at the door keep talking. Thais draws down a set of tools. She reaches for my arm, and I flinch, but I motion for her to get on with it, rubbing my ignit to distract myself. She sets to work. The metal bites into my scales, fresh blood oozing, but the pin holding the clamp together slowly comes out. The ping of it hitting the ground is dampened by the creak of the door closing.

I yank the clamp off so quickly it grates, but this burn flares with the good kind of pain, reminding me that I'm alive and free. Free. Thank the mists, I'm never letting another piece of metal touch my skin again.

Thais's hands flash. "Are you okay?"

"Yeah, yeah, I'm good. Let's go." Blood drips along the sliced rim of my scales, and the nerve-rattles threaten to descend again at any moment, but my own honesty cuts deeper than either, because I am good now, despite it all, and damn do I want to get the fuck out of here.

The pipe bearer walks back toward us, and the eyes of the other two humans turn our way. I glance down, my muscles tensing. Thais's fingers wrap around mine. The slightest tug from her springs me forward. I shove by the hat woman, knocking her and her companion to the side with my tail as I drag Thais through the hallway. We fly out the back door and down the tight path.

I almost freeze at the sight of the main street. The scent of humans precedes their hazy forms, extra lanterns shining through the mist and weapons waving like deadly limbs. Thais tugs me forward. I squeeze my new ignit until its pulse settles in my veins and follow her lead. If she meant to hurt me, she could have done it back at the mechanic's shop, and if she meant to sell me, she would've been smarter to keep the clamp on my arm. For whatever crazy heroic reasons, she sincerely wants to help.

We dash between the buildings, Thais leading the way, but barely two intersections pass before we stumble into a loose troop of humans turning a corner. We push through them. Their shouts sting my head like a knock in the skull, and the pounding of their feet follow us through the streets. A net hurls past me, trapping someone deeper in the mists instead. Gunfire rings through my spine, but I launch us around a bend.

Our pursuers multiply, forcing us to turn ever farther from the direction Thais tries to flee. Her breath grows heavy. My muscles burn, the wooden road tearing into my belly, and the drying blood from my arm wound cracks against my scales. We veer onto a wide path. The lights burn brighter but farther apart here, nearly overcome by the mists. At the end of the road rears a massive wooden wall. The soft vibration of rippling water fluctuates from beyond it.

Water, like the river. We're almost safe.

I sling my tail over the wall and pull Thais up with me. We run headfirst into an ornamental fruit tree. I slide through the branches, toward the trickling, but when I drop, I find myself not in a stream at the village's edge, but surrounded by a dark courtyard.

Thais lands beside me. Wood paths wind around flower boxes with orchids and ferns, and the water vibrates from a little waterfall over a pond on the other side of the fog-laden space. The whole place holds such a stillness that it feels like we have passed into a different world, as though the boat village has its own private boat-human Murk.

Lovely crimson rocks litter the planters. I snatch one, giving it a quick glance. In the shadows, I swear they look like uncut rubies, but with this many so casually placed, they must be the more common red garnets. I pop one into my necklace beside the ignit to look at later.

Thais steps forward cautiously, surveying the unlit windows of the surrounding rooms. "I don't know where we are— I never came to this part of town."

"It doesn't matter. We just have to get into the river." I move toward the decorative waterfall, searching the ground. "Are there grates? Doors? Anything leading down?" I slide to a stop. The mist swirls away from me, shifting over the stone-lined pool built into the wood. Clear water drains down to it from a pile of rocks. I lean in, and a small caiman scoots away, hiding in a gap between the rocks.

A gentle breeze carries forth the scent of wine and one so much like the heat of the sun in the afternoon that the night seems to pull away. I freeze. In an archway beyond the pool, a bug net billows, and the leader of the Fang Cartel, Rubem, steps out.

FOUR

---⤳---

PRECIOUS STONES, PERILOUS POISONS

When does bravery become stupidity?
That's a trick question: all bravery is stupid.

RUBEM HOLDS A VIAL of luminous green and a glass of dark wine red, but his preoccupied hands drift in a motion that mimics the budding flowers in Lily's name. He stops when his eyes settle on us. He sets down his glass and places the vial into the front pocket of his shirt where it glows beneath the thin fabric, gently pulsing with an ignit's soft heartbeat. With one fishnet-encased hand, he flicks a switch on the courtyard wall. The hum of a machine starts up, lighting lamps throughout the garden.

A shudder runs through my bones, and I clutch my necklace-bound ignit, letting the thrum of it sink into my heart. I feel Thais gasp beside me.

"I was expecting someone else, but I suppose you'll do," Rubem says.

Her hands fly into motion. "You're not taking us."

A twist comes over Rubem's lips. "I admire your spirit, child." Each gesture is as dark and fluid as the alcohol he smells of. The long red flaps of his coat and the loose bundles of his beaded braids flare silently as he works his way around the pond. "Perhaps I was too impulsive, having you hauled to me like a captive. We could be working together in this—should be. I must have your mother's ignit hoard, one way or another, but if you're willing to help me, to hear me out, then you'll be under my protection. Not prisoners, but partners."

My breath catches, my darkest fears throwing me visions of Thais stepping to Rubem's side and the two of them turning viciously on me. I doubt she would, but I slide backward anyway, coiling my tail. I hit a flower box. The scrape of scales on wood to my right lures my attention just long enough for me to spot the shape of another one of Rubem's pets plodding closer, this one a massive crocodilian, as though the caiman from the pond has somehow grown to be twice my size. I go still, refusing to give it a target to snap at.

"You can return to your performing, Thais, with my protection and funding for your travels. No other cartel will dare seek you out. You'll have boats, instruments, a mansion to return to—anything your heart desires. You can even continue your friendship with the boiuna, if you wish." Rubem pauses, his stare digging into me. "I know you both have no one else."

"You're not planning to do anything bad to him, then?" Thais asks.

Rubem's brow does a funny twitch I can't read. My heart recoils. *No.* No, Thais tried so hard to save me. She's a fucking hero. She can't—

But I would. I would hand her to Rubem in an orchid wreath if he promised me a hoard of ignits and a safe life to lead with them. The understanding jerks my heart anew.

"What I will do with him is still to be seen." The fishnet gloves on Rubem's smooth brown hands make terrible sickly patterns as he waves one into the lamp light.

I nearly can't watch, gripping my ignit tightly.

"But I would never hurt him," Rubem continues, "if that's what worries you. I've no desire to harm anything that comes from the Murk. Quite the opposite, in fact."

Just words—lies, I'm sure of it. What does a boat shit cartel leader care about those from the swamps?

Thais glances at me, but I can't hold her gaze. Her features shift as though she's trying to tell me something, but I don't know what. *Run? Stay? Are you really worth this much to me?* I know the answer to the last one. I'm not worth that much to anyone, even a person with a moral compass as pristine as Thais's. I bunch my muscles, tracking the monstrous crocodilian at my back as I prepare to flee, but something stops me, some twinge in my chest. Will Rubem take Thais captive again if I run? It shouldn't matter.

It doesn't matter. If she decides to work with him, he won't hurt her. And I wouldn't care if he did.

The beast at my back lurks a little closer, its ridged tail sliding like a tree trunk across the wood. I spring over the caiman pond. One hand holding the ignit in my necklace tightly, I grab for the roof on the other side. I whip my tail around, splashing as I climb, but my fingers find no hold on the roof tiles. The weight of the moving crocodilian shudders the wooden courtyard floor. It snaps for my tail, missing by a scale.

I slip from the roof and leap again. I need both hands to pull myself up, but I can't let go of my ignit. I can't.

I feel the vibration of the beast's teeth descending a moment before they drive into my tail, pushing through scale and piercing flesh. My grip on the roof fails. I hold my ignit tightly and tuck my head in as I smack against the wood like a wet towel. My belly burns from the impact, but I force myself to writhe, wrapping my body across the crocodilian's. I encircle its thick neck. It tries to whip me off, clamping harder on my tail in the process.

The vibrations of Rubem's shouting rattle along my ridges, but they feel distant and unimportant.

I jab my thumb into the beast's eye socket. It hisses and rolls, my tail still caught in its jaws. I loop around its body and tighten my hold on its neck and legs, latching my thumb farther into its skull. It snaps its mouth open, careening in a panic. I yank my tail out from its teeth and twist tighter around its neck, waiting for it to go limp.

The scent of Rubem's fear and anger surges through the air with burning intensity. He slams into me. One of his fishnet-covered hands touches my scales, and I jerk away from him. My grip slides down the crocodilian's body. The beast rolls once more, pinning the lower half of my torso between its rough hide and the wooden deck. It struggles inside the coils of my tail.

Rubem lunges for me again, but Thais appears on the other side of the crocodilian. She chucks an uncut gem from the planters at Rubem's face. He ducks, but the motion distracts him. His pet monster whacks into him from its blind side.

I tense my muscles with everything in me, forcing the noose tighter around the crocodilian's neck. Its movements slow. Rubem screams again. His hands shake, and he launches a punch to my head, straight for the lines of my ridges. Just the sight of his impending fishnet gloves tears my world into strips, and I can't move. I can't move.

Thais leaps over the crocodilian's side, barreling into Rubem. They go down in a twist of fabric and limbs. The soft glow of Rubem's vial gleams as it falls from his pocket. It cracks against the ground. One of Thais's flailing hands slams into it. She yelps. When she lifts her arm, red oozes in a thin strip. From the cut, a glowing trail of green traces its way through her skin, pulsing. She shudders, and I feel the tremble so deeply in my bones I think I might be mirroring it. Then she goes limp.

I unfurl myself from the crocodilian like lightning, rolling it off me in the process, and spring to catch her before she can hit the ground. *Thais!* Don't be dead now. Don't be dead because of me.

Her corpse can't sit at the top of everything else I've fucked up in my life.

Her chest rises and falls, ragged. She jerks out of my arms, and bile pours from her mouth in heaves. Rubem stares at her, then at the broken vial. His senses seem to return with a wave of emotional scents too chaotic for me to distinguish. He stumbles.

Grabbing Thais beneath her armpits, I drag her away from him, toward the wide wooden door on the other side of the courtyard, the door back into the town. As I slam it open, I coil my tail beneath me and hold on to Thais's waist, preparing for more cartel humans, for fishers, for hunters. But the only people in view of the little path to the doorway catch me off guard: the older two from the mechanic's shop, the redhead and the feather-hat woman.

The hat woman draws her pistol, but she aims it at the ground, trying to see past us to where a wet-faced Rubem trembles, his arms around his bleeding crocodilian. With her flowing red cape and broad chest, the hat woman looks far more intimidating than he. Her companion rushes to my side. Together we help a weak Thais into the street, the hat woman covering our backs.

She barks something, and Thais answers, shaking her head. Her limbs drag heavily as she stumbles between us. After a moment of hesitation, the feather-hat woman holsters her gun and picks Thais up like she weighs no more than a palm branch. Curling my tail back and forth beneath me, I watch her and the redhead walk through the fog. The redhead glances over their shoulder. They wave for me to follow, but when I don't move, they shrug and leave me be.

Both of them seem to want to care for Thais far more than they want to catch me or kill me. I cup the ignit Thais gave me at the mechanic's shop, rubbing my fingers over the smooth blue stone. The glowing veins of sapphire and cyan pulse gently, a deeper version of Thais's eyes.

Still clinging to it, I follow after the humans, climbing from roof to roof. The streets hold a few stragglers, but most of the hunting parties have moved on. No one bothers to look up.

My muscles feel like they've been stripped and roasted in the sun and then sewn back into place, scorched and tenderized. The river calls to me from beneath the village. I'll leave. I will. I just have to know whether or not Thais is going to die first.

The memory of her knocking into Rubem crashes through my head like a raging river. Why did she do that? Fucking hero. Why does she have to be so damn good?

I swish my tail in frustration, and it stings where the gashes from the crocodilian rub against the roof tiles. The hat woman and redhead enter a two-story building with a sign outside bearing a picture of a hammock and the stiff lines the boat humans call writing. A light comes on in an upper room, shining through the redhead's cloud of hair as they wrap the curls at the top of their head and stick a long piece of metal through the bun. The hat woman yanks the curtains closed. I coil across a pole connecting this roof to theirs and hang from the edge, watching them upside down through the crack between the fabrics.

The humans lay Thais on a small bed. She breathes heavily. The redhead meets my gaze through the slit, and I try to yank back up, but my muscles refuse in a tantrum of pain. Their bun bounces as they open the window and wave for me to come in.

"They're good people." Thais moves sluggishly, her deep-olive skin an off color.

I balk, clutching my ignit.

"I can translate for you—"

I cut her off with one hand, "No, you're hurt."

"Not—not *that* hurt. I feel just fin—" She curls, clutching her stomach. Her shoulders shake and she leans over, but only spit comes out. Slowly, she lies back down.

Stupid boat human.

A stubborn hunting party approaches from down the mist-strewn street. I make one last feeble attempt to pull myself back onto the roof before giving in to my exhausted muscles and slipping the rest of the way through the window. The redhead tries to help, but their reaching hands give me a burst of new strength. I dart into the corner, my tail slapping against the wall. Teeth half-bared, I coil up.

The hat woman ignores me. She says something to her companion, who turns down the light and sits beside Thais. I watch. And I wait.

Fatigue curls itself around me in the shadows, deepening as the once ruckus-filled town subsides to tranquility, then to a stillness so heavy it could be a grave. Thais dry heaves twice more before the exhaustion overwhelms my senses. I descend into darkness with my head propped on one hand, and my thoughts still lingering on Thais.

FIVE

—————— ⟋⟍ ——————

MY KINGDOM FOR A CURE

Sometimes we are what we think,
and sometimes we're the things we say
when we're not thinking.

BRIGHT MORNING LIGHT AND achy muscles wake me. I lie crookedly across my coiled tail. Peeling my fingers off my ignit, I stretch my arms over my head and scan the small room. The redhead works at a little table near the window, a contraption of metal and wires stealing all their attention. A soft breeze sneaks through the curtains, a sliver of blue sky and rooftops beyond. Thais's bed is empty.

That jolts me to life.

I burst upright, and the redhead startles, dropping her tools. I sign Thais's name. They sign something back, but their hands use foreign motions, some kind of siren seas version of sign language. Whatever. I'll figure this out myself.

I rub the ignit, sliding toward the door of the room. It opens before I reach it. Thais enters, her soft curls braided across her shoulder and her loose outfit clean once more, her scarf twirling at her back. She lives. My chest warms. Not because I'm glad. Or maybe it's because I am glad, but I'm only glad because I didn't want it to be my fault if she died. That's all.

She holds two plates of human food, each with a few slices

of bread and a mix of cut fruits. It barely looks like a meal. No wonder humans have to eat so many times a week.

I draw back into my corner.

Thais hands one plate to the redhead and sits on the bed with the other. "Good morning."

"You're alive," I sign.

"Why wouldn't I be? I'm strong and stubborn." She snatches a piece of her bread and shoves it into her mouth in one go, as though that will hide the scent of her fear, so stark I can pick it up for once.

"What's wrong with you?" I have to know, because . . . because I have to. Not because I care whether she hurts.

"Nothing."

Something on Thais's face must suggest she's lying, because the redhead waves a metal tool at her and interjects.

I glance between the two, not meeting either of their gazes. "What did they say?"

Thais tears into her second piece of bread, yanking it apart without eating it. "She, not they. Her name's—" Thais tries to describe the syllables, like the beginning of my species' name combined with my pronouns and the word for eel, because somehow, she refuses to understand that none of those things have a sound to me. "Murielle is here with her wife for their anniversary. Her brother's partnered to a siren, apparently, so they're cool with all kinds of mer."

A siren? I roll my eyes. Sirens eat humans, like the fishers do the boiuna, only twice as bloody and incredibly more deadly. But if the predators of the Murk can work together, then maybe even sirens and humans can cohabit. "Who cares?" I snap. "I asked what's wrong with *you*."

Thais crosses her arms over her stomach.

"If you don't tell me, I'll eat you. Then I *will* know what's wrong because I'll be digesting it."

"No!" Her hands fly through the sign like they're on fire. "Then you'll just be poisoned too."

"That green stuff's still in you?" I creep a little closer until, somehow, I end up sitting on the ground beside the bed, leaning my head against its wooden frame. "Isn't it going away?"

Thais shakes her head. "Murielle's an expert in ignit-related technology. According to her, the poison is a substance made from a powdered version of a rare activated green ignit."

"The green ones are nasty," I sign. "When pressed to the skin, a whole green ignit causes blisters and heaving, and then you die pretty much immediately. The Murk banned them a long time ago. Throws them into the sea near the deepest part of the drop-off." They even tried to destroy the individual ancient notorious for making them. Thais doesn't need to know about that, though. Since the Murk's ancients are producing far more ignits than usual this century, the stones often spill into the rivers, but most boat humans still don't know their creators are mangrove-bound parasites.

Thais's nose pinches.

Maybe referencing the green ignit's effects was the exact wrong thing to say to her now that the stuff flows through her veins, no matter how small the quantity.

"Anyway," she continues. "Murielle was able to track the movement of the poison through my body. It's congregated in my bloodstream but still far too dispersed to deactivate or remove."

"But you're not throwing up anymore?" The question barely leaves my hands before I answer it myself. "Because the powdered ignit still has to recharge itself, just like a normal stone, doesn't it? That would make the sickness it brings come in waves."

Thais nods. "It's been taking a lot longer than a full ignit stone, even a small one. I had two episodes while you slept." If she feels anything about this, I can't tell—the scent of her fear has dissipated now that she's composed herself. "But it doesn't matter. I'll be fine. I'll be fine." Her mouth moves with the repeated signs.

Murielle throws a cog at her.

Thais's lips turn down. "I *will* be fine! Murielle is making me a reversal mechanism."

"A reversal mechanism?" I ask, even though I absolutely do not care, not even a little bit.

"You know how both sirens and yellow ignits give out trance waves? Decades back, ago pirate in the siren seas used yellow ignits to cancel out the siren's songs. Murielle thinks we can do the same thing with the toxic waves making me sick. I'll just need a green ignit for the device to function. So, I get one from my mother's hoard, and everything will go back to normal." She gives the motions an extra flare.

Now, *there* is something I do absolutely care about. "Your mother's hoard?"

"Unfortunately." She brushes a wisp of her curls behind her ear. "My mother had a few of them. I'd bet Rubem has another as well, but we've proved we can't steal from him even if the ignits are sitting in plain sight."

"Who said anything about we?"

Thais shrugs, drumming her fingers on her leg. "No one. Nothing. You're not coming with me. I can manage the Murk on my own."

The Murk. My heart clenches. I rub my ignit, only letting go to sign. "If you're traveling through the Murk, you'll need a guide. Boat humans don't come out of the swamps alive." I saw to that personally before. "Even the cartel won't send people in unless they've got a really good reason."

"Yeah, well, if you see a Murkling offering their aid, send them my way."

"I'm a Murkling, and I *am* offering." The words come out before I think them through. They chill my spine and wrap tight claws around my lungs. I shiver the sensation away and trace my fingers over the stones of my necklace.

I know the Murk well enough to act as an escort, but if the council learns I've returned, there won't be enough left of me to guide a flock of vultures. And Thais's safety isn't my problem. She can go with Murielle or Murielle's feather-hat wife.

But as my thumb brushes the surface of my humming ignit, the ignit Thais took for me when I couldn't steal it myself, I know what I need to do. "I'll guide you through the Murk. But only if you give me the rest of your mother's hoard."

Her face slackens. She smells like a void, emotion hiding behind layers of mist my senses can't infiltrate no matter how far I submerge in them.

I choose to make my point as clear as possible. "I can get you wherever you need to go, as long as we have a boat. I grew up in the Murk. I'm the best bet you're going to find, and I won't sell off your mother's ignits like Rubem would."

A shudder runs through her, trembling her hands. "I know you won't. You're a selfish hoarding slung-drain. Someone would have to pry them from your grimy fingers."

"Exactly." Fire boils in my stomach, but it feels more natural than the heat my chest held earlier. It turns out I didn't have to hurt Thais. I just had to wait for someone else to. "Good to know we understand each other." I clutch my ignit. I'll have an entire hoard. An entire hoard. It feels unreal. Slowly, I force my fingers to detach. "Where are we headed?"

"Straight through the Murk, to the crescent peninsula."

"You can't just sail along the coast?"

Thais shakes her head. "Rubem controls the river system from here to the sea, and it'll take too long if I have to waste my time trying to avoid him."

"What do you mean *too long*? Are you . . ." I hold my ignit a little tighter.

"I'm fine. I'm just dying, that's all. But we'll go through the Murk, and we'll get to my mother's hoard in time. No more poison." She lifts her chin, giving a rhythmic rap of her hands. "This is just a momentary inconvenience."

"An inconvenience for *me*," I grumble. But the signs bite back a thought that hurts like the breaking of bone: Thais is dying, slowly, painfully, the light being drained away from her eerie ignit eyes. Because she took a poison trying to save me.

But she won't die, I remind myself. I'll get her to her mother's hoard and get my ignits, and I won't have to think of her again.

That goal settles in me like great stones landing on the bottom of a still lake.

Murielle pops up from her seat, bringing her little mechanism with her. It fits perfectly in her wrinkled palm, flat and oval, attached to a long bronze chain. Tiny gears and wires run through the inside, and at its center sits space for a large ignit. She loops the necklace around Thais's head.

Thais tucks it into her flowing shirt, not letting go until she finally speaks to Murielle, signing her words for my sake. "Thank you. This means a lot to me."

She translates for Murielle as the redhead replies, "Glad I could finally use that damn tech for something good."

"Well, thank you all the same."

Thais's rain-cleaned scent fills me up, and I can't help but look at her, my gaze catching on her eyes. They shine with the purest blue, brighter and truer than the sky and the sea. But they send a buzz of agitation through me as they meet mine, haunting my bones, and I look down at my ignit instead.

"We'll need a fan boat," Thais signs.

A dry grin slips over my face. "We know someone who has more than his share of those."

Violent banging from the downstairs entrance breaks my smile.

SIX

———————⌗———————

THIS IS OUR TRAVELING SONG

Touch is a dishonest silt-breather.
It means a million different things
at a million different times.
And all of them fuck you over.

MURIELLE'S WIFE BURSTS INTO the room, her pounding boots clashing like thunder against my head ridges, and I nearly jump out of my scales. As she speaks, Thais translates.

"Someone's here looking for you two. Murielle is going to try to distract them, but they're adamant." She turns on her heels, her hat feather flaring, and guides us out of the room.

I sign to Thais, "Are they Rubem's?"

"No, fishers." After a short exchange with Murielle's wife, Thais adds, "The light-skinned orange-haired woman leads them."

"Lily." I press against the hallway to keep Thais's hands in my line of sight as we follow Murielle's wife.

At the stairs, I pull to a stop, glaring at them angrily. Thais waves at me, her motions turning aggressive as the voices from the building's entrance escalate. I bare my teeth and shake my head, but with a tight jaw, I plunge down the steps, half falling, half rolling. The floor below meets me with a thud.

"Quiet!" Thais grabs my arm, yanking me after Murielle's wife, away from the shouts at the front door.

My panic catches up to me a moment too late, as though the trauma of last night had stunned it somehow. It slams through my muscles, trembling them into action. I burst through the hallway, curling around the feather-hat woman. She ignores me and pulls up a grate in the floor. Above her, water drips from a shower head with dozens of tiny holes in the bottom. Too many holes, the sort that crawl up my spine the way netting does. I look down at the grate instead, rubbing circles into my ignit.

Murielle's wife pulls it away and loosens a sloping bit of metal to reveal the river slipping lazily by beneath us. Thais grabs my tail and drops it through the hole.

It falls, dragging me down with it. "Muck—"

I splay my body as I hit the shallow murky water. Thais wavers over the opening. She catches herself a moment too late and topples, belly first. Her landing creates a silty splash.

"Cacao!" She climbs to her feet, drenched once more and sputtering like this is somehow my fault. The water comes up to her waist. Her new necklace hangs like an amulet beneath her shirt, round and heavy.

I shrug. "Yes, boat shit?"

But I feel the tremor of the fishers' feet charging down the hallway above us. I grab Thais's arm, pulling her along. The river slides gracefully by me, my tail barely riding along the surface as it beats back and forth, my torso low. Thais stays upright, sloshing through at half my speed. She trips and collapses into the water before pulling herself up again.

I flick my tongue at her. "As amusing as it is to watch you make a fool of yourself, we have to hurry."

"I'm fine, Cacao. I've got this," she snaps.

I lift my hands. "Whatever, boat shit. It's not like I *wanted* to help you."

Light streams through the gaps in the village street above us, cutting shocking golden walls into the dimness. Drafts of spicy human food and pungent oil mingle with the damp stink of the covered water. We keep to the shadows, moving slowly toward the bobbing hulls of the fan boats at the edge of the village. Every time Thais falls, I stare at her, but she doesn't ask for help, and I don't offer it.

I focus on the vibrations around us, glancing back every now and then. No angry fishers appear in the water, but someone seems to keep pace on the walkways above, always just a little behind. We need to move faster. I glance at Thais. Her pinched face and determination not to look at me make the comment fall from my hands.

We slow when we near the docks, scouting along the undersides for something small, painted with a scarlet fang on the front. Even the larger riverboats are fairly flat underneath compared to the deep-bedded canoes of the Murk, and with the river low for the dry season, the humans climb down onto bobbing decks to reach them. Thais pulls me into the shadow of a small fan boat, tapping the fang as she passes. Her clammy grip slides against my scales, but I don't ask if she's all right. She's not.

She's dying.

Stupid hero human wants to look brave or something, I guess. Her legs shake as she pulls herself onto the fan boat and ducks behind the simple wooden railing. Water drips from her curls, pooling at the tip of her chin. I rub my ignit once and don't look at her eyes.

"Do you know how to work these things?" I ask.

"My mother had one."

"That doesn't answer the question, muck-face!"

"Get your useless complaining ass up here, Cacao."

I slip my tail over the side of the boat, grimacing as my bite wound's scabs catch, and slide in beside her. The flat wooden deck lifts slightly near the front, with a bench-style sitting area in the center and a giant fan at the back. My full tail barely fits within it, and I slide awkwardly over the old blankets and empty canteens that litter the floor.

Thais fiddles with a steering lever beside the driver's seat. "Check the engine."

"Do I look like I know anything about human machines?"

But she twists her hand in the bitter two-fingered sign for *fuck you* while she watches a group of cartel humans mingle on the other far busier end of the dock.

I rustle my tail aggressively at her as I examine the engine below the fan. Pipe and metal and cogs form a block of human nonsense inside a wooden casing. I peel back a little insulated trap door. A subtle red glow comes from the ignit at the engine's center, the scale-sized stone fully charged with heat and ready to launch this thing into the Murk once activated. Or to sit neatly in my palm with my other glowing stone. My fingers twitch. A canteen hits the back of my shoulder, and Thais stares at me.

"You're getting an entire hoard of them. Lay off, you greedy parrot dropping."

"Yeah, yeah, silt-breather." I wiggle at her and slam the little door back into place.

She thrums her fingers against the side of the driver's seat. The scents of sun and leather and wine hit me, paired with the harsh musk of Rubem's monster crocodilian. Beyond the slits in the boat's giant fan, the crocodilian plops, one clawed foot after another, onto the lower floating dock, its missing eye covered in a bandage. Rubem strolls after it. His fishnet gloves vanish into the short-sleeved vest of ruby red he wears over his browns and blacks. Wolf walks at his side, head bandaged but otherwise looking no worse for the wear since his fall last night. Shame.

Lily charges up behind them, shouting something without signs. All three of them turn toward the boats. Their gazes find me first, then Thais.

I grab Thais's arm, yanking her down, but the shot of a pistol rings before we can hide behind the low railing. My heart ricochets like the bullet that scatters wood chips along the dock at my side. My side, specifically, as far from Thais and her precious hoard knowledge as possible. Thais screams all the same. I coil backward and accidentally smack into a knob. It must activate our engine's ignit, because the machine whirls to life.

Our boat's fan flies into motion. We shoot out of the dock, careening to one side. Thais screams again. We knock into the vessel next to ours, and she rights our course, aiming us out onto the main river.

"They're shooting at us!" She signs it with one shaking hand, steering us through village canoes and mat rafts. We whip up water as we swerve past a confused merchant boat.

"Shooting at me," I sign huge sweeping motions to make sure she sees me. "They'd want you alive. For now."

"And the shooting doesn't bother you? You're just—" Her final sign must require two hands, because she flings her free one out obnoxiously instead of continuing.

"It's kind of been my usual life since leaving the Murk." Not that I want to talk about that. I slap the engine. "We have an hour before the ignit needs a recharge. Probably."

"Probably?"

"I'm familiar with the ignits, not the human machines!"

About five boat lengths behind us, a dozen vessels zip onto our foam stream, creating a mismatched diamond formation. Most of them bear the cartel's symbol, but the nearest three are all dark wood and netting. Lily wields the helm of one, her flaming orange hair billowing out behind her as Wolf preps their weapons. She draws closer, two extra fans giving her small arrow-shaped vessel an extra boost. The nets draped over the bottom send shudders along my spine.

I clutch my ignit to my chest. My eyes meet Thais's for a heartbeat, and they settle me like a sweep of mist and a dosing of rain, an ignit glowing from within them, all power and light and peace. The boat pulls up across from us, and Wolf launches a net, barely missing our railing. A volley of shots follows.

I wrap myself around Thais, leaning over her shoulder.

"Faster!"

But it's not my panic that saves us. Rubem draws up on the other side of our boat. He shouts at the fishers, and his hands follow a fluid pristine series of motions: "I have them. Back off."

Lily stands still as a shadow, her chest barely moving. She pulls her boat off to rejoin the others. Rubem does not follow them. He swings his vessel closer to ours, but Thais swerves away, dodging a floating log. I coil tighter around her seat.

She brushes me off with a frazzled pat-slap on the tail. "Go! Help! Lazy coward!"

I want to snap back that I'm neither of those things, but I have very little proof to the contrary. Unfurling slightly, I cling to the bottom of the boat. Rubem's bearded crewmate draws out a grappling hook, their sweaty muscles gleaming in the sun as they hurl the metal toward us. It hits the deck and scrapes a deep groove through the wood before catching on the rail.

Our boat twists. I grip Thais with my tail, keeping her in her seat as the momentum flings me against the far railing. Pain shoots through my shoulders, but over the spray of the water and the ringing in my head, I faintly sense the vibration of a machete hidden under our boat's center seating area. I unhook the weapon and dive for the grappling hook. Its rope takes three swings to sever.

Rubem shouts as our boat careens away from him once more.

"We have to get into the Murk!" I sign.

"Yeah, you think?"

The dense line of the Murk rises like a wall of green and grey not far to our right, but in our peril, the fisher boats slipped between us and it, making a small moving wall a few boat lengths away. With a yank of the lever, Thais turns us straight for them. They lift their guns, and Wolf mounts the net shooter on his shoulder.

I drop to the deck as the fishers fire at me. The shots ring through my skull, swaying my vision. I want to dive into the water, to block out the crazy rush of the world, but I steady myself as best I can, focusing on the thrum of my ignit. If I don't do something about the fishers and their nets soon, it might not be enough of a distraction.

Bunching my tail beneath me, I spring at the boat beside Lily and Wolf's. My tail thumps against the deck and slides, nearly spilling me over the other edge, but I grab the boat's driver, using my momentum to help sling myself around them. I squeeze their neck. They collapse. The boat's second fisher rushes me with a half-loaded pistol and a spear gun, but I shove my shoulder against their belly and knock them into the river.

I bare my teeth at Lily and Wolf as I turn my stolen boat toward Thais. She curves her vessel around. I aim the stolen boat to zip back toward the rest of the fishers' wall and jump back to Thais. My lungs burn, and last night's bruises ache afresh, but I grin as the now driverless boat forges us a path through our attackers. Grin, at least, until I focus on the edge of the Murk.

The small riverside mangroves on the far bank look like hatchlings compared to the Murk's towering swamp trees, their branches interwoven in a canopy so thick only the dimmest light peeks through. Their roots create a similar barrier beneath, strangling boulders to pieces and forming pools of salty stinking water that flicker with sheens of rainbow. The last hints of the night mist still linger between the thick groves. Within, a series of wide rivulets form paths through the unbreachable trunks, one running so near that the deep green and blue water gleams amidst the trees. But the line of mangroves along its outskirts creates an impassable divide at this spot in the river.

Thais points to where a partially underwater boulder separates two of the trees, letting half a boat's width of water flow from the river into the Murk. "We can enter through there!"

"No, we can't!" I protest. "Thais, we can't fit—" But she watches that tiny break in the trees instead of my hands, veering us toward it so quickly I scramble for the railing to keep from falling.

"We'll make it," she replies. "If we tip the boat."

I slap the very flat bottom with my tail, the tip bouncing off the solid but slim railing. "If we sink the boat, you mean?"

"We'll only need to lift one edge enough to scoot over the rock's high point on the right." She points to the grappling hook.

"Do I look like I'm made of muscle to you?"

She stares at me a moment longer than feels comfortable, especially with our probable death speeding toward us. "Actually, yes." Her gaze snaps away, settling back on the split between the trees. "Ready?"

"No."

But all her attention fixes on the tiny gap she's determined to drive us through.

Motherfucking Murk mist. I tweak the grappling hook free and wrap the remaining bit of rope around my wrist to stabilize my grip. "I hope you know what you're doing," I half sign, half glare.

She waves dramatically at the quickly approaching trees.

Fixing my tail through the large metal latch on the side of our boat, I add a quick "I hate you" and prepare to jump.

The gap flies toward us. I leap for the branches intertwining above it. Slipping my grappling hook between them, I drag upward with all my might. My muscles blaze and bite, and my side of the small boat lifts out of the water. The hull scrapes along the rock, but we barely slow.

I loosen my grip on the hook. Before I can drop onto Thais's head, the latch I wound my tail through snaps free of the boat. I hang, disconnected from the vessel that zips under me.

The subtle vibration of a weapon firing turns into that of Wolf's net opening in the air behind me. It slams into my side, wrapping its terrible biting lines around my arms and head.

Thais's boat skims past the rock with a grind and a splash, and I drop a moment too late, falling into the river behind it.

I struggle to reach my necklace beneath the netting. Too much fire runs through my being. My lungs catch, drawing in water. I writhe. The surface falls away, the bottom of Thais's boat fading into the distance. From beyond the Murk's edge, a spear shoots through the water, narrowly missing me as it latches into the net. It drags me into deeper water.

I fight the net's confines, but its agonizing sensation against my scales tears into me like a toxin, my body reacting in a range of reflexes and fears. A cord attached to the net jerks taut. It pulls me along. The netting and I break the surface, and Wolf's spotted pale hands yank me onto a black deck.

I gasp in air but it feels like water, like fire, like fear, polluting me from the inside out. The slight brush of Wolf's skin when he lets me go hurts worse than a hundred bruises. My lungs clench, and I writhe on reflex alone. I concentrate on the heartbeat of my ignit, trying to block out all else. Wolf vanishes, my world caught somewhere between darkness and pain. He reappears with a knife.

With his free hand, he signs the continuation of a conversation. Not a conversation. A death sentence. "—get rid of this one."

Lily must concede, because through my scale-shattering haze, he grabs hold of my neck. His fingers dig, shoving up my chin, revealing the weakest scales where my jaw meets my ear. The blade comes down. I jerk, and he repositions, one foot on my chest. He rolls his eyes from something Lily speaks, and this time I can't move, I can't breathe, I can't—

Rubem leaps onto the boat at my side, his footsteps eerily soft. He knocks Wolf out of the way with a quick jab from his elbow, stealing the knife in the same motion. I barely have time to flinch before he cuts the top of the net down the middle. More still entangles half my hips and wraps around one of my wrists like a cuff. I roll frantically away from it, straight into his fishnetted hands.

He traps me against the deck, his leg across my waist, and his knee putting pressure on my shoulder, like he's pinning down his massive crocodilian. "None of that, now," he signs, the fishnet distorting his words into a fever dream.

I snap my tail around, but the crocodilian tackles it, keeping it in the water despite my frantic wiggling. I cling to the ignit on my necklace with my free hand, as though my world will fall apart if I let go. It might. Half of me believes it already has.

Over the side of the boat, the crocodilian bares its jaws. The wound it left on me last night aches in response, but Rubem signs a few simple words, "Stay, girl," and then, "Close mouth."

His pet obeys.

I stare at his hands, and my body protests the sight, rolling my eyes up to the overhanging mangrove branches above him, until his fishnet blurs with his skin.

Lily appears like a bullet. "What the fuck?"

His reply comes swift and smooth. "The boiuna is mine—that was the deal. Everything from the Murk—"

"A deal you keep expanding upon without ever fulfilling your end of the bargain," Lily snaps, jabbing a finger toward Rubem on the *your* like she can spear her long nails straight through his chest. "You refused us an ancient because you claimed this hoard was the *easier* target, yet I'm still stuck here in your despicable jungle because you can't even hold on to the damn girl who's meant to bring us to it."

An ancient. The motion of the sign—both thumbs linked, fingers like claws, pounding like a heartbeat—sends skitters along my scales. How the fuck do Lily and Rubem know what those are?

Rubem shoots to his feet, the beads in his braids tingling together. "She's not gone far! I can get her back. We can still make this work." His motions come out sharp and small and deadly. "We *will* make this work. And you'll give me the damn boiuna. In one piece, I should add."

I wiggle, so slow and slight the two fools arguing above me don't notice. The netting falls away, little by little, but each brush of it makes my skin scream and my bones cry. I cling to the ignit in my necklace all the harder, to its gentle soothing pulse, and try to keep from writhing out of my own scales.

Lily's jaw pulses. "Fine. Just keep it out of the way. For whatever goddamned reason it seems to be helping the girl." She wheels around. I barely make out her final signs. "There's a bigger opening to that foul swamp a little ways south. Take the snake. We'll meet you there."

Motion from the trees draws my attention. Thais drops from a branch, landing her heels straight into the back of Rubem's head. He grunts and collapses over the side of the fisher boat, into the water. His crocodilian shifts. I prepare to dodge its jaws, but it only shoots to Rubem's rescue. From the other end of the boat, both Wolf and Lily charge Thais and me.

"Come on!" Thais clutches my arm. She dives with me into the river, toward our idle fan boat drifting just within the Murk.

I glance behind us as we flee, expecting shots or nets or crocodilian teeth. Glares greet me, hands on guns paired with eyes tracking the inches of space between Thais's body and mine, likely calculating their chances of hitting me and not her. They break for wheels and engines in a lagging attempt to chase us down, leaving only Lily staring. As we scramble over the rock, she takes aim.

Thais slumps.

My chest feels pierced from the wrong side. I search for the smell of blood and a cloud of red in the water, but instead Thais curls around her stomach, her face twisted and sickly. Her empty healing necklace presses against the inside of her wet shirt. My lungs release. It's just another poison spasm.

I dip into the water to scoop her up, and a bullet whizzes past my head. It rattles my skull, throwing the world into a disarray. But I plow forward, swimming Thais to the boat. She flails with her hands, but she's too weak to fight, too weak to do anything more than lean over the railing and heave the rest of her breakfast into the river while I restart the fan. The boat zips forward. We leave our pursuers behind, Lily as red as Rubem's scarlet accents, and the cartel leader climbing, dripping, back onto his boat.

As we drive deeper into the Murk, Thais curls up beside the middle seat, lunging for the side every few minutes. Her hair frizzes into messy waves in the muggy air. But her haunting eyes slowly go from a fogged-over grey to their eerie ignit glow, dancing across our surroundings.

The sun rarely breaks the canopy, its touch a golden spotlight between endless dim green. Birds call from all sides. The branches liven with snakes so large they could be trees themselves and sleeping monkeys patterned in poisonous colors, their blind eyes and oversized teeth a terror at night. A spider as large as my face works through a web that spans the entire river. I bat it away with a branch when the top of our fan tears through its silken creation.

The water is no less populated and no less dangerous. I hold in my scent name, turning the boat onto a new rivulet every time I smell a boiuna in the distance. Despite my best efforts, we still sneak up on a youngling, less than half my length, looped over a root and yawning, their tiny baby fangs as sharp as they are cute. They stare at our boat. When they spot me, the smell of their fear turns to confusion.

"Fuck off!" I sign.

They poke their tongue out but flop to the water, swimming deeper into the roots. A branch overhead vibrates from the steps of something too large and agile to be a mere monkey. Through the leaves, I glimpse feathers and leather shoes.

I coil tighter around the driver's seat and poke Thais with my tail. "There's someone here."

"Another boiuna?"

"Not unless we've evolved *legs* since I left." I shift my eyes back to the trees, searching in vain for the person. By the time the boat's fan pitters to a stop, I give up looking.

I check on the ignit. "It should need about fifteen minutes to recharge. The grains are good, close together, and the deep color contrasts imply hefty ignetic strains. Rubem's cartel has good stock."

"How do you know this stuff?"

With a shrug, I lie out along the deck, my tail still twisted up in the driver's seat. I tug my ignit out of my necklace to rub it before I sign, "I like rocks."

The gentle lap of the peaceful Murk water vibrates against the side of the boat, small animals romping through the trees around us. Thais stares at me, her expression a crinkled mess. Then her chest shudders violently.

I bolt upright, half-annoyed and—well, fully annoyed, and not the least bit worried that the poison in her veins might be giving her some kind of spasm again. "It's true. I just like rocks, okay."

"No—I—" She keeps quaking, and it finally hits me that the vibration might be *laughter*. "I think it's funny. You say you just like rocks while wearing a rock necklace, playing with a rock, traveling through the Murk to get more rocks. Your entire life revolves around rocks. Of course you would know so much about ignits."

"Fuck off, boat shit," I grumble. "I can *love* rocks if I want to."

"I think it's nice, Cacao." She brushes her wiry curls back, tucking her feet beneath her legs. "You have something that means a lot to you. Most people go their entire lives and never find a passion like that." Her hands lower, and she raps out a rhythm against the center seating block. She repeats it three times before her words finally sink in.

"You're the only one who feels that way."

Thais pokes me in the shoulder. "Hey now, I never said I approved of your actions. It's nice—good—that you love something. It's not nice that your love hurts other people."

I roll my eyes. "That's called greed."

Her cheeks puff out and she shakes her head. "Fungus

brain."

"Yeah, yeah," I grumble. "Hey, did your mom also love rocks?" It stirs my chest to think that there was someone in the world who would have listened to me ramble about how rocks have cycles just like water and replied with a detailed analysis on the formation of geodes.

"Only the ignits," Thais replies. "She didn't care for rocks, just hoarding something powerful and beautiful all to herself, and she only learned as much about them as she needed to make that happen."

My imagined connection crumbles. Better luck never.

Thais slaps the wood twice and pops onto the seat. "So, you think we're safe here? From Rubem, I mean. He might enter the Murk after us."

I lean back, staring at the canopy. "He can't be *that* crazy. But he does seem to have some weird deal with the fishers, and they're definitely crazy enough." My thoughts wander from there. "I'll finally move out of his territory once you give me your hoard. I won't have him and the fishers breathing down my neck for the rest of my life." The far edge of the Murk butts against another river system under the control of a lesser cartel who goes by some kind of fruit symbol. A banana or a plantain. I could try there.

Thais's eyes pierce into me with such intensity that I can barely keep my gaze on her hands because even the peripheral haunt of her irises hurts. "You never plan on living in the Murk again, do you?" she asks, then returns to tapping the wood on either side of her.

"Are *you* ever planning to stop that incessant drumming?" I scowl.

"Nope." Her shoulders roll like a slithering snake, and she gives three more raps. "I want to create music endlessly, for all my days."

It makes a stupid amount of sense. "That's what you meant, about being a dancer. You're one of those damn street rumblers."

"Street what?" She cocks an eyebrow at me.

"Street rumblers," I repeat. "You play your instruments in the streets and create so many vibrations the wood rumbles. It's annoying."

"I do street performances, yes, but also inns and festivals and other things. I was part of a group for a few months, but they didn't like my objection to the cartels' tyranny, so I left." She barely looks at me.

My hands move before I can think to stop them. "They must have turned your departure into a brand-new holiday."

Thais stiffens, but she replies by popping open a compartment in the center seating area. As she digs through it, her hips wiggle to the beat that still echoes through my head. Curiosity gets the better of me. I sit up.

The compartment holds a few light blankets, spare parts, a rope, and a container of dried meat. Thais's fingers graze the edge of the food, and her stomach gurgles. With her human eating habits and her last two half-digested meals populating the environment, she must be dying for nourishment, but her lips bunch and she lets the dried meat go. She moves to the blankets, pulling them out, still folded, and setting them to the side. A hand drum lies beneath.

Thais's ignit eyes gleam as she grabs it. She sets it between her legs and raps her hands against its taut top. A rumble starts up in her chest and rises into her throat. Her lips move. She sways rhythmically. Her eyes close, long lashes resting against her light brown skin. A spiral of her dark hair slips along her graceful jawline. Her rain-cleaned scent sparks with happiness.

I rub my necklace in time to her vibrations, moving my shoulders to the beat.

Thais's snaps her eyes open, haunting, terrible, beautiful. She blinks. "You can dance?"

I realize how long I've been staring. A rush of heat sweeps over me, and I glare at the deck instead. I never disliked dancing until this moment, but suddenly my annoyance burns like a torch in my gut. "No. Dancing is for fools."

Thais's soft smell bursts with something extravagant, and she leans toward me. Her hands find my shoulders and hips, the tips of her fingers nudging my body to a phantom beat as they move. The soft motion comes with the needling pressure that arches through my bones, her touch too light. I jerk away from her. My tail hits the railing, and my torso falls over the edge.

Water floods up my nostril slits. I yank myself back onto the deck, sputtering and dripping. With a shake of my torso, I scoot a little farther away from Thais. A puddle forms beneath me.

Her scent vanishes, and her new beat overflows with ungainliness. "I'm sorry, I didn't mean to—do you not like to be touched?"

"With all the pulling me around you've been doing, if I couldn't stand physical contact as a whole, I would've said something already, boat shit." The truth sticks to my chest, though, terrifying and horrible. I don't like that *particular* touch. I don't like the shiver it shoves along my ribs or the stupid way I suddenly crave her palms pressed there firmly instead, my side raw and empty where her skin only brushed, as though she ripped off the scales as she removed her hands. I twist away.

My nose floods, a mess of scents running over me like a shudder. I flick my tongue out. Approaching ridges form in the water as a pair of tails oscillate back and forth below the surface, and two unique boiuna scent names separate themselves.

SEVEN

———— ⌁ ————

PUTTING THE PAST IN THE FUTURE

Maybe the curse was actually me.
Or maybe it was both of us.
Either way, this sucks.

I GO STILL, TRYING not to breathe, not to exist. The larger boiuna draws her torso out of the water, revealing herself to be just a bit smaller than I—not small enough to eat. In the moment I meet her irises, they tighten, her name dark and pungent, like the stink of rot. A loop of fungi drapes over her shoulders. The boiuna at her side looks similar enough to be her kin, splashes of deep red blossoming over their dark scales, metallic and bright, sanguine.

My gaze jumps to the engine. The light of its ignit shines through the open front. Grabbing Thais's arm, I nudge her toward it. She nods and slips slowly from my grip.

"We know you, Bittersweet," Rot signs, her distaste flooding my nose.

"Funny, because I've never met either of you," I reply, baring my teeth. "I would remember people who stink this damn badly."

Sanguine bobs in the water. "We were at your trial." Their words come with a reflection of my scent name, leaving no doubt they speak of my hearing.

"So were a lot of people. Get the fuck on with it." My fingers creep toward the machete as soon as I stop signing.

"You're not supposed to be here," they accuse.

I shrug, pulling my lips back farther. "Where might here be?" But that question just triggers my mind to reply, bouncing the thought like a million black-nosed monkeys: *here is home.*

Sanguine only flicks their tongue, swimming around Rot's back, their tail twisting into the tree roots.

But Rot stares me down as though I'm a piece of fresh capybara meat instead of an equal-sized predator. "I'm not the sort to care about your little stunts, but you're floating by our home with a boat human and one of their disruptive machines, and I won't go against the elders." She flings the words with sharp motions and a sharper scent. "Leave the Murk, or they'll come for you."

A chill settles over me despite the muggy afternoon air. This is real. *Someone here will try to kill me.*

Not Rot or Sanguine, but the elders for certain, if not a band of hunters or a mob. My fingers flick to the ignit Thais pressed into my hand last night. "Then I die." I sign the commitment, small, one-handed. Next week, either I'll lie on a hoard of ignits or the Murk fish will swim circles through my skull.

The boat's fan whirls to life, and we shoot forward, clunking over Rot's tail as we fly along the rivulet, Thais steering us through the tight bends between the trees. We soon pass out of Rot's range, the boat too fast for a boiuna her size to keep up. But the movement takes us deeper into the Murk, closer to the elders and all the other terrible dangers this place holds.

Thais tries to catch my attention with her hands. I ignore her in favor of our surroundings, watching for other boiuna. Thais's distraction allowed Rot and Sanguine to sneak up. If she would just shut up, maybe we can make it through this place in one piece. But Thais being wordless or still—the rains forbid, both at once—might never happen, even in death.

Her stare nearly bores a hole in the back of my head, and when the fan cuts out again, she scrambles across the boat, plopping onto the railing so near that I can't ignore her flinging signs. "What *was* that, you insolent self-loathing bug?" She jabs her finger at me accusingly. "Explain!"

With her bastardized boat language and utter inability to smell, she must have missed pieces of the conversation. I shrug. "They want me gone."

"From their territory?" Somehow, Thais leans closer.

I scoot away. "Boiuna don't have territories, we aren't sirens or some muck. We have individual central dwellings, and from there we go wherever we like."

"Then from what—the Murk? They want you gone from the Murk?" Her motions rage like a storm. "That's why you left it? They kicked you out?"

"Hard to kick when you have no legs."

She reeks of something so frustrated and determined that I concede.

"Banishment." I touch my ignit, sliding my thumb smoothly though the worn grooves, before adding, "The elders banished me for the crime of being an absolute pile of garbage."

Thais stares at me. "What did you do, Cacao?"

"Fucked some muck up, mostly." Rattling from above draws my gaze, but I see nothing through the leaves. "I'm a greedy insolent bottom dweller, like you're so very fond of proclaiming. Honestly, I would've thought you'd figured it out already."

The smell of Thais's anger fades. She slumps onto the deck, rapping her nails in quick succession. "What will they do if they catch you here?"

"I don't know." The lie slips easily through my fingers. I don't *know* if they'll manage to kill me. I *might* escape dramatically in the middle of my trial.

"They banished you already," Thais says, as though I need a reminder. "You boiuna don't happen to have some funky root prisons somewhere? Are your elders known for granting second chances?"

"Banishment was my second chance. Or fifth, if you count the lesser council meetings."

"No more chances, then," Thais concludes. She blows air through her lips. Her haunting eyes go as cloudy as the midnight mist. "What's your plan to avoid them? How can I help?"

I grin, but my fingers curl tightly around my ignit, refusing to let go when I sign a one-handed, "Plan? I don't know that word."

"It's like a strategy you create to—" Her gaze narrows, and she whacks me in the shoulder with one of the folded blankets. "Cacao, you treacherous child of a tapir! You haven't even made a *plan*?"

"I made a plan! The plan is to go through the Murk without dying, get a ton of lovely ignits, and be happy forever." The last part sits in my heart like a weight.

When Thais draws a breath, her chest vibrates once, and she presses her hands to both sides of her snobby nose, watching me. "Well, then that's where I'm going to get you!" She pulls her thumbs across her fingertips, making a sharp vibration with them. "Are there routes we can take that are less likely to run us into these elders? What if we travel at night instead? Boiuna have those scent names, right? If we load our boat with things that smell strongly—"

"If you expect me to burn out my nose for this, I'd rather die first," I grumble.

"—then we could—"

But the purr of a downriver boat fan flares along my head ridges, and I grab her hands. "Boats coming!" I sign, scrambling toward our silent engine. The red ignit holds a glow so weak I can only see it when I cup my hands around its casing. We're dead in the water.

Thais wheels around and yanks a long simple pushing rod off its railing hooks. The full wooden pole towers over her head, but she spins it and shoves the edge against the nearest root. Her muscles bulge, and the boat drifts ever so slowly away from the root.

"Good try, weakling. Now do that another three thousand times in the next thirty seconds."

"Why don't you get off your scaly haunches and help me?"

Even with my strength, we're nowhere near the next break in the rivulets, and the boat—two boats now—approach fast, a blur of them visible through the distant trees. "We fight and hope we can kill them all?"

"Cacao!"

"Right, fine, those are bad odds anyway." I scowl. "If our ignit can't carry us anywhere, then we steal theirs." Stealing ignits is the only thing I'm useful for anyway. Though useful might not be the right term, considering how many times I've been caught.

"Well, go on, then!" Thais picks up my tail and dumps it into the river.

But this time I anticipate her jostling, and I bunch up my muscles around my hips to keep from sliding after it. "What about you?" The question bubbles up from some strange place in my chest, filling the space of the approaching boats, lingering there like a palpable danger.

"I'm fine, you silly fool."

"Hey, hey, don't be rude. Soft insults are bad for my health!" I roll over the edge of the boat and slip beneath the surface before she can form a snappy reply.

The water wraps around me, dense with flecks of greens and greys. The brown silt coating the bottom lifts in swirling clouds as a catfish meanders along it, smaller fish darting out of its way. The lairs beneath the tree roots create their own little worlds. Pumping fins and paws and flippers tickle my head ridges while ripples churn the world above.

I sink until I blend with the shadows, letting the haunting rhythms of the Murk fill me up, soothing my soul. This is home. This *was* home.

The first boat nears, a clear symbol of the cartel painted on its side, but when the second stalks around the bend after it, my gut twists. This one's dark wood projects a daunting shadow. A blaze of orange hair rides above it. My skin crawls at the thought of the fisher's nets, and I sink a little deeper into the water, focusing on the gentle thrum of my ignit where it slides like a heartbeat along my collarbone.

As the cartel boat nears our stolen one, it slows. Down the river, the fisher boat mimics it, slipping along the far edge of the trees like they anticipate a trap. All the better for me.

Shimmers of silver catch deep within the translucent grey rock as I draw it off my necklace. I swim beneath the cartel's stopped boat and come up on the side farthest from the fishers. The humans' feet vibrate the wood toward the front, so I slip around the back, peeking over the railing. Both the driver and the crewmate hover as near to Thais's boat as they can, weapons drawn. She must have ducked behind the center seats, because I don't see her anymore.

I sneak over the railing and pop open the engine. Their ignit glows at half power, about the same size as the one on our boat and just as gloriously beautiful. My fingers twitch to grab it, but the still-active rock radiates the kind of heat even my scales would be unhappy with, and I have no time to figure out which of the boat's switches will deactivate it with a shock of electricity. Instead, I press my clingstone to its edge. The rocks stick together, and when I draw the clingstone back, the activated ignit comes with it.

Relief rushes through me, but the cartel humans smell none of the scent that comes with it, just as ignorant to my existence as before. Grinning, I slide my torso back toward the water. Before I hit the railing, my ridges spike with the vibration of the fisher's spear gun. I roll to the side. The tip of the projectile scratches a long burning scrape over my bicep. My grip on the clingstone slips. I grab for the pair of rocks, my mistake registering a moment too late. My fingers brush the activated ignit. Its heat flares against my scales like a well-warmed pan, so hot I instinctively launch it away.

It flies at the face of one of the cartel humans. Their delicate flesh sizzles. They shriek and stumble over the middle seating, scrambling for a canteen while the ignit rolls along the wood, leaving an unhappy tingle of brown in its wake.

The other human turns toward me, machete raised. I lurch at them, my teeth bared. Somewhere in my spinning mind I think up excuses to shout at Thais: *Mostly dead isn't actually murder* and *If I eat the corpse, it doesn't count.* But as I lunge past the center seating, the distracted human steps into the path of a fisher's next spear shot. It blooms through their stomach, blood spilling from the wound, then slipping from the corner of their mouth. I jerk away.

Their companion scrambles to their feet, lifting their pistol. The tip of a pole hits them in the back of the head. They sway, and another smack knocks them into the river. Behind them, Thais leans over the railing of our boat, holding the pushing rod.

The fisher vessel speeds toward us. With one hand, I attempt to rub my panic into the ignit on my necklace while I snatch my clingstone off the deck with the other. The cartel's active ignit comes with it. I fling myself into our boat, nearly taking out Thais as I do. Shoving past her, I reach the engine. I press the new ignit to the old one, ripping free a small green sharestone from my necklace and tapping it between them. The red glow moves from one ignit to the other with a flash.

I slam the engine's start knob, and Thais grabs the driver's lever. We shoot forward. The fishers knock into us from behind, and Thais bounces in her seat. I coil my tail around her, holding her in place, and latch onto her shoulders.

Wolf props his spear gun up for another launch, the tip bloody with the dead human's insides, his aim low enough that it would have to go through the bulk of my muscles before having a chance of hitting Thais. As he pulls the trigger, I shove Thais's steering arm, jerking the boat to the left. The spear sails harmlessly by.

Thais elbows me in the side, fighting to poke her head over my back. She yanks one hand out from under mine to sign half a mangled, "Do you want to drive or should I?"

Insults spring to mind, but a jump in the boat knocks them out of me, and me off of Thais. I unfurl part of my tail, grabbing the center seating instead. The speed blurs my senses. I judge our path based on my knowledge of the trees and my fear of our pursuers, pointing out directions in quick succession.

The fishers slip just out of sight as the light dims. The thickening canopy looms far overhead, blocking out the evening rays. Mist pools in nooks and wells like a living beast, rising to consume the Murk and—if the weather is right—the rivers beyond it.

The branches rustle above. Leaves rain in a little storm of green. A giant black feather falls with them.

My heart picks up speed. "Faster!"

Thais waves one hand in a motion I can only interpret as distressed ire, but she wiggles the lever. Somehow, she presses it down a little farther. The front of the boat lifts clean out of the water, nearly blocking the branches that churn along the side of our curving rivulet—churn from the motion of something huge and sleek. My muscles scream *run*.

I crash into Thais, slamming the lever to one side and diving us into a mist-cloaked offshoot that veers away from the shifting brush. The fog overtakes us, turning the world into a ghost, and us to mere memories. I cut the fan.

"If we don't move, it won't find us."

"What won't—"

I clamp my hands over Thais's and slow my breath until my soft exhales no longer stir the thick haze of white. Thais mirrors me. Our boat slides to a glide, then a stop. Stillness descends.

The vibration of a giant fan still prickles my ridges, so much like an after-feeling that I can't place it as real until its form blurs through the white wall. My hands freeze around our steering lever. I wrap my tail tightly around Thais as the oncoming fisher boat collides with us.

EIGHT

———⌇———

THE HUNTERS BECOME THE HUNTERS
BECOME THE HUNTED

Different isn't bad.

But sometimes bad is bad, and the different is irrelevant.

Basically, boat humans are dumb.

LILY AND WOLF'S BOAT crashes into us, and the wood of both vessels crunches inward. The sudden impact flings Thais and me headfirst onto the fishers' deck. I cling to her. We roll across the dark wood of their boat, part of my tail slamming into Wolf.

There comes an instant that could almost be stillness, if stillness were a type of existence instead of a lack of motion. Our crushed boat, far more decimated than the fishers', slips beneath the surface while the fishers' engine putters, then dies entirely, the vessel gently tipping toward a river grave as water spills into the gash we made in its front. Through it all, Wolf and Lily stare at me, so stiff they could be made of bark and wood. Through the fog to our right, branches rustle.

"Stay," I sign, so sluggishly it barely counts as a word anymore.

But the fishers don't know the Murk like I do, and, probably, they don't care. Wolf scrambles toward his spear launcher.

A feline blur of green and black shoots through the mist, feathers and fur ruffling, giant paws extended and gleaming white teeth bared. It snatches Wolf's shoulder in its jaws and carries him into the grey. The vibrations his lungs produce make my stomach sick.

The water spilling into the cracked end of the boat splashes over my tail and onto Lily's boots. She sways from one foot to the other, twitching like she can't decide whether to launch for Thais or rescue her brother. With his cries still rattling the air, this doesn't seem quite the time to bring up how Thais did in fact save him barely a day ago and the fishers should very much repay us in turn, please and thanks.

It matters little, because as her brother's vibrations fade, her focus directs firmly onto Thais and me. She steps toward us.

I bare my teeth. "So, coming south just for the murder and butchery wasn't enough for you. You're trading in fancy rocks now too?" As I sign, I slide in front of Thais and nudge her toward the side of the boat, hoping she has the sense to swim for the nearest roots.

Lily's lips turn up, but the scent she gives off holds only bitterness. "You barbarians, you could change so much of the world with these ignits—you could make things better, lift up your heroes, decimate your villains—but here you poke them into simple machines and gamble them around without a thought."

"So, you're going to take them, then, is that it?" I snap. The thought sears into me, dark in a way that settles behind my eyes and turns the world red. After all the boat people have stolen from the Murk, here comes this northerner storming in to demand the rest. But the rest is *mine*.

"You can't have them!" Thais adds, as blunt and obvious as always.

Lily's teeth almost glow in the dimness. "Don't worry. I'll put them to better use in the north." A dagger flashes in her hand.

She swipes for me. I dodge, whipping my tail around her legs and leaning away from her blade. Her dagger slices the air where my heart had been. I tighten my coils, working them up her waist. But as I prepare to dive with her into the water and cut the blood from her brain, the feline form leaps back through the mist—a dreaded penajuar, giant and black, three times as large as a jaguar, its feathered mane flaring and its dagger-long claws extended.

I drop Lily as it swats her with its great black paws. She flies into the mist, splashing to the river between the roots. The penajuar vaults after her.

Thais wavers at the edge of the fisher boat, the water up to her knees as the vessel sinks. "You're a scary predator, right?" Her hands fly through the signs, blurring them together. "That cat won't eat *us*."

"The elder boiuna are terrifying, but I'm so tiny even *humans* hunt me. I can't fight a penajuar on my *own*!"

She hits my shoulder. "You're not on your own, you have me, you coward's piece of—"

I catch the rustle of the trees just before the penajuar pounces. Grabbing Thais around the waist, I yank her into the river. Her chest vibrates as she shouts or screams, likely some kind of insult. I return it with a one-handed *fuck you* and shove her toward the nearest roots.

The penajuar hits the sinking black boat, and a rush of water floods in under the monster's weight. Feathered mane flaring, it scrambles in surprise, knocking into the engine. Its sleek dark fur turns it into a shadow in the thickening mists. Beyond it, I sense no frantic boat-human motions, only a couple small manatee-like creatures escaping the area with great flipper paddles. The fishers must both be dead.

Thais climbs up between two thick roots, clutching a branch like a sword. I try to join her, but my tail catches around a bundle of netting from the fishers' half-sunk boat. My insides crinkle and I clutch my ignit, wriggling. The penajuar's ears swivel toward me. It boosts itself off the boat's engine and lands on the roots in front of Thais. Its tail flicks as it prowls, haunches tightening.

A barrage of exclamations fight to jerk my hands around, *no* mixing with *stupid boat human* and *oh, muck*, my heart churning them into one panicked scent that burns through my lungs.

Thais prepares her branch, lifting it to swing. A leaf falls on her head. From the canopy drops a human, their leather shoes making no vibration when they land in a crouch in front of Thais. Slips of metal-embroidered leather cover their left forearm, palm, and first finger. With it, they hold two small activated red ignits. They drop the stones into jars attached to their flaring boiuna-scale shorts. Steam boils out.

A ghastly smell accompanies the vapor. I gag, clutching my necklace. The penajuar's maw wrinkles, and it stumbles, rubbing a paw over its nose. Thais grips her branch tighter. She steps forward, but I grab her ankle, yanking her between the roots. Her chest vibrates.

"Stay down!" I sign.

The human slips off two pairs of curved shell bracelets. They clamp the shells together, stepping toward the penajuar with knees bent, placing the ball of one foot delicately in front of the other. The penajuar's feather-tufted ears snap back. I feel its pain, the sharp vibration of the shells ringing along my head ridges like gunshots.

The penajuar shakes its feathered mane, throat rumbling. But it refuses to back down. The human slides their shells seamlessly back around their wrist, trading it for a crossbow of dark polished mangrove wood from their back holster. They fire a bolt fitted with green and brown feathers. The projectile sinks deep into the penajuar's chest. Dark blood drips from the wound, and the beast roars.

It won't be enough. The knowledge touches me like the kiss of an elder. No one our size can take down a penajuar alone.

I scramble my senses together and lurch back into the water. The sunken cartel boat Thais and I stole rests peacefully against the riverbed, a curious fish already exploring its crannies. I swim straight for the engine. Carefully, I press my clingstone to the two quarter-charged ignits resting in its center. Both of them come out when I pull. They thud a steady beat into the water, heating the layer just around them so near to boiling that I can barely hold on to them as I burst back to the surface.

The change in our situation hits me instantly, sharp with the smell of fear and fury and the shakings of a proper fight. Thais lies beneath the penajuar, pinned to a hollow between the mangrove trunk and its knitted roots. Only the branch shoved in its mouth stops it from tearing her open. Bolts graze it from the canopy, but it twists too quickly from side to side, forcing the human hunter to make precarious shots to avoid hitting Thais by accident.

A tremble runs through my hands. I grab the penajuar's tail feathers, pinning them between a root and a piece of driftwood. As it bucks its hips, I jab the active ignits into its fur. The stones sizzle it a nasty welt. It shrieks, its eyes rolling. The human leaps from the branches, their crossbow already loaded, and lands gracefully on the penajuar's shoulders. They fire three bolts into the back of its head before vaulting off.

The active ignits fly from my hand as the beast teeters, claws scraping wood. Then it collapses. Its back heaves in a final great breath, and the penajuar goes still, a mound of cooling flesh and dark fur and giant green feathers.

The human fidgets beside it, their own chest rising and falling heavily. They stand at least a head taller than Thais, their torso slender and their bare arms and legs thick with undefined muscles. Even in the twilight, their brown skin gleams of red undertones. Black makeup elongates their slim curved eyes, every line of their face contrasting the hard angles of the boat humans with fluid soft shapes. A boiuna-scale vest clings to their chest, buried beneath ropes of orange and green beads, strings of feathers, and strands of their dark straight hair.

Their gaze drops to the dead penajuar. They crouch, and their hands fall through a death proclamation. "We are all one in the mist. Though your death was not foretold, it will not be in vain. You bless us with your life. May your kin be blessed in turn."

The penajuar's face seems to bob in response as Thais shoves it to the side and climbs out from under. She shakes. Her fingers ball into fists.

The sight of her breaks something within me, like a reed pulled too far. "You damn piece of—of *muck*! What the fuck did you do to make it attack you?" My cruder signs blend with the others, creating a language all its own.

"I hit it! I had to do something, Cacao," Thais snaps back, her lower lip trembling.

"You weren't supposed to engage!"

"Why not? You vanished, and the strange person was fighting like—like some crazy heroic jungle warrior. I had to help."

"Silt streams, Thais, you can't help in things like this. You're not a Murkling. That's why I'm here, isn't it? Because you might be a little river-born human who thinks they're so brave and strong out there in the soft graces of the rivers, but there's real danger here! The Murk will eat you alive, boat shit." The words slip from some constricted dark center of my heart. "Don't fuck up like that again." I bare a hint of my teeth. "If you die, I don't get my ignits."

That's all this is about. That's all I want. Not Thais, not her touch, not her haunting eyes alight like my precious stones. I don't not want Thais to die because I don't *not* dislike her. I run those ideals in circles until whatever else I feel sinks under a layer of nonsense.

All the while, Thais's face shifts through a series of tight wet expressions. She shoves her shoulders back, but they tense again as she fires a few sharp signs, "I just wanted to help."

She swivels toward the Murkling human, who examines

the dead penajuar, their back to us. Thais signs a hello, her mouth moving in tandem. They ignore her. She steps toward them, repeating the greeting. The human doesn't look up until she enters their periphery. Their chest vibrates, and they spring a few steps back, bobbing uncomfortably. Their gaze meets mine. We both look away like the visual touch is a poison.

"I'm the Bittersweet Earth, male, he." The signs tingle along my fingers, missing something. I point to Thais. "She—the One Who Drums, undecided—calls me Cacao."

They give a little nod. "I am the Way the, um, the Mist Falls in the Morning, all, and, uh, they." Their hands stumble between certain words, like a beat of hesitation.

Thais stares at their signs with a tight brow. "What did that mean?"

"They're . . ." I pause, because the boat human's dialect has no word for the ways the fog moves. Finally, I just sign the name again, drawing my fingers smoothly in an expanding circle. "Xera—that's what they're called. They're both boy and girl."

"Is there something wrong with them? Are Murk humans like boiuna, without any hearing?"

I shrug. "There's nothing *wrong* with them. They're probably just deaf. It's common here."

Xera nods. "Yes, that's—that's me. Deaf." They pause only a moment. "I must tell my councilors to send collectors for this penajuar. Someone else will, um, come help you." Their light feet spring them along the roots in the direction of the deepening swamp.

Panic grips me. "Wait, wait!" I wave my arms, tearing in front of them. "You're from the Bright Bark village, right?"

They nod.

"Don't tell them about us." I realize how uncomforting that sounds once I finish signing it.

The corners of Xera's curved eyes narrow. "Why?"

Because you'll tell a single councilor, who will tell the other councils, and they will tell the elders, and the elders will come rip every scale off my body and make it into a very nice pair of shorts for some other Murkling to wear. I choose a different version of the truth. "My first forebearer is an elder. We aren't on the best of terms right now."

"I understand." Their gaze bounces between me and Thais. "But you are odd, from the, uh, river. You do need help."

"No. We're *fine*," Thais cuts in.

I sign larger to block her out. "We're trying to get to the coast, but the boat we stole from the river cartel sank." Along with the fisher boat and probably those ignits with the clingstone the damn penajuar shoved from my grip, because I can't see or feel them anymore. "If you have lodging and food for this one," I point to Thais, "that would help. But we don't want to cause any problems." *Or be pointed out or noticed by anyone, at all.* I've somehow stayed in the respectable lanes of proper conversation so far, though, so I hold the last bit in. I can't break down yet.

The stink of Xera's vapor has faded enough that I can finally make out their scent name, their indecision riding on a smell like cracked nuts and wet bark. "Then, you come with me," they sign finally, slow and a little twitchy. With that, they turn, continuing along the roots, their footsteps so light I sense no vibrations.

Thais grabs my arm. "You don't trust this Xera, do you? They seem twitchy. What if it's a trap?"

I shrug. "They're a flighty person."

If they suspect my crimes, running away now will just confirm things. Besides, if Thais continues without food, she might not recover from her next poison spasm. And a village means boats. Boats we can steal.

"Come on, we're losing them," I add, sliding from one root to the next.

Thais's throat vibrates, but she follows. Her bare toes point as she jumps over the gaps, her arms swinging out like a bird taking flight. "I don't like this," she signs. "How can that flinching coward be the same warrior who took down the penajuar? It doesn't make sense."

"Not everyone who's brave is loud about it," I reply, giving an eye roll for good measure. "Being able to shut up is a virtue. You should try it sometime, boat shit."

A whiff of her annoyance catches in my nose slits when she shoves past me. She bounces along the roots as though pounding out an angry beat, but her feet slip in the darkening landscape. After plunging into the river one too many times, she finally sticks to my side, her arm wrapped around my elbow like she might squeeze the blood from it.

"What's this thing with the council?"

"Doesn't matter. You won't meet them."

Thais stupidly takes my reply as a cue to keep talking. "They're like the boiuna elders, aren't they? But they work with your elders, right? You were worried they'd find out about you? Because one of them is—" she repeats my signs for first forebearer, though hers are sloppy and they look more like *first anger brain*. Not a totally inaccurate statement. "What's that mean?"

I pretend I can't see her hands in the darkness.

She elbows me.

"Hey, fine!" I elbow her back, skipping right over her last question to explain, "Each of the four Murkling species chooses a group of leaders for their skill and wisdom. For humans and hoatzis—"

"Wait, what? I don't know that sign."

"That's because most of you ignorant boat humans think there's just boiuna in the Murk, and maybe some remaining native humans, but there's actually four primary intelligent species here. The hoatzis are two-legged people with feathers on their arms for gliding and bird feet that make prints like backward human footsteps, like the legendary curupira." For their name, I make a motion like a footprint with the back of my hands. "They and the humans have councils: small groups of adults nominated by the village's young people. For the boiuna, our leaders are the oldest and largest among us, called elders. The dolphin-tailed botos are so few they have a single leader known as the intermediary. The leaders guide their own kind and convene regularly to share news and plans. In matters where a decision would affect the other species, they make a cooperative choice."

Thais stares at her hands for a moment, rapping her fingers against my arm. "That sounds a lot better than what the cartels do."

"We're a civilized people." The *we* drops like a rock in my stomach, and I nearly slide off the edge of the root. No *we* anymore. Just me and them.

The thickening mist creeps in, stealing our conversation away. In the darkness, Thais's presence at my side becomes acute. Her grip on my arm sparks a flame beneath my scales, and I pull her up at the slightest stumble. The feel of her compared to Xera strikes me. Somehow, they are both water, but Thais is the pouring of it, both the blinding moment of the first downpour and the still sigh after it ends, while Xera is the fog that swirls around us, their grace the kind that makes them fade, untouchable, barely even there.

We nearly lose Xera in the deep mist and shadows, but they return to guide us every time I wonder at our course. Soon, the roots grow large enough that Thais no longer slips. A distant light emerges, so dim I think I might be imagining it until Xera reappears, their hands visible once more.

"I have to check something." They turn, then turn back. "Wait here." They scamper into the fog, leaving Thais to stare at me.

"They say they're coming back." But as I sign it, my scales tingle unnervingly, a chill riding down them. With the light ahead, we can't be far from the village. "But it might be better to scout than wait here, where we're easily ambushed."

"Let's go." Thais steps forward.

I pull her against my side to keep her from moving too far ahead. "Follow my lead, boat shit."

"You palm-headed—"

I ignore the rest of her insult, letting my ridges lead us through the trees, sweeping toward the light in a roundabout way. It spreads into two, then five, and finally ten small flames piercing the fog. More dim glows appear farther on and up, their colors a chaotic rainbow of different hues spread among the trees. I slip with Thais behind a trunk and focus on the vibrations around us. Nothing moves.

Slowly, I peek out. The original lights come from a dozen candles in holders made of glistening bone, hanging from branches and embedded into the sides of roots which sweep themselves in an unnatural circle around a large pool of river water. Scattered throughout the trees in neat arrays sit larger bone bowls and troughs and a few skulls. Colorful flowering plants grow out of them, vines weeding through a rib cage, and an orchid blooming out the eye socket of a complete caiman skeleton.

Thais vanishes from my grip. Before I can scold her, she slips around the side of the tree and reaches the edge of the pool. My head ridges spike with the sense of motion from the water. A green boiuna larger and thicker than me shoots out like a bullet, wrapping around Thais's legs, and yanks her under.

NINE

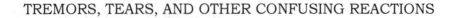

TREMORS, TEARS, AND OTHER CONFUSING REACTIONS

Imagine there's a language everyone else knows,
but to you it sounds like gibberish.
We wear that language on our faces.
And I see only nonsense.

MY HEART SLAMS AGAINST my rib cage. I burst after Thais
as though the force in my chest propels me forward. The
candlelight reflects off the surface of the pool like a glimmering
array of scattered stars, leaving the water dense and dark
beneath. Thais squirms at its center. Her hips and shoulders
twist furiously as the green boiuna coils around her. Panic
floods my senses—Thais's or my own or both—but not quite
enough of it to mask my opponent's scent name, musty as the
ferns growing from one of her bone bowls. Fern's thick muscles
ripple beneath the bone jewelry adorning her arms and tail as
she tightens her hold on Thais, her body longer and heftier
than mine. Maybe long and hefty enough to eat me.

Here goes something.

I dive at them, winding myself around Fern's back and
catching her neck in the crook of my arm. I yank her toward
the surface, squeezing. She loosens her hold of Thais and
turns on me with full force. We spin once, tails thrashing.

Suddenly, she jerks back. I grab Thais and drag her to the nearest root, heaving her over the side between two bone planters. Her shoulders shake as she coughs.

Fern coils into a crook across from us. "I'm so sorry, I thought this was a... no, no I was right." She props herself up until she stares down at us, her irises narrowing to thin slits as she scrutinizes the fabric clinging to Thais's body and the light dusty brown skin it covers. "Why did you save a boat human? What's going on here?"

Thais tries to sign some kind of defense, but she shakes too much.

I coil in front of her. "What's it to you?"

Fern's pinched expression is as unreadable as any Thais has ever given me, but her anger smells sharp and bright despite the dampening mist. "You're that asshole thief the elders banished last year!"

Motherfucking— "No? No. That's not me. I just smell like him."

"Like greed and mud."

At this rate, she'll be best friends with Thais in no time. "There can be two greedy brown boiuna born in the same swamp."

"So, you aren't the one who stole the heartstone from the Leaf Song village?" She plucks a small yellow ignit from a bird skull with a vine curling out its nose socket.

I twitch toward the gently glowing rock and wrap my fingers around my own ignit. Fern's lips pull back, revealing a mouth that could swallow my entire head once dislocated, probably my shoulders too. My mind flashes to the sizes of the elders' jaws. I wonder if they'll let me hold my ignit while they strangle me.

Thais moves behind me, one hand pressing against the curve of my waist. Her skin trembles, wet and cold. She needs food and rest and probably other things I can't give. I signed up to get more ignits, not to take care of a dying human.

"Yeah, fine. It was me! But I had no idea that ignit was

supporting the power system for the whole damn village. It wasn't my fault that family died."

Fern shrugs. "Sure, thief." She tosses the ignit once.

My eyes follow it like an invisible cord ties them to the stone. "I'm just helping this useless human to the coast. Once she's there, I'll be gone for good." With a hoard of ignits. An entire trove of them. So many I don't need that single tiny beautiful stone Fern tosses around carelessly, like she doesn't even want it. So many she would be the one jealous of me. "I have better places to get ignits now."

"The boat human, you mean?" Somehow, Fern put the pieces together, or maybe her shot in the dark got lucky. Her scent turns smug. "Where will your ignits come from if I eat her?"

I bare my teeth. "Silt-breather."

Thais presses her fingers to my back. I twist to see her blue eyes, ghostly and dark in the candlelit mist. She tries to scoot around me, but I block her ever so slightly. I catch a whiff of her annoyance before her scent fades.

Fern's gaze wanders over me. "You might not fit in my stomach, but I could use a skeleton like yours in my collection."

I unhook and rehook my jaw. "I would have every rock you own before you could even—"

Thais slips her hands around my side. "Cacao, you fool," she signs, small and pointed. I miss her touch in a stupidly delirious way, like it's some fucking ignit. "Let me—"

"Shut up, boat shit." I lean in front of her, as if that will somehow make her soothing caress return. "Haven't you done enough already?"

Thais drags in her breath too fast, almost chaotic, but she quiets when Xera whisks through the fog, landing agilely in front of a massive tree, one hand on their crossbow. Their gaze darts around, and they slowly let the weapon go. Nothing moves but the very distant vibrations of planks far above and the occasional dart of a small animal through the mangroves, the stillness so complete that I swear I can almost feel Fern's plants growing.

Xera leans against a trunk. They sign, soft and small, "Are they bothering you, Fern?"

Fern replies with a question of her own. "They're friends of yours?"

Xera looks at us and nods once.

"Then they're not a bother. Not yet, anyway." Fern wiggles her little glowing stone along her knuckles, bouncing it from groove to groove. "But don't let the bittersweet one near your hunting ignits."

Show-off. I rub my thumb along my own ignit, clutching it too tightly in its necklace to attempt any cool tricks.

Fern flicks hers into the air and catches it. "So, why'd Xera pick up an odd pair like you?"

"This helpless lug had to be saved from a penajuar," I sign. Thais shoves against my shoulder. I lean over, blocking her again. "Clearly, she can't manage the Murk on her own."

Thais clambers to her feet. "I'm not helpless!"

"Yeah right, boat shit." I don't know why I say it, the words just come out, because it's the sort of thing I do often say.

"I'm not. And I could get to the coast just fine on my own, thank you very much." Thais's eyes moisten. She juts her chin up and whips around, storming along the roots to sulk. I feel her slip, then right herself before moving deeper into the mist. She can go throw her temper tantrum on the other side of the tree for all I care.

Fern's ignit hits me in the back of the head, shooting pain through my skull.

I flinch. "Hey!"

The stone plops into the pool, and I move to grab it. The tip of Fern's tail twists into a circle, catching it and yanking it away before I can.

"You're going to let that boat human run off to cry? You really are just in this for a payout?" A heavy scent of annoyance backs her signs, paired with hints of confusion.

But my chest catches on one motion in particular. I repeat it with jerky movements. "Cry?"

"Yes, cry. Did you not see their face? It looked like they took your disregard pretty hard. They're crushed. Shattered. Decimated." She pauses, shaking her head and spinning her ignit on the tip of one finger. "Didn't you notice?"

Oh, muck. I don't know if I sign it or not, my numb hands shifting senselessly. Clunking over the first few roots, I dart in the direction of Thais's distant falling, leaving Fern and Xera to stare numbly after.

She doesn't like me—she shouldn't care what I think of her. I hadn't meant to block her out. But maybe I had, in a way, taken over for her because these are—were—my people, my place. I just hadn't realized it would hurt her like that.

But I don't care. I don't like her. I shouldn't have to fix my mistakes.

The word *mistakes* catches me, regret clinging to my chest like a leech. Mist hangs heavy between the roots, cascaded upon by the lights shimmering in the canopy above and the fading pinpricks of candles behind me. As I move, Thais's vibrations vanish, or maybe the humans and hoatzis and the few visiting boiuna in the village far over my head block them out with the thump of feet, the occasional rhythm of music, and the gentle thrum of ignit-powered machines.

The ability to speak and hear with words rarely interests me, but in this moment, I wish I could call Thais's name so loud the entire swamp would quake. The waters below a Murk village should be safe, but the sort of safe that almost got Thais strangled a few minutes ago. The safety that comes from putting the most intelligent predators of the Murk in one place, predators with an ingrained dislike for the boat humans.

"Thais!" I sign her name as wide and sweeping as I can, but the mist barely budges around my shadowy hands. When my root plunges downward, I wrap my tail around it to keep from dropping into the dark water, and rub my ignit. Its gentle heartbeat fills me.

Rhythm.

Thais can't smell me and I can't call to her, but she can still distinguish a beat. I flail around for a fallen branch, finding a long piece of wood wedged between two roots. Breaking it in half, I thud one of the same tunes I've felt from Thais over and over again the last few days. *Buh-bum, buh-bum, buh-bum.*

My wrists hurt after the third chorus, and I slow the motion. Something moves deeper into the swamp beneath the village, the slip of fur through water. This was a stupid idea. Thais has no reason to come to me anyway. If she's not already drowned or partially ingested.

The creature nears, poking its large round head out of the water. Its eyes reflect red. The great otter's scent rips open my memory hoards, churning up everything I want very badly to forget. The Elder Acai, third oldest of the Murk boiuna, brings great otters with them everywhere. This one's terrible white teeth gleam in the dim lights above us, a slip of fabric caught between them. Thais's scarf.

The world seems to drop away beneath me. I twist up the side of the nearest tree, bracing my tail in the deep grooves and nubs of the bark. The branches fan, giving me more holds to wrap around as I weave onward, but I slow to hide my movement from watchful eyes or nearby boiuna. The small lanterns cut halos of every color into the mist, reds and blues, purples and greens, oranges and pinks, turning the wood of the village walkways into paths of rainbow that wind through the canopy. They flow with the natural lines of the trees, rising and falling and cutting together and coming apart. The intricate maze of streets guides from one treehouse to the next, the most massive mangrove trunks wrapped by circular homes, colors gleaming in the veil of mist.

I wind myself above pathways and across roofs, keeping to shadowy corners and deep fog. The council room shines in the night, a solid glow of yellows, oranges, and light blues. Its floor hangs from the canopy by chains made of strong metal links, poles propping it above a stretch of clear water. No walls or roof constrict the round room, only ornate wooden rails and a ceiling of carefully manicured tree branches. I wind through those branches, hiding in the darkness and peeking out over the floor. At its center, between the four pedestals representing the union of the four species, sits a stool I've curled around in other council rooms time and time again.

Thais huddles there now, her otter-bitten scarf hanging off one shoulder. She grips one of the pedestals, but every time she tries to stand, her legs tremble and give out again. I doubt she can heave up anything at this point, but she stinks of bile.

The room's occupants seem to notice too. The dozen council members all keep to the edge of the otherwise bare room, their hands flying. Sharp shouts of agitation accompany the humans' signs, and the humanlike hoatzis fluff their head feathers and ruffle their deep-grey and orange arm plumes. I recognize none by name, but a couple of the older, more wrinkled councilors who hold the higher positions in the hierarchy look familiar.

One of them—a hoatzi with deep-brown skin and feathers going white—leans toward the only boiuna in the room, their red eyes gleaming as they sign, "If your otters found this one, could there be more?"

A muddled scent of deep thought comes from Acai. "Perhaps."

The elder boiuna lies with their massive torso barely peeking into the council chamber. Trees block all but flashes of their green and purple scales, but I know their tail would barely fit in this space if they coiled across the entire floor. I hold in as much of my scent as possible, though with the condensation fans along the edges of the room eliminating the fog, Acai isn't likely to smell anything from the canopy right now.

Other than Acai, the entire village's bone-, feather-, and scale-crowned council seems to have gathered save for one or two members. A few young servers in beads and flowers and soft fur skirts pick up abandoned desserts from what must have been a leisurely festival planning committee prior to Thais's arrival. Off to one side wait a handful of warriors wearing scale and leather chest bands over flaring shorts.

I curl tighter around my branch and rub my ignit. How the fuck do I get her out of this? The council alone would stop me, but with trained warriors and an elder in their midst, I stand no chance.

A whisper in the back of my mind taunts me: *If you were selfless, if you cared about her, you would go down and plead with the council, your life for hers.* But I feel some part of my subconscious already calculating the chance that this village's primary ignit energy sources are guarded when there are so many warriors casually present with the council.

"Where there is one boat human, there are always more!" an older human signs, each motion dramatic as the feathers of their colorful necklace.

"Please, there's just me." Thais's hands shake. The councilors ignore her.

A middle-aged hoatzi ruffles their plumage, and the half-dozen small white strips running near the tops of their otherwise deep-grey feathers glimmer. They sign with clawed fingers, their scaly grey skin wrinkled around their knuckles. "You find threats where there are none. This one is barely more than a child, weaponless and sick."

"A ruse, to distract us from the invading force!" another hoatzi puts in, red eyes bright.

"They may be cruel enough for that, but we've seen no other scouts, witnessed no reason the boat humans would have grown needy for the Murk."

"Please—" Thais tries to interrupt again.

"Those savages need no reason! They took from the native river peoples and the overly friendly botos until both were forced inland to the wilds, and they will take from us as soon as they find a way."

Xera creeps up the walkway, their head bent and a lock of

their straight black hair falling across the center of their face. Barely noticed by the council, they huddle beside the entry arch, picking at a flower like it's their entire reason for being here. But their gaze flickers through the branches of the roof and locks on me. Their body tenses, and they step into the council chamber.

I feel made of sludge. But I have to grab Thais, before Xera exposes me. I have one chance at this.

I prepare to spring on Thais. The cool scales of another boiuna slide around me, Fern's smell hitting me too late. She pins me to the branch with her large body, her teeth bared.

"Wait!" We both sign it at once.

I stare at her, and she motions to Xera.

The flighty human raises their hands over their head, clanking their bracelet shells once. The room turns. Xera shifts between their feet, edging backward. Their eyes dart to Thais, and they swallow.

"There is a, a, a penajuar, in the swamp north, the north swamp. A dead one, I mean, just the, uh, the body. For up-pick, or, um, pickup." Their hands keep moving, but the chatter in the room returns to its original topic, and Xera's trembling takes over their fingers in little bursts and flinches. They repeat a muddled sign for boat three times and finally give up.

I smell Fern's agitation.

"I have to help them," she signs. Unlooping her tail from around me, she slides along the branches, vanishing into the shadows. Her soft vibrations fade, and then the sound of her body plunking onto the pathway floor tingles my head ridges. She bursts into the council chamber.

"Would you drop your damn hands? You're drowning Xera out! This isn't just a penajuar retrieval, they saw boat humans." Her tail swims around Xera as she speaks, coiling protectively. The flighty human seems to melt into Fern, giving a small nod and a signal for Fern to continue. "We were out in the south swamps, and three vessels came up, brimming with boaties, weapons, and ignits. The whole lot of them will be here soon if we don't act first!"

My suspicion of Fern vanishes as she continues to paint a picture of a dangerous invading force, only half a lie. I can't quite make out the signs the eldest councilor shoots to Acai, nor the reply they receive before the great boiuna plunges back into the river, the council floor shaking as their weight leaves it. The warriors rush down the pathway toward the southern swamps. Half the hoatzis follow. Both servers usher the two oldest councilors toward the nearest house, Fern guiding them along.

Only three people remain to guard Thais: two humans and a hoatzi. She tries to stand again, but her knees give out, and she slumps over her seat. She heaves. Nothing comes up. The hoatzi presses scaly knuckles to their lipless mouth, looking away, but the humans watch her. One tugs at their hair.

I finger through my necklace stones and finally yank off the uncut ruby I collected at Rubem's house. The rock has bad memories anyway. Weighing it twice in my palm, I chuck it in a perfect arc over the three onlookers' heads. It clatters along the far path.

As one, they all swirl around to look. In a place that puts such value on stillness, clatter always gets a reaction. Before they turn back, I drop from the branches like a spring, scooping Thais up and carrying her back into the trees with me. Anger and fear clog my nose as she wiggles in my arms, but I clamp my hand over her mouth, and my arm around her back, her motions far too weak right now to do anything to me.

"Calm down!" I manage to sign after a moment, "You stink so much every boiuna beneath the village must smell you."

Thais's breathing steadies, and her scent fades back to the barely decipherable smell of soft rain-cleaned air. "Thanks." She forms the word so small that I almost miss it. "Not that I needed—"

"It's fine," I cut her off, signing into her space.

"Yeah."

I don't know what that means.

As we move slowly away from the council room, I can almost feel the poisonous waves of energy coursing through Thais, twinging a little in my stomach and weakening my grip. I catch her from falling into the mist-cloaked river when she heaves up a glob of burning saliva. It hits something scaly below, and a small boiuna flinches off a root, splashing into the water. I grin, but Thais stumbles, and my smile falls too. Her face glistens with sweat.

Fucking hero. I want to snap her out of this, to knock her over the head or hug her, but she yanks away from my touch, pulling her feet under her once more. This time she only wavers, managing to stay upright.

Xera lands in front of us, and our branch sways. "Come," they sign. "We'll go to my, um, my house. They won't check for her there."

"You don't mind?" Thais manages.

"It's just me there, otherwise," they explain. "It's what a, um, a good Murkling would do, isn't it? A good person."

"A hero," I grumble.

They dart back toward Fern's pool and vanish into the mist, only reappearing to check on us.

Thais ignores me, her eyes glued to the branches as she fights to stay upright. I twist myself in awkward ways trying to be on all sides of her at once. We near Fern's pool, but instead of dropping toward it, Xera continues up the largest trunk on its edge. A dark circular treehouse of open spaces, palm roofs, and wrapping vines shadows the fog.

Xera slips in through one of the many massive glassless windows and stands on a bench to flick on a chandelier lamp. The light sparks through the lower hanging lanterns, one for each color of the rainbow. Their dazzling glow illuminates a comfortable half-circle living area. A dining table curves along the side of the bench Xera stands on, while a pile of cushions creates a cozy sitting place across from a desk with miscellaneous paint supplies cluttered around a metal-and-wood record player. A hall along the tree trunk leads to another large room, maybe the kitchen or the main entrance, and a ladder beside it extends to a curtained area.

Xera sits down on the windowsill and leans out over Fern's pool. Thais shuffles into the room. Her shoulders shake, and she drags her scarf over her head. With a tremble that rattles my chest, she collapses into the pillows.

TEN

---∽---

EVERYTHING AND NOTHING

Seeing something and not having it
is like losing it with every breath.
But having something and being sure you've lost it?
That's somehow worse.

THAIS QUAVERS. SOMETHING LURCHES inside me, ten different thoughts all compiling into one: stupid me, I'd assumed her spasms were over. But this shaking comes in quiet shudders and hitches, more controlled than when she heaves. She wipes water from her face. It dawns on me: she *is* crying.

My impulses tell me to run, but Fern's accusation bites me like a crocodilian, refusing to let go. I have to make this right, even just to relieve the ache in my chest.

Carefully, I curl my tail around her pillows, sliding closer bit by bit. "I fucked up," I sign. The colorful light casts rainbows across my scales.

"Yeah." She leans against me, slowly at first, then like she wants to bury herself into my scales. "Yeah, you did." Her hands linger in the air before she wraps them around her stomach, grumbling something in her human vocals.

"What?" I poke her shoulder.

"I just—I don't know. I thought I was some hero. I thought I could do this." Fresh tears slip down her cheeks, and she pauses to brush them off. "I'm strong—was strong. I've never failed before and, I just, I don't know. I'll shut up now."

"Don't shut up." I need her to say something, her and her ignit eyes. "Don't ever shut up."

She looks at me. I hold her gaze for one perfect heartbeat, and when I glance away, I feel warmer and lighter, as though one perfect heartbeat from her lasts a lifetime.

Thais's fingers shake. She continues, slowly, "Now, a little stupid poison and a new place and suddenly I'm the one who needs saving. I couldn't even get that council to listen to me. I was useless and pathetic, and you and Xera and Fern had to come to my rescue. A thief, a coward, and a liar. What does that make me? A hypocrite?"

"A person."

"Yeah, a person you can barely put up with."

"What?" I loosen my tail in confusion and trail my fingers over my ignit.

Thais's shoulders bounce. "You don't have to be like that, I get it. Ignits are your thing. My life isn't really important compared to that."

I rub the stone a little longer, trying to sort through the chaotic mess in my head. Thais wipes her nose and tries to stand. I wrap myself around her, pulling her back down. She tenses, but she doesn't squirm or tell me off, simply runs her tear-dampened fingers along my tail, tracing the patterns.

And it hits me, like a torrential downpour, like the crash of a waterfall, like an ancient mangrove toppling in the dead of night: this is trust. It's my body wrapped around hers, and her confidence that I have a reason for pulling her back, and I think, her knowledge that if she asked, I would let her go.

I've had first dates, even seconds and thirds. I've grown close to my first forebearer and then been sheared off. I've had friends. At least one or two, I'm pretty sure. But I've never felt this before—this need to wrap around Thais, to protect her even when my anger could almost, *almost* strangle her instead. But I couldn't ever strangle her. I couldn't hurt her, not just because she hasn't harmed me, but because the pain of it would tear open my chest and spew my bloody heart onto the ground.

"You're half-right," I sign. "I want your ignits, and I'll have them. I wouldn't have come here without knowing I'll get them. But I also came because you saved me, when you didn't have to, when I meant nothing to you. And because even when I can barely put up with you, I kind of like you." What else do I call the warmth in my chest? Or the way her eyes soothe me, even though I never know how to react to them. Or the fact that her being near is easy, even when it's a challenge. "You're almost cool, boat shit."

Thais runs her palm along my tail, her touch strumming a perfect beat as though each draw of her hand plucks at my heart. As her fingers close, she leans against my chest, melting there with a heavy breath. "Well, you're still a greedy scaly bottom dweller. But an almost cool one." She flicks my shoulder hard enough to make me swat at her, wrapping her tighter by accident.

"What was that for?"

"Calling me boat shit! If you do really like me, you shouldn't name me after something disgusting."

I don't point out that she just called me three less-than-nice things, because I can't say they aren't all true, and I think maybe she *was* right in her original lineup. A thief, a coward, a liar, and a hypocrite. "Yeah, yeah, fine boat—ignit eyes." I switch at the last moment, choosing the new nickname on instinct. "That's a compliment, you know."

Thais blinks, watching my thumb swirl around the little blue ignit. Its gentle glow competes with the gleam of the chandelier for the honor of turning my scales a new color. "Do they really look like ignits?"

"Yeah, super eerie and as confusing as all other eyes, but they're really pretty." Looking over her nose like this, I catch every line of her face, every curl her wavy frizzing hair makes against it, the hints of the curves beneath her now-dry clothing. "You're really pretty." The words spill from my hands before I can stop them.

But Thais studies Xera too carefully to notice, watching as they lean over the railing to sign to Fern in her pool below. "That council had an elder in it."

"Yeah?"

"They weren't there for my sake—they were already meeting when I arrived. I understand that the Murklings work together because the Murk is dangerous and you need cooperation to survive, but—" She waves her hands, stinking of frustration. "The human and hoatzi warriors wear your scales. Fern has their bones made into flower pots! And you're just all okay with this?"

"You boat people really are idiots, aren't you?"

When she lifts her hands to protest, I plop my ignit into them.

"The boiuna whose scales Xera wears was a few decades larger than me, so they probably died in a hunt with Xera's first forebearer—Xera's mother or father," I explain with an odd mixture of annoyance and affection, one squarely taking over the other as I continue talking, warming me from the inside out. "In their death, that boiuna would have wanted their hunting companions to live on. Xera wears the scales for protection so they might in turn protect the ones they hunt with, and to carry on that boiuna's legacy, to honor their life and their sacrifice by making the most of what remains."

"And the bones? The feathers?"

"Life isn't just about surviving." I snatch the ignit back from Thais, pressing it into the empty space in my necklace so it sits against my collarbone. "It's also about enjoying that survival. I like stones, Fern likes skulls and plants, some humans like beads, and others like feathers. The Murk shares what it doesn't need any longer." Except for with me. The greedy bottom-dwelling ignit thief.

"Your species are really close, then." Thais's scent floods my senses, not wracked with any emotion, but simply cleansing. She runs her hands along my tail again, quiet and dragging, as though she lives in her head and her arms only mimic her thoughts. "Do you ever intermingle?"

"Inter-what-le?" I ask. Fern must smell my confusion all the way down in her pool.

Thais tips her chin up, pointedly reiterating. "Is it possible that Xera and Fern are *dating*?"

My tail unfurls partially as I jerk up straighter, bewilderment turning to shock and then back. "Dating?" I pause. "It's possible, yeah. Less common than same-species relationships, but I went out with a really gorgeous hoatzi until he insulted my rocks—the silt-breather. No one cares as long as everyone involved in it is a Murkling." And not a banished thief.

Thais's lifted brow drops, her lips bunching.

"Why the fuck do you think Fern and Xera might be dating?" I ask. "Do they even like each other?"

"You can't tell?" Thais's ignit eyes pierce through me.

I trace my thumb over my stones, looking away.

"Well, then I'll teach you. The first time we saw them together, Fern's expression changed. She accepted us based on whether Xera liked us, she started showing off with her ignit tricks, and she glanced at Xera even when you were talking. Xera blushed, tried to watch Fern without looking, wanted to speak but didn't. And then at the council meeting, Fern stood up for Xera, fiercely. She wrapped around them even though they were safe." She pauses there, like it should mean something to me.

"Uh-huh."

She gives me a meaningless look. "And here, watch Xera talk, the way they tuck back their hair and their ears turn a little redder when they smile, and the fact that they're having this long laughing conversation with Fern even though Fern is so far below that Xera has to make their signs huge just to be seen through the mist—Xera, who barely signs anything bigger than the length of their own fingers!" She grasps my chin gently as though my face will tell her something important.

The touch feels nice, but I look down, lingering on her lips instead of her eyes. She's an enigma, and the things she sees in Xera and Fern are equally odd and foreign. Yet, I still feel utterly content in her presence.

"You really don't see it?" she asks.

I grin at her. "I think they're both just doing normal people things." I touch the tip of my finger to her nose. "You're silly, ignit eyes."

"I'm *right*," she grumbles, but she relaxes against me, setting her head on my shoulder. She feels like an ignit, warm, alive, soothing. Her body moves all too quickly though, popping up to a sitting position once Xera finishes their conversation and meanders our way. "You should invite Fern to join us!"

Xera takes three steps back, looking over their shoulder as though Fern might suddenly be there just because Thais signed her name. "Oh, no, no, uh, she doesn't—she might not—"

"I'll do it for you. I want to talk to her again before we leave tomorrow, anyway." Thais stands. I tighten around her, grabbing her legs in a vain attempt to make her stay, but she just pats me away, her fingers lingering along my shoulder. "As long as that's okay with you, Xera?"

Xera gives a nod so tiny I wonder if I imagined it, and zips down the hallway.

Twenty minutes later, we all curl up around the table. The humans sit on the bench, bowls of soup steaming in front of them. Across from them, Fern and I knot our tails beneath us, making our own makeshift seats. I rest my elbows against the wood, flicking out my tongue. A mild and meaty smell floods my senses, maybe snake flesh and fungi, though the mixture in Thais's bowl seems mostly broth.

She sticks her tongue out at me in return, not touching the food. "If you want it, it's yours."

103

I roll my eyes. "When I'm hungry next, I'll eat a proper meal, like a caiman or a catfish or an annoying cartel leader."

"Just make sure you take his gloves off first," Thais points out. She watches Fern and Xera's conversation about mushrooms for a moment, before I nudge the soup closer to her.

"I might not need food, but *you* do."

Her motions come small, weak. "But when the poison hits me again . . ."

The weight of her worry builds in my own chest, a phantom pain mirroring hers, but it can't equal the horror she must feel, to hate the spasms so much that she would rather starve herself than risk more burning food launching back up her throat. "If you don't, and you pass out, will that be better?"

A shudder runs through her. She holds the bowl to her lips, taking a tiny sip. Her cheeks pinch, but she slowly drinks more before waving for Xera's attention. "This is good. I hope I don't throw it up on your floor."

Xera shoots to their feet. "I will bring a, uh, bucket."

Thais's chest rumbles and she holds out a hand. "Later, later. I'm fine right now."

Their brow tightens, but they sit back down. "What, um." They circle their hands between all of us. "What is this?"

I have no idea what that means, but Fern translates the question from Xera language into less vague terms: "What are you and the boat human planning to do?"

"Thais. My name is Thais, like the beginning of taunt and the funny ice from—"

"Don't care, boatie," Fern cuts in. "Didn't your rock-headed friend not tell you that boiuna don't do ridiculous things like sounds?"

My lips tug up. "I did, she's just stubborn."

Thais looks at Xera. "Are all of them like this?"

They shake their head so hard their beads jangle. "About that, though. When are you leaving? Not—not that I need you to go—you seem like you really need help, and if, um, if I can help, I'd like to—but you shouldn't stay past morning. They'll start looking then. In houses."

"We'll be gone before the mist clears," I reply, glancing out into the fog-veiled night. We need a canoe, but the more I bring Fern and Xera into our plans, the more chances they might decide to turn on us.

"Are, uh, are there more boat humans chasing you?" Xera asks. "Other than the ones that, um, crashed, I mean."

Fern looks at Thais, and Thais looks at me, and I drop my eyes to the center of the table, rubbing my ignit to soothe the tingle in the back of my skull.

"There's really more of them?" Fern swings her hands so hard her bone bracelets rattle. "Dredges, I'm good."

Xera's throat vibrates and they cover their mouth.

"You didn't know?" I ask Fern.

She shrugs. "I told the council what I figured would make them leave but couldn't be traced back to me as a lie. But this is better! I'm still hiding in thin fog after the weavers kicked me out."

"This is not better," Xera protests. "Boat humans are bad for us. I mean, not Thais—Thais isn't bad—but others, probably."

Fern's motions soften. "No, I know. You're right, Xera."

Thais sets down her half-drank soup. "These boat humans just want Cacao and me, but I doubt any of them will find us here. It's amazing the two on our tail lasted that long. If the cartel is attacked by the village warriors, I think Rubem will back them off. I doubt he's all that interested in fighting anyone in the Murk."

"Then we're safe?" Fern sticks her tongue at me as though daring me to lie.

"Unless you put out 'Hey, cartel humans, come get your poisoned prisoner and a boiuna here' signs?"

"Nah. They say, 'poisoned prisoner and idiot thief.'"

"Fuck off."

A pleasant stillness falls over the table.

With a cringe, Thais picks up her bowl and sips the rest of

her soup down. "What was that one sign, the—" She repeats what I assume is meant to be the motion for a weaver, sloppy and wrong both times she makes it.

I show her the proper version, a motion that mimics plaiting but formed near the side of the head. "A weaver is a storyteller who memorizes and reenacts the legends we pass down through the generations. Each village has one or two, but they all meet and train in the northern village of Endless Shadow."

"I joined them because I wanted to create new stories," Fern explains. "But I kept making the old ones better, too, and the master weavers didn't love that particularly."

"You tried to convince Cupuaçu that the tale of the first mist started with a skeleton war," Xera adds with their small gentle signs.

"Maybe it did! It's not a lie if you can't disprove it."

Thais's face pinches up. "Skeleton war?"

"Oh, yeah. But to truly tell the tale, we must start from the beginning." Fern bares every one of her teeth, rising up over her tail with her arms spread wide, like the most malevolent storytelling actor to ever live.

As she launches into a tale of woe and living bones and spontaneous jokes, I slip back toward the pillows, sprawling out along them. I stare at the ceiling, letting Fern's story become a distant wave of arms and an occasional tingle along my head ridges. My eyes slip shut for a moment. When I open them, I find Xera leaning over me, staring.

They stumble back, holding their hands to their chest. "Sorry, sorry."

I stretch my lips into something almost a grin and almost the moment before a strike. "What were you looking at?"

"Um." Xera's fingers tangle together before they manage, "Y-you. Looking at you."

"I got that, yeah. *Why* were you looking at me?"

"That stone." They point, their finger hovering in, nearly tapping the wiring cover of a tiny veined rock on my necklace, the elaborately wrapped metal keeping it from touching the other stones. A fissure down the middle reveals a glimmer of color that isn't color, a rainbow that's only there if you don't look at it.

I lift my hand to the necklace, blocking their view of the rock. "What about it?"

"I have one."

"Cracked open? There's a spectral fissure exposed in it?"

Xera nods.

"And you never took it to the mechanics?"

"It's pretty."

I like Xera a lot more suddenly. "It's called an eruptstone. It makes active ignits *explode*." Not that I would ever destroy a perfectly good ignit with it. "Bigger the ignit or the eruptstone, bigger the boom. No one knows why, and nothing is ever left in the places the flash touches, like everything there's been disintegrated straight out of existence, but beyond that blast radius, nothing's affected, like the energy is reflected back in on itself. It's brilliant. Metaphorically, anyway. Wouldn't want to see one actually go off."

Xera's brow shoots up. I think that means they never knew, but they say nothing. They glance over their shoulder, toward the table, but look back so fast I might have imagined it. "Fern says you are not a, uh, not great person."

"Fern's right." I coil my tail beneath my back, propping up my shoulders like a lounging seat. "But Thais *is* a great person, mostly, so you shouldn't kick us out for her sake." With that, I close my eyes again. I sense no vibrations from Xera, no sign of their leather-soled feet along the wood, but a brush of skin against my arm jerks me back to life, sending awful shudders through my bones. Yanking my tail farther under me, I sit up and rub my ignit.

Xera crouches at my side, their dark irises shadowed by sloping lids and a thick line of black makeup. "Maybe you're both wrong." They sign the words like a pair of twisting butterflies that scatter into the forest. Their hair rushes in a wave behind them as they seem almost to fly out of the room.

My brain needs a kick in the gears to start up again once they vanish. I shake my head. Strange cryptic human. I respect that. But their stillness sends a shiver down my spine. It reminds me of Rubem. Nothing else about Rubem and Xera seems the least bit similar except that creeping quiet, as though both of them are wary predators, always on the lookout, always ready to flee or give chase. What sort of a life is that, to be so cautious of attack at all times?

Once Fern wraps up her story, Thais wanders along the edge of the room. She pokes at the desk and moves the cluttered painting supplies off the phonograph. Her nails click as she taps them against its flower-shaped sound horn. After digging through the drawers and a nearby trunk, she finds a sleeve with a large flat disk and sets it on the record player's box. She searches for something—a crank, maybe. Her hands drop to her hips, and her lips bunch.

I wave at her. "It needs a blue ignit, either small or midsized."

Xera appears beside the desk, leaning against the wall as though they've been standing there since the beginning of time. "I don't have it. I mean, not anymore. Music was mostly important to Father, and he died."

The lines of Thais's face droop. As if they're three heads of the same hungry monster, Thais, Xera, and Fern all turn toward me. My bones crinkle under their gazes, and I clutch my ignit. I scowl. Thais looks away first, her shoulders slumping.

"It's fine," she says. "The reader is probably dusty by now anyway."

Releasing a gust of air through my teeth, I yank off my ignit and wave it in Xera's direction. "You have a transitioner?"

After a moment of staring at my one-handed signs, they slip a little box out of a pouch in their belt and flip open the top. The wiring beneath produces a spark that will activate an ignit, while another set of wires exposed on the bottom can dampen the power and return it to its inactive state. A weakly pulsing red glow illuminates its inner mechanisms.

I rub my thumb over the back of my own ignit. I don't need Xera's tiny red one too. I don't, because I'll have more and far larger ones when I receive Thais's hoard.

Giving my ignit one last caress, I hand it up to Xera. "Don't get any big ideas," I grumble. "It's still mine."

Xera takes it without comment, plucking it from my fingers with their leather hand protector, veins of a protective metallic substance running through the glove. They hold it to the lighter. A spark shoots through the stone, brightening the glow until it shines like one of the colorful lamps. The force inside it grows as well. The air sweeps away from it, the furniture rattling, Xera's hair flying out behind them. They wrap it quickly in a cloth woven from their glove's protective metal and hand it back. Its vibrations still stir a steady breeze and send trembles up my arm and tingles along my head ridges, but the cloth quiets its earth-quaking effect and keeps it from tearing into my scales.

I open a compartment in the phonograph's side and press the ignit into the empty coils, where the layers of dampening and receiving metals quickly direct all the ignit's power to one side. With the tap of a switch, it starts to spin in a circle. It blurs into a happy blue ring of light, and the phonograph's disk moves. Thais's eyes light up. The sound rolls over me in soft vibrations, creating a subtle beat in my head even though I can't hear the words or instruments.

Thais grabs Xera's wrist as they pass. Their brow lifts, their body going rigid, but Thais waits for their permission before pressing their palm to the side of the great metal speaker. Slowly they relax.

"You feel that beat?" she asks.

The corners of Xera's lips tug and they nod. When they slink away to sit with Fern, they move with a little more ease than before. Fern takes their hands and pulls them into the loose coils of her tail, but she pauses to wave me aggressively toward the phonograph. Toward Thais.

"Mind your own business," I snap back. Yet my muscles strain without my asking, sliding me up to Thais. Traitorous body. A flare of warm desire traces the space her hands touched when she tried to move me to her rhythm back on the fan boat.

I almost turn around, but she notices me and grabs my arm. She tugs, but I draw away. My tail knocks the back of her knees as I do. A soft vibration wobbles up her throat. She stumbles into me, catching herself on my chest.

A rush of warm nerves spreads along my scales, and a grin infects my face. I wiggle my fingers between us. "How clumsy, ignit eyes."

"Oh, you—you sneaky little tormenter!" But Thais remains so wonderfully close, staring up at me, her lovely haunting irises bright with blue fire. The moment I rip my gaze from hers, her hands move again, snatching back my attention as though she's saving my life in the quietest moments. "Could a clumsy boatie do this?" Her whole body sways, serpentine and fluid, then pops like a firecracker, her hands twirling out near her sides.

I swallow hard, following the roll of her waist in her loose fabric, down to her hips, along her legs, to the little jut of her twirling ankle, and back up again. Each motion sets a fire deep inside me, somewhere I had forgotten even to look since leaving the Murk. I lean my face into her hair, breathing in and out in time with her dancing, her rain-cleansed scent filling me like a fresh beginning. I could be anything in this moment. I could steal the world or I could give it away.

"Not a clumsy boatie, then," I say. "A clumsy serpent."

"You're one to talk!" Thais's chest trembles in a laugh. "What are these? *Hips*? You move them like a flailing palm branch." Her fingers drift toward my waist, but she pauses, her face pinching.

Last time, I jerked away, and she clearly hasn't forgotten that. Neither have I, for very different reasons. Reasons that haunt my scales like a hunger. Casually, like I overestimated a twist of my tail, I slide my body into her grasp. "Time to shut up," I tease. Then I loop my arms over her shoulders.

Thais closes her eyes, and I don't need to read her expression to sense the joy sweeping off her, clouding my mind and warming my chest and coursing through my veins, a blissful poison I can't fight. She runs her hands along my scales, one tracing up my side and the other drawing down to my hips, making me sway to her beat, to her life. I let her. I let her gentle fingers strangle me from the inside out.

My own hands filter into her hair, twisting carefully through the soft waves, brushing the frizzy bits into silk. I follow the lines of her silly human earlobes and her jaw and neck, caressing her tender skin. Such stupidly tender skin. If Thais is a fucking hero, I'm far less decent, far viler, yet I suddenly yearn to protect this ridiculous breakable champion. My body has its own desires, too, the thought of my lips on Thais's skin and my hips pressed against hers burning through me, bright and eager.

She leans closer.

Her toes slip over the tip of my tail. She pulls away, her eyes springing open like I jolted her out of a daze. She taps her chest to signify herself, but her hand lingers at her chest, her sentence falling to pieces.

"Hey, dancers!" Fern waves at us from the cushions. Xera lies in her coils, a blanket folded around them and a pillow tucked between their arms. "We shouldn't play that music for too long. There's another house three trees over, and they'll wonder what's going on after a while."

Thais nods, scrambling to turn off the record player.

And like that, the beauty of the evening vanishes into a droopy melancholy. I retrieve my ignit with the cloth and use the transitioner to deactivate it. My scales tingle as I slip it back onto my necklace, and my fingers knock numbly together. Thais wraps her arms around a bowl Xera must have brought out in case she has to heave again, looking everywhere but at me.

Well. That was that, then, I guess. Everything and nothing.

I flop across some pillows and poke Thais with my tail. "Come sleep, ignit eyes. You need it."

Grumbling something in her verbal tongue, she crawls over me, purposefully stepping on every bit of my tail she can. I wiggle, shoving her shoulder when she pokes her knee into my stomach.

"Hey, hey, fuck off with you, taunt ice," I say, mocking the silly way she tries to describe the sounds of her name.

She catches my hands and pins them to the cushion at my side, lying on them. "Your turn to shut up, chocolate bean."

I flick my tongue at her, tapping it against the bridge of her nose. She smells lovely. She *is* lovely—here, in the stillness, the passion that beats through her entire being reverberates on some subconscious level. When I tug my hands from under her, I leave them lying between us. I drift off to the faint scent of a fading rain.

Thais wakes three times during the night. Her first spasm empties her stomach again, creating such a stir that Xera rises to clean the bowl for her. Her second returns to bile. By the third, the only thing that leaves her are her tears as her body shakes.

She doesn't look to me for comfort, and I don't offer it, but I hold her hair back and wrap a blanket over her shoulders when she finishes. I can't recall how many spasms she had while at the river town. This feels like too many, though, and Thais weakens with each cycle, the slump of her shoulders building like a chain around my own.

I wonder if she would tell me her ignit hoard's location so I can retrieve the stone for her and return with it. I don't ask, not because I worry over what she will say, but because I feel the draw in my chest every time I glance at the belt pouch where Xera keeps their tiny red ignit. And that scares me. If I went to Thais's hoard alone, would I ever come back for her?

ELEVEN

THAT WHICH GOES BOOM IN THE NIGHT

Life is like an explosion.
It gives and then it takes away,
and somehow makes both those processes
really,
really suck.

I AWAKEN TO A glimmer of red against the mist. With everything cloaked in shadow, this single hint of light traces the large living space, rimming the table and desk in a faint red sheen and turning the hallway behind us into an open maw. My hazy mind thinks first of a red dawn, but the color comes from below, not above. Like lanterns.

I slip out of the cushions, careful not to wake Thais as I wiggle my tail from under her head. She rolls over, her throat rumbling, but her eyes stay closed. A stray slip of hair blows away from her lips, then slides into her mouth. Gently, I brush it behind her ear.

Something vibrates below the house: a stomp, then a sharp cry. Leaving Thais to sleep, I slide to the far window. Through the mist shines the glow of red-glass lanterns held by two humans perched on the tree's massive roots a few stories down. One carries a device with what looks like it might be a compass. The soft lantern light illuminates their fishnet-gloved hands.

Rubem.

The cartel leader nods and offers his bearded companion the compass. His entire body wavers like fabric in the wind, his feet slipping. The other human catches him by one arm. Rubem steadies himself with both hands. He signs, and the bearded human replies, their words blurred by the mist and muddled from the mixture of my odd vantage point and the lanterns they still carry. I decipher just enough to put a few sentences together.

"Not—boat—away!" Rubem's usually fluid hands move with sloppy slurring motions.

The other human shakes their head, the gold clams in their beard bouncing. "—too much wine. Let us do it."

Rubem fumbles around with his hands but manages to make something that looks like, "I want all of them *alive*—all of them!"

"I'll rein the crew in," his companion replies.

A heavy vibration echoes through the wood from the front of the house, tingling along my head ridges. I whip around. Thais, Xera, and Fern still sleep peacefully in the cushion pile, the hallway beyond them dark. I feel nothing more. Leaning back out the window. I catch the end of Rubem's signing,

"—after the fishers—"

"None of us would turn on you, sir," the bearded human assures him.

"You turned on your last leader, didn't you?" He wobbles in place, as if the root shifts under him, though his companion seems sturdy.

Another vibration hits me from the front of the house, this one stronger and nearer, but I still see nothing when I glance over my shoulder. I miss whatever the human replied with, but Rubem shakes his head in response, motioning them away. As they leave, he turns toward my window. His chin lifts.

I yank back from the sill. My heart thumps like a creature

bent on escape. I burst to wake the others, but before I can, the vibrations return, clattering down the hall. Two boat humans appear in the archway, pistols already drawn.

My muscles set themselves alight. I spring at the cartel thugs, half sliding over Fern and Xera in the process. Wrapping my tail around both humans' legs, I yank them together. They topple into each other. One of their guns goes off, tearing a clunk of wood from the floor.

I grab hold of the other weapon and pull the trigger directly into the opposite human's chest. A burst of blood pours out their back, just another shade of red in the maroon-tinged light. The stew of liquid and flesh reminds me far too much of Thais's stomach contents, though. I put both pistols down instead of bothering with them again, swimming my tail around the living human's neck and tightening. The human goes limp.

I catch Thais looking at me, Fern and Xera waking behind her. She stares, and her hands form my name. Too sharp.

"They shot at us," I snap, "I have every right to kill them."

As I untangle myself from the bodies, Rubem's wine-reeking scent floods the room. A fishnetted hand clutches a grappling hook embedded in the windowsill, and he pulls himself inside, a lantern swinging dangerously from one elbow. He stumbles. His chest vibrates and his lips twist. An odd gust of emotions tickles my nose, a heat like the sun, not anger and not joy and not determination, but somewhere in between, a dramatic drunken mix of life, swirling around something dark and dead, like a sweet flower masking a sickly rot.

"I was very, very much put out by your running away," Rubem signs, sluggish and then too fast.

I stare at him. "Are you drunk?"

"I am high tipsy, I'll have you know," Rubem counters. "I'm here to capture a pair of teenagers who've done nothing to deserve it, I'm allowed to dull the experience." He ends the sentence with a sloppy middle finger. It's almost funny.

"You're here to be annihilated by a couple teenagers, you mean?"

Coming here compromised shows a level of bravery I hadn't expected from Rubem. It's convenient that bravery is just another word for stupidity. This shouldn't be too hard, fish-nets or not.

I rub my thumb over my ignit and dash for the intoxicated cartel leader. Behind me, the hallway vibrates once more. A third human sprints into the room. The ring of their pistol trembles the air. I duck, and I swear I feel the bullet graze the very edge of my scales. My head cracks from the vibration, my world spinning into too many pieces, but I can still make out the projectile when it smashes through Rubem's lantern. The glass gleams, its fire a falling snake of spark and light. It hits the ground.

The flames fade. Then they burst, dancing along the wooden floor with terrible ferocity.

Rubem seems not to notice. He marches toward the human with the pistol, the top of the broken lantern still clamped to his arm. "Alive, dammit!"

He slips around the bench and desk like he's made of nothing but mist, drawing a thick rod from his coat as he walks. A short rope spirals off it. He tugs away a metal-lined cloth at its end, revealing an active purple ignit—a paralyzing variety, harmless in the air, but a single touch can make whole patches of a boiuna's flesh go numb and stun a human from head to toe for near a minute.

"We are not fishers." His signs twirl the ignit disastrously near his own face, but somehow, it never hits, his chin tipping out of its range so precisely that it seems beyond what even a sober human should be capable of.

It hits me like a blast of seawater: I underestimated him. Rubem possesses the sort of ingrained skill that clings to him even with the alcohol. A chill races across my aching skull when I realize how close his plan had been to succeeding—how fucked we would all be if I hadn't woken when I did. And how fucked we still are.

I tense, trying to shut up the pounding that bullet left in my skull so I can attack him before he reaches Thais. But Rubem ignores her and Fern. Instead, he swings the ignit end of his weapon at the other cartel member. It smacks them in the head. They collapse.

Complete stillness reigns for half a moment as everyone stares at the limp human who is unconscious but still breathing. My confusion overrides my better instincts. Rubem paralyzed his own fighter. Paralyzed. His own fighter.

Xera recovers first. They rush at Rubem with a small blade. Both of them are silent cautious predators, but Rubem, despite his intoxication, is older and more experienced. He moves just as fast and twice as quietly. His ignit flies straight for Xera at a speed too fast for their knife to compete with.

Thais leaps at the weapon, sluggish and bungling in comparison, yet she stretches out her arm just in time to grab the paralyzing stone before it can hit Xera in the chest. Her clumsy body crashes to the floor, pulling Rubem's weapon with it. Her eyes flutter closed, and the ignit slides from her grip.

A spasm wracks her. The fire spreading along the floor-boards lights the spit gurgling out of her mouth as she heaves, half-conscious. My chest tangles itself into knots. Into fish-nets.

Whether the sudden wave of sickness is brought on by Rubem's ignit or just a bad twist of fate, I don't know. I don't care. Either way, I have to get her to safety. My gaze slips from the fire now licking at the far wall and catches Fern. I sign for her to take Thais and go.

Baring my teeth, I launch myself at Rubem.

I hit his waist, yanking him to the ground. He struggles. Every movement is bizarre—perfect and yet entirely wrong—as though Rubem knows what I'm about to do and has the skill and control to react, but forgets his own intentions half-way through that reaction. I wrap my tail up his legs and over his waist. Before I can reach his neck, the fire hits the ceiling with a crackle. Sparks rain down. I jerk away from them, rolling us both toward the windows.

Fern rushes through the space I just occupied, Thais in her arms, and slides into the hallway. In her wake, the human Rubem knocked out earlier stands with heavy shaking steps, still holding their pistol. They ignore the fire raging along the room to one side of them and aim for Fern's back.

Like the mists of their namesake, Xera appears from nowhere. Flame lights them from behind as they plunge their little knife into the back of the human's skull. Blood washes over their hands. The body falls. Xera flicks their fingers twice, forming the phrase for *not here*, a death proclamation which leaves no blessing or curse, because the dead is not of the Murk and therefore those of the Murk are not the ones responsible for acknowledging it. It's more honor than I've ever given the boat humans I've killed.

Rubem reclaims my attention, gripping his weapon again. Its ignit flies toward me, forming a lovely purple streak over a background of orange flame. My fascination fades when it hits my side. A wave of energy tingles through my muscles, making them too tight, then too loose. Rubem fumbles beneath my tail loops, shoving my body off. I reach for him, but he's too far away and my arms are still too heavy. Smoke fills my lungs. I hold my breath.

A tremor from the ceiling hits me. One of the great wooden beams that holds up the palm-laced roof creaks where the fire consumes one end. Then it falls. It crashes onto me, pinning my chest and stealing my air. An excess of pain shoots up my ribs and down my spine. It tosses back and forth within me.

I writhe through the agony, pushing it aside enough to steel myself and swing my tail around the beam. I heave with all my might. It rolls off my upper chest, down to my waist, but from where the room meets the mangrove's trunk, another three giant planks of the roof collapse, dropping on the end of mine and immobilizing it. Trapping it here. Trapping me beneath.

I twist and squirm, but the wood sinks into one of my arms and most of my torso, as if a penajuar lies across my body. The flames lick closer. Nausea grips me, fueled by the rapid rhythm of my heart and the tingle in my bones. *Oh muck, oh muck, oh muck.*

Two sets of hands reach around me, one with fishnets and the other with leather bracers. They both try to lift the beam. They both fail. Xera gives me one last look and darts away. My chest hurts more from that than from the wood pinning me down, but I respect their choice. Heroes are idiots. Xera shouldn't die here with me.

But Rubem stays. His weapon forgotten on the floor, he shoves at the wood in frustration, as if confused why it won't move. His fishnets gleam like gashes in his skin, like he's falling apart, reality falling apart, *me* falling apart. I can't reach my ignit to soothe myself, but I can't look away from him either.

"You—you and Thais could fix everything." He pauses to push at the wood again. "If I had that hoard." His hands slur together, and he coughs. "I could make those damn fishers leave."

The fishers you made a deal with are penajuar lunch now, I want to sign. But the searing rush of fire overwhelms that, though. I roll my tail away from it, but it chases me, leaping along the beam to lap at my scales.

It catches hold of Rubem's sleeve. He stares as it licks at the baggy brown material, jumping toward the ruby rim of his long vest. His eyes widen. He stumbles, smacking the burning material against his shirt.

Xera darts in from the hallway, a cloth pressed to the lower half of their face. My surprise makes my head light, or maybe that's the smoke. They came back. But why?

They snatch Rubem's discarded weapon off the ground and toss it toward the trunk of the tree that forms the far wall. The active ignit bounces against the wood. It lands on the chunk of burning ceiling that immobilizes the beam pinning me down. Xera unravels a slingshot and drops a stone into its crook. As it falls, I catch the glimmer of color, flashing like a fissure down its center.

What a fucking hero.

Without hesitating, they launch the eruptstone at Rubem's ignit. Their aim strikes true, and the dark rock clicks off the luminous one. Both explode.

Light spreads from them, disintegrating all it touches. It ripples out in a perfect sphere from the ignit's center, consuming the blankets and pillows, the floor, the ceiling, hollowing out half the room and half the mangrove's trunk. It stops suddenly, the explosion of light vanishing as quickly as it had come. All that remains in the space the light touched is a dull useless stone, which falls out of sight, nothing left to weigh down my beam.

I heave the wood off and scramble away from the flames. They blaze through the room like it's a furnace, and we're the only kindling left. The massive tree creaks, starting from the great hole Xera's explosive left in the trunk. Slowly, the portion of the tree above the hole tilts. Then it tips, sluggishly splintering through the burning ceiling.

All my previous pains vanish in a burst of horror. I grab Xera and launch into the hall. Rubem's feet pound behind us. The floor starts to fall away, chunks of the walls breaking apart as the tree topples. We crash through a room that might have once been a kitchen and out the front door. The house tears off its supports, bowing away from the elevated front path. Pulling Xera into my arms, I spring through the gap, the river stories below us. We tumble across the pathway. It rocks but stays sturdy. Xera bolts from my grip and rushes down the street to Fern and Thais.

Only then do I notice Rubem. He clutches a plank that hangs out from the broken edge of the path, his shirt sleeve still smoldering. He drags his torso onto the wood, propping himself on his elbows. The crash of the tree toppling behind him drowns out any other vibrations.

"We want the same thing!" he signs. "We shouldn't be fighting."

I bare my teeth, rearing over him. "Yeah, well, if you haven't noticed, both of us wanting ignits means we'd have to share."

"Ignits? No, not only ignits, but—" The crumbling wood beneath him splits in half, cutting his ramblings short as it spills him into the mist. The splash of his body hitting the water rings through my head. I barely feel him break the surface again because approaching footsteps pound down the pathway to what was once Xera's house.

Xera tugs at my arm, then leaps like a monkey for the nearest branch. They swing themselves higher into the canopy. I take Thais from Fern's arms and follow them. The lighter looser fog of the early morning doesn't quite cover us, but the approaching Murklings whip past all the same, dragging a water pump and hose toward the orange smear of fire and black billows of smoke.

Thais struggles out of my grip. "Let go, I'm fine."

I lower her to the branch beside me, but I move too slowly for her pride. She rips out of my grasp, her curls snagging on my hand. The hair stays there as she stumbles away, barely keeping her footing. I move to catch her, but she glares at me. Her gaze lowers to the locks in my fingers.

"You tore it!" Her arms shake, and she takes another step back.

"Because you wouldn't be patient," I snap. But as I loop the hair around my wrist and tie it there, her accusation turns my stomach. I didn't tear it. It came out. It came out into my hands, already torn. Whatever that means, it can't be good.

"Come on," Xera signs, motioning us higher into the trees.

"But your house—my pool—our things, our *tree*," Fern objects, her hands drifting shakily through the signs.

Xera grows so still they seem to stop existing for a moment. "Cacao was more important," they say finally, their hands unusually sure of themselves. They turn away, continuing through the canopy.

Their words hold me in place like tiny claws. Me. More important. Xera saved *me*, not because of some heroic nonsense or a stubborn abidance to right and wrong, but because I was more important than their home. The notion clings to the inside of my skull. I don't know what to make of it yet.

TWELVE

———— ⌗ ————

THE HEART HAS A COMPASS TOO

It's in the moments between that we find ourselves.
But finding oneself is like finding a point on a map
with a million steps separating now and then.

WE CLIMB SPEECHLESSLY through the canopy, met only by
the sudden rushes of startled birds, the gleam of giant monkey
eyes, and the occasional scattering of a tree snake from our
path. The fog fades to a haze and finally to clean fresh air as
the leaves above part for a deep blue sky and distant pink
clouds. I coil myself three times around a branch just thick
enough to hold my weight. Fern does the same a little to my
right. Thais settles in the groove between us, and Xera's
leather shoes peek out from the leaves above. We all seem to
heave the same sigh.

"The fuck was that," I grumble.

"My thought exactly," Fern replies, shoving my branch with
her tail so hard it bounces. "You said those boat humans
wouldn't find you with us."

"They couldn't have!"

Fern bares her teeth. "Yet they did somehow!"

"Yet they did somehow," Thais repeats, her motions slow
and controlled. "Somehow, Rubem has to be tracking us."

I jerk upright. "That's it, that's what he was doing." When

the others only stare at me, I continue, "I saw him, just before the attack, handing off some device with a compass. What other reason would he have had for a compass there, at the base of our tree, if it didn't point toward us?"

"How is that possible?" Fern cuts in. "Unless he planted you with something he can track—"

"The poison." Thais flips over her palm at the end of her signs, staring at the cut where the green ignit powder first entered.

I nod. "Could be the poison, yeah. All active ignits send out multiple kinds of waves. Even the trace amounts in Thais's body can be tracked with the right calibration, especially for a stone as rare as a pure green."

Thais gives her hand a little shake. "Well, how do we *stop* it from being tracked?"

"We don't, not unless you have enough wardstone to make yourself a full body shield." My fingers dance across the little red-brown square of it on my necklace. "The boat humans ship it down from the base of the mountains, but we won't find more than scant traces anywhere in the Murk. If your mother was smart, she's probably lined her hoard with it to stop someone like Rubem from tracking any active ignits in her hoard and taking them, but that doesn't help us unless we can get there."

"And we can't get there if Rubem is constantly on our tail," Thais concludes.

In the stillness, the sun's touch drifts across my back in a threatening caress as the leaves sway above me.

"Destroy the device," Xera says finally. "No device, no tracking."

"They're right," Thais agrees. "As long as Rubem has that device, we'll never make it to the hoard, and if we did, he'd be on our tail the moment we arrived."

"Then we find his boat, break in, and take the compass." If I can steal a few of his ignits in the process, then all the better.

Xera nods. "I can track him."

"Why should we help them, Xera?" Fern lunges out of her branch in annoyance, grabbing hold of the trunk to bare her teeth at the other Murkling. "Our homes are *destroyed* because of these two. Isn't that enough sacrifice for one day?"

For all of Xera's flightiness, they hardly flinch at the sight of Fern's outrage. Instead, they touch their forehead to hers and ask, small but confident, "Is there a limit to how much good one should do?"

The question makes Fern's mouth snap closed. She leans against the trunk, her face pinched and her scent name clouded with bitter annoyance.

Thais takes this as her cue to interject. "We don't need you guys. We can do it on our own. We've—"

"Got this?" I finish. "We don't *got this*. You've got poison running through your body, and I've got a host of elders who would strangle me if they caught me, and a crazy cartel leader is after us both. We need help." Xera sacrificed their tree for me. I live because that ignit exploded and a colossal mangrove fell, and I'm sure as fuck not dying yet, not if I can help it. Determination burns in my core like a tiny heat ignit. I'll have that hoard and my own hide and Thais's life. All of it. I look to Fern and Xera, meeting their gazes as long as I can bear. "If you stick with us until we're out of the Murk, you can have something in return. Not ignits, something else."

"I want your bones," Fern replies.

Thais's brow shoots up. "What?"

"When you die," Fern explains, each motion calm and controlled, "whenever that happens, this week or in five or fifty decades, if I can get to your corpse, I want your bones."

I tip my head at her. "Deal."

"Hey—" Thais protests.

I poke her with the end of my tail, spearing it into her stomach. She shoos me away, muttering something in her spoken language. I look at Xera next.

They fidget. "May I, uh, choose what I want later?"

"Whatever." I lie back along the branch, propping my head

on my tail so I can still see the others. "Because the ignits are too hard to track while inactive—not producing energy—we should be safe until Thais's next spasm." A leaf lands on my nose. I pick it up, flicking it away. "I guess this is where people usually make plans or something."

"You guess?" Thais swings her arms as she signs it. "This is why you went to trial so many times, you catastrophic mess of whimsy."

"Things worked out, mostly. More than they didn't. I wasn't a *total* disaster."

"A hurricane is less disastrous than you."

I sit up in a burst, sliding toward her until I hover in front of her face, my teeth bared, my tail curled beneath me. She smells fresh and light and a tiny bit electric. "Say that to my face, why don't you."

"You," she pokes me in the chest, "are a scaly hurricane."

I clutch her fingers, pulling her forward. Her chest vibrates in a noise of surprise, but I catch her in my coils just before she can fall, curling around her tightly and burying my chin in her neck. My signs form stunted and off to the side but every bit as authentic as usual. "I am that exactly."

With her arms against my chest, she rumbles in her vocal language, laughing or scolding or both. She relaxes against me, and a peaceful scent slips from her, filling me up. I could almost kiss her neck. If I were braver. If I thought this moment could carry us anywhere.

It hits me then like a slap in the face: even if Thais lives, we won't have this much longer together. I'll take her hoard and flee somewhere safe with it, toward the inland rivers maybe, and she'll go back to performing for the village people. The deadline for reaching the ignit hoard is also the deadline to my time with Thais. And I selfishly want to make the journey take every day possible, to keep Thais near me as long as I can, to feel her fingers trace my scales and her gentle sigh against my chest one more time.

I really am a scaly hurricane, a selfish one too.

Fern hovers above me. "I'm more than happy to get your bones by sitting around here until you turn into a skeleton, but I'll be hungry again in a few days, so I'd prefer to get this over with. Possibly eat this Rubem person along the way."

Thais wiggles in my grip. Grudgingly, I loosen myself, letting her pull her hands up to sign.

"We don't kill people unless we absolutely have to," Thais says, each hand motion fiercer than the last.

Fern bares her teeth, the branch trembling as she strangles it. "He's the only one left I can blame for crushing my pool. I will eat him if I damn well please."

"You—you—" Thais pokes her finger at Fern's chest. In the end, she settles on, "You damn boiuna."

I nudge Thais in the sides. "Hey, hey, don't be speciesist! I, for one, try not to eat too many humans. The adults make my throat hurt, and it feels like a weight in my stomach for weeks." The pinched expression Thais gets means little to me, but I know her well enough to follow up with, "And no, I don't eat *children*. That kind of horror is reserved for savages, like fishers and sirens."

A rush of tense sadness leaves Thais, clouding all my other senses until the gentle wind carries it away.

I brush my palms up and down her shoulders a few times, absentmindedly. "We'll worry about killing and eating later, though. Right now, we just need to *find* Rubem. When his companion took the device away, they went east. We can start looking there. He must have at least a few boats, so someone would have noticed them go by."

"You should stay out of sight," Xera says, pointing at me and Thais.

"No way. We're help—"

I gently probe for her to stop and circle my arms over her shoulders, snuggling against her back. "We'll travel with you a ways, but we'll stay *very* out of sight. When you find the boats, come back, and we'll all go attack together, with one of those plan things. To make Thais happy."

"Useless muck-mouthed leech." Thais sighs a great heaving gust of air and goes limp against my chest, her head tipping backward onto my shoulder. Relaxed as she is, with her warmth pressed against me and her scent in my lungs, I almost want to stay like this, to let Fern and Xera do all the work for us. But Rubem might have more ignits.

As I detangle myself from Thais, she signs a grumbly "You're terrible" at me.

I reply in haste. "You, too, ignit eyes."

She smiles, and I stare into her shining blue irises, just for a moment, until the vibrations of a distant shout interrupt me. In the stillness of our small group, the rumblings of a much larger crowd sifting through the trees nearer the village's heart finally come through. A crowd looking for us, or the cartel, or both.

Fern unhooks and rehooks her jaw as she puts my worries into words. "Someone must've realized it was more than just a freak fire."

"We should start moving." Xera's hands tremble once, quiet and small. They set off back into the canopy.

Thais follows. I trace my necklace stones one by one, slipping after her. The mists linger between thick roots and on still pools, but most of it has faded, the world giving way to the hazy grey and green light that filters through the thick foliage above. The distant whiff of smoke comes and goes, but even when we near Xera's old tree to retrieve their little canoe, we see no new damage or flames. Uncontrolled mangrove fires can be terrible monsters. The villagers did well to extinguish this one quickly.

We row the canoe past the place where Rubem's boats must have come through, since it's the only wide enough rivulet on this side of the village. Fern trails behind to watch for village tracking parties while Xera scouts ahead, the canoe tucked into the foliage to keep it out of sight.

I lie in the lower branches of the canopy, the lazy green water far beneath. A pair of dragonflies the length of my arm sweep along the surface, and the leaves vibrate to my left as a flock of parrots hop through them. This close to a town, there would be days when a few hoatzi children and a human teenager playfully catch the parrots, maybe a small boiuna looped around one of their shoulders, clinging to their hair and grinning. In my forebearer's youth, a little pink botos might have swum below them, whistling and clicking in tune with the birds. But there have been only two baby botos this decade, both raised in the safety of the centermost village.

Still, this is home.

Was home. My gut hurts. If I can't live here, in the place I was born and raised, a place I love dearly, then these cartel humans most certainly aren't allowed, especially those as unwelcome and aggressive as Rubem's.

I run my fingers over my ignit, slipping it out of the wires so I can roll it around in my palm. The veins shimmer as though a thousand stars run through them, threaded by streaks of glowing indigos and sapphires and azures. Its gentle heartbeat fills me, soft and soothing.

Thais shifts at my side, brushing her fingers against mine. I freeze, but then I open my palm to her. She touches the ignit, narrowing her eyes. Pulling her hand back, she taps her fingers on the branch, her beat a little faster and more anxious than normal.

"Where did you live, before you were banished?" she asks. "Did you have a pool like Fern's?"

Her question surprises me. I press my ignit back into my necklace as a dismissal rises in my fingers, but the urge to snap it out never comes. I held it back so many times, and now I can't, as if the truth has piled up inside me and Thais is the fissure that can finally release it all. "Sort of. For a long time, I had a den beneath a little tree in a northern village. When I first started getting into real properly greedy trouble, I moved through a bunch of places, mostly on the outskirts of the villages that had a high supply of ignits, but some months I'd travel through the Murk, checking the trees that make the ignits— the old ones with parasites in their centers, which we call ancients—for fresh growth."

Thais's eyebrows come together. "Do the Murklings not harvest them?"

I roll my eyes. "Of course we do, especially now that they're producing so many. But not like the muck-faced cartels. We have three days once every season when the whole community harvests. Whatever's found is brought back to the villages and distributed as needed."

"No one tries to take the ignits early? Other than annoying hurricanes." She prods my ribs, sending a little tremble of pain and joy up my side.

I wiggle, batting at her hand and grinning. "Not anyone who values their life. Most ancients have some nasty guardians— penajuars and the like. And ignits aren't bought and sold here like you barbaric hagglers do it. If someone stole an ignit and tried to sell it, an elder would eat them, no questions."

"And if they used those ignits instead?"

"That's a matter for the council. If it's determined that the distribution wasn't fair and the thief deserved their ignit, they can keep it, and the distribution itself is put under trial instead, to weed out any who might be working against the betterment of the whole. If they didn't deserve the ignit they took, they must return it, along with any others they may have."

Thais stares at me. "Do you not believe that's a good system?" Her hands wiggle as though she's searching for the right signs. "You just know it so well, and you say it like it's the right way to do things, but you don't follow it."

I shrug. "And I never will." But the question prunes back through the forest of my greed to the very first root. "It's a good system, but there's something broken in it too. I need an ignit for the way it thrums. I need one every time I feel the brush of a net or see the bark pop out on a veiny piece of driftwood, or come too near to a tortoise shell. That wasn't always greed; that was a child whose bones hurt and whose skull itched, who just wanted to feel like everything inside him wasn't shattering into little pieces all day long. But for all the councils and the elders factored into their distributions, not one bothered with a little boy crying for a pretty stone when there were hunters needing tools and families needing food and whole villages needing light."

Thais holds her hands up as though she might reply to that, but after a moment, she only wraps one arm around my back, pulling the other to her chest in the motion for *I'm sorry.*

Her touch alights and soothes all at once. I set my chin on her head. "But now I also want them more than everyone else ever will. And I'll keep hoarding them until I have so many that I can't possibly lose them again. Ever. I don't care if a few villages have to go dark to do it."

She can't like that, because she's *Thais*, a hero, a good person. A savior. But somehow, I don't mind that she's the person she is, with her stupidly pure morals.

She shakes her head and leans it against my shoulder. Slowly, she rocks us, as if listening to some distant melancholic rhythm. When she finally pulls away, her shoulders bounce a little and her signs grow larger. "You're telling me things finally, you grumpy ridge-headed hermit."

I roll my eyes. "Yeah, yeah, well don't get too used to it," I grumble, looping my tail around myself so I can huddle into it. "And my head ridges are damn gorgeous. Some boiuna would kill for these patterns." I pull that line clean out of my silt-strewn backside. Not a lie, exactly, because it might be true.

Thais stares at me, and I think she must see straight through the half fib. But she draws one hand over my head, hovering it just above my ridges as though tracing the risen boxes and swirls. With her other hand she signs. "Damn gorgeous."

That lights up my heart. I want to be gorgeous to her. "Fucking ignit eyes." I brush my thumb over my own ignit, not looking at her. But I feel the draw of her haunting rain-cleaned soul through her stare, or maybe through the subtle pulse of her heartbeat in her wrist as it comes so near to my skull that her skin almost touches my scales.

With her free hand, she signs. "I hate that you kill people." The statement seems so contrary to her actions, but the whiff I catch from her ties them all together, beautifully sad with melancholic yearning.

"I don't always kill them," I grumble. "Sometimes I don't use as much pressure for so long and just knock them out. Not lately, but, you know, I could. If I wanted to."

"Wait, really?" Thais perks up. She shoves me in the shoulder. "You ridiculous glop!"

"Hey! I haven't had a lot of love for intelligent species in a while—blame them, not me." I stick my tongue out at her for good measure.

"Ruthless idiot." But she loops an arm through mine. "How do you do it then—the whole strangling business? So I know how to avoid it in the future."

"In case I try to eat you?" The tease earns me a snort.

"In case one of you Murklings tries to knock me out. Or someone else for that matter."

Slipping the end of my tail up, I nudge it threateningly against her neck. Instead of the stiff panicked struggle of those I've strangled in the past, Thais loosens her shoulders, nuzzling her nose against my scales. The warmth of her breath spreads through me.

Gently, I lift her hair away from her skin and tap two fingers to her pulse. "The blood flows to your brain in a vessel along both sides of your neck. If I squeezed hard enough, too little blood will reach your head. First, you'd go unconscious, then you'd die. Somewhere in the middle there, you'd get a nasty case of brain damage." I slide my tail off her shoulders and encircle it lightly around her middle instead.

She raps her hands against it a few times. "Could a human or a hoatzi do that too? Do you need a tail, or can you make it work with just hands?"

"Hands, no. Arms, maybe? I've seen human warriors

practice it while training. They wrap an arm around the person from behind, elbow down, and squeeze. It's slower though." I pause, my gaze on her ever-moving fingers as they continue their incessant rhythm. "You want to try on me? For fun."

"Sure." Thais faces me. Her fingertips brush too gently against my neck, sending unpleasant tingles through my spine. When she presses harder, the firm touch eats away at my momentary discomfort. But she draws back. "Well, turn around then."

Before I can, her chin snaps toward the canopy. The rustle of branches pricks along my scalp, and I follow her gaze. Only a monkey drops out of the leaves, swinging by us and climbing higher into the trees. When I turn back toward Thais, though, Xera sits on her other side. I startle, rubbing my ignit to soothe the scattered sparks twitching beneath my skin.

"I, uh, found Rubem's boat," Xera says.

At the same time, Fern pokes out of the water below us, giving a quick wave before signing, "There's a scouting party a ways back, heading straight for us. If we're going to do this, we'd better hurry."

Stretching out my back, I detangle myself from the branch. "What are we waiting for, then? Let's give one silt-breathing cartel leader a damn bad morning."

THIRTEEN

———— ∽ ————

THE FUTURE IS A GEODE

A thief, a coward, a liar, and a hypocrite walk into a boat.
Only three of them walk out.
(You thought this was going to be a joke, didn't you?)

THE SILT SWIRLS AROUND me. It settles once I do, the occasional coppery fish stirring up a fresh trail of it. I stare up at the shadows of three cartel vessels. One of their two small flat-bottomed fan boats sinks a little deeper into the water, a massive crocodilian tail hanging over its edge. The larger boat sits between them, its hull plunging halfway to the riverbed.

It possesses no fans or sails or motors, but a twistable device at its back harbors a massive blue ignit, all its would-be power directed out one side. The stone lies dormant now, taunting me with its faint glow. I sweep my tail in agitation, stirring up more of the loose bottom dirt and making a catfish dart away in confusion.

An ignit the size of this boat's would be impractical to carry and all but impossible to remove from the boat. And we didn't come for it. We came for the compass device in Rubem's cabin, where there will likely be more ignits of many sizes and colors which I can take instead. I refuse to try anything Thais would call stupid bottom-dwelling hurricane behavior. No matter how the pulsing rock tempts me.

Near the back end of the large boat, a tiny amethyst hits the water. It sinks straight down. Relief rushes over me at the sight, both because I missed its presence against my collarbone and because it means Xera made it.

I snatch the stone before it hits the swamp bed and fit it back into my necklace. Following its path upward, I poke my head out of the water to find an open cabin window. Xera crouches within, so motionless they nearly fade into the background of the tiny room. I search for any dangerous vibrations, but I only sense the rattle of something dice-like across wood in the nearest small boat and soft rumbles of human speech after it. No warning signals from Thais or Fern.

I grip the window and pull myself into the boat, drawing my tail after me. It fills almost the entire bathroom space. Xera climbs onto some kind of toilet to avoid me.

"Quiet," they sign.

They arch over my bundled tail and open the door, landing beyond it with such light feet I barely feel their leather shoes touching the deep-red wood flooring. I slide out after them into a much wider main cabin. We both go still, two trespassers on a new planet.

The red wood stretches everywhere—floor, walls, and ceiling—framing the double-wide windows on either side of the cabin and reappearing in the tables and counters and shelves. Maroon stones line the bottom of a giant fish tank mounted across the back wall where an assortment of Murk-dwelling fish swim, including one mighty green bass nearly as long as my torso. A caiman relaxes on a bundle of scarlet blankets in the far corner, but it scuffles beneath a stool when it notices us. A blossom of brilliant red marks the back of a palm-sized spider locked in a ventilated glass jar beside a number of other small but terrifying creatures: beetles with horns, butterflies with bone markings, a lizard with two heads, and a bat hanging upside down, nibbling on a piece of fruit.

Only the bed diverts from the color scheme, its frame an ordinary tan. A mess of browns, reds, and blacks spreads across it, Rubem a part of them, sprawled on his stomach. His eyes twitch behind closed eyelids, and his mouth hangs open slightly, deep-purple stains in the cracks of his lips.

I creep closer, holding my breath. The cords of his braided hair tangle over his back and shoulders, gold beads gleaming throughout. The arm with his singed shirt hangs over the side of the mattress, fishnet glove torn away. His limp fingers cradle the top of an empty wine bottle. He smells less of alcohol now, and more of bile and misery, with a hint of cracking leather and smoke.

Despite my nearness, he doesn't stir, his back rising and falling gently beneath a billowing brown shirt, vest crooked. One of his hoop earrings bends at an angle. With his chin kinked over a pillow, his neck lies open, vulnerable. I could squeeze my tail around it, a quick tight pressure against the veins coursing beneath his skin, and he would barely wake long enough for the life to leave him.

I hold my hand out, calculating the best way to do so. But then he shifts, small and tired. A twitch of his fingers knocks the wine bottle off-balance. Xera catches it before it can fall, gently sweeping it out from under his grasp and setting it off to the side.

If I kill him, then what? The thought feels like Thais's smooth skin and exuberant motions. I have to answer it.

If I kill him, pathetic and asleep, then maybe the boat humans will leave Thais and me and the Murk alone. Or maybe they'll keep coming. Maybe I'll just have strangled the only one of them who's ever tried to help me instead of shoot me, even if it was a weird, probably selfish kind of aid.

Selfish. My gaze darts through the room, hovering over all the creatures in Rubem's collection. His own little hoard. A tremble runs through my outstretched arm as though my muscles can't hold it there any longer.

Xera places their hand over mine, gently guiding it back. In the moment their fingers pass near the harsher boat-human lines of Rubem's face, it hits me that his skin holds more of the red of the Murk than the river's dustier brown. His ruby accents conceal it, but it remains: a hint of some past that once weeded with my forebearers.

I swallow down the weird lump that forms in my throat and turn my attention back to the room. "The device is handheld, mostly metal. If you find something like it, I'll look." I pause. "It may be on the deck, or with that bearded human."

"That's tomorrow's waterfall," Xera replies, but they move in jittery leaps, as though every vibration they keep from their surroundings is being used up inside them instead. They poke through the shelves and lean to check the clutter beneath the tables. It seems to be mostly animal supplies and alcohol, along with a music box surrounded by shark teeth and a broken clock.

I open the chest at the end of Rubem's bed, and my heart leaps forward. An opaque box lies within, gleaming of ignits. I stop looking for the tracking device and jiggle its lock. It stays clamped. My attention settles back on Rubem. He must have keys. If I can get them.

Carefully, I slip my hands through the pockets of his half-discarded vest. Nothing. Twisting my torso upside down, I inspect the fabric of his shirt, trapped between his body and the bed. A piece of metal hangs from his belt, and the edge of a pocket pokes from his vest near his chest, another barely visible on his pants.

Xera taps my shoulder. They wave a little mechanical box at me, but I motion them away. "Bigger than that. Keep looking."

"You, um, you know what it looks like. Shouldn't you . . ."

But they sign too slow and fumbling for my patience. The ignits in that box call me back. I shoo Xera away. With the care of a parent tending their newborn child, I loop my tail beneath Rubem's limbs, staying as far as I can from his gloved hand. His throat vibrates. I freeze. His eyelashes flutter once, but go still. Painstakingly, I keep moving, twisting my coils beneath him and elevating him off the bed.

I slip my hands along his belt and find a ring of keys, all far too big for the ignit box. His pant pocket yields a crushed paper with scrawling human words on it, the ink bleeding together from his dunk in the water. Twisting awkwardly to reach around Rubem's fishnetted hand, I feel through Rubem's drooping shirt pocket. My fingers hit metal. My heart leaps.

I yank out the little key so quickly that Rubem's body drops back against the bed like a wet sack back.

His throat vibrates again and his face pinches. He presses his cheek into the blankets and curls his arms tighter, bumping a loop of my tail in the process. His motion stops. Slowly, he wraps his arms around my tail and snuggles it to his chest.

My lungs catch when the fishnet of his glove rides against my scales. The insides of my bones ache. I clutch my ignit in one hand, waving my other arm aggressively at Xera.

They cock their head to the side, and their shoulders shake. "I think he, he likes you."

Motherfucker. "Get him off, get him off!" I make the one-handed motions aggressive enough that the constant stream of cursing in my head must come through.

Xera leaps to my side, gently sliding Rubem's hold off of me and around a pillow instead. Between his unreadable expression and my shuddering bones, I have no idea what the sleeping cartel leader feels about this, but from one greedy silt-breather to another, I imagine his looser grip must mean the switch disappointed him. I can almost smell his melancholy.

Xera leaps back across the room to finish going through the final shelf while I slide the key into the ignit chest. It vibrates with the very soft bounce of metal against metal. I lift the lid.

The glow of the stones burst like a rainbow, glimmering off my scales and warming my chest. The colors come in more blues and reds than yellows or purples or oranges. Nothing green.

My heart drops, first, because there are no poison ignits,

but second, because I didn't even think about Thais and her needs until now. It never occurred to me that finding new ignits could help her—save her. I can almost feel the subtle press of her cool necklace chain as I showed her the blood choke, and the glimpse of the pendant through her sopping clothes when she pulled herself out of Fern's pool the night before. Selfish. Selfish stupid hurricane.

The brush of Xera's hand against my shoulder makes me jump. They flinch back as well and wrap one arm around their chest. With the other, they offer me a new machine to look over. I need only one glance at the compass-like system attached to it.

"That's it." I fit the compass device into my wire necklace, behind its largest stone, securing it firmly, out of view. "I'll keep it with me for now. We can find a way to destroy it later." I'll sink it into the river with a bag of rocks if it comes to that.

They nod, a tiny quick bob of their head. "Time to go."

"Wait, help me carry—" Too late, I sign the words at their back as they slip through the cabin. With a little lunge, I grab for their arm, sliding my tail to gain the momentum. It knocks against a pedestal with a cage of giant beetles perched atop. The enclosure topples. It hits the floor, creating a vibration that feels all-consuming and sending the bugs into a frenzy.

Xera continues moving, oblivious to what they can't feel or hear. As the cage finally rolls to a stop, they slip out the window, leaving me in excruciating stillness. I barely breathe, waiting for Rubem to burst from his bed, or his cartel subordinates to rush down the stairs. Footsteps clomp across the deck above the cabin, but they stop near the railing. I can almost feel the air moving out of the way as the human looks over. Instead of stomping down the stairs to check, though, their boots track back the way they'd come.

Rubem groans and wraps an arm over his head. At the foot of his bed, the ignits call to me once more. I slide toward them. But as I reach for their case, Thais and Fern spill through the open back window.

Thais rushes me, almost stumbling over her own feet. "You're safe, thank—" Her haunting eyes fall to the stones in the chest before me, and her whole face goes slack. Then it pinches. "Cacao!" She signs my name like her hands are on fire. "When we heard the crash and Xera came back without you, we were worried—but spare ignits? You, you, you—" She pokes me in the chest in a repetitive sign for you, and I don't know if she's building toward an insult or just releasing her anger. "We thought Rubem had awoken and captured you or, or worse!"

Those last sentences cut like a knife into the slits between my scales, letting all the other accusations flow in. She's not mad for her sake, or for Fern's or Xera's. Her hot terrible fear-stained anger that stings in my nose swathes off her because she worries about *me*.

My fingers jolt toward my necklace. "I'd feel better if I had these ones too. Just in case." Guilt wraps around my stomach in sickening knots. I want to get rid of the feeling. I want to go back to not caring.

"You don't really believe we'll make it to the hoard?"

That's not a question for me, not a phrase about me or for me. It's Thais's own fear now, for herself, so small she barely touches it, like it's a ghosting breeze that will pass her by if she ignores it long enough. But it won't be gone; it's just circling back around.

"I believe it less and less the longer we stand around and talk," I snap. She deserves a better answer, but this is all I have.

"Exactly." Fern says it without signing, the scent of her agreement and determination so strong that it paints a picture of the word. But she ignores the way out, her gaze fixed on Rubem.

She springs at him, the muscles of her powerful tail tense and her jaw already unlatched. Thais slams into her. Together, they hit the bed, falling onto Rubem's legs. Thais kicks Fern in the chest. Fern recoils, and they stare at each other, tight and stiff.

Rubem screams. He jerks upright. His gaze darts around the room, and his chest shudders. The scent of his fear blisters, acidic. He moves like a bloated corpse, groggy and red-eyed, as though he hasn't quite reached a state of consciousness yet.

Outside the boat, his massive pet slips into the water. It feels like the rattling of our entire plan falling to pieces. Fuck plans anyway.

Rubem says something to Thais, his throat vibrating rough and sluggish, but she replies before his lips finish moving. The boat rocks as though it hit a log the size of a huge crocodilian. Or a crocodilian the size of a huge log hit *it*.

I wave to Thais, "Silence him!"

Her lips bunch together and her eyes widen obnoxiously, but she grabs the terrified half-asleep cartel leader and wraps her arms around his neck, just as I showed her earlier. She squeezes. Rubem's brow shoots up. He gives half a thrash; then his limbs drop.

Thais lets go like he might burn her if she lingers. He slumps onto the bed. His eyelids flutter and his fingers curl, but his post-alcohol brain seems unable to fit enough pieces back together to do much more yet.

Fern rises up on her tail, her tongue flicking toward Rubem. "He still lives!"

"He'll keep living," Thais shoots back, sliding off the bed to stand in front of it.

As they argue, I dart into the little bathroom to check the window. Another small rock of the boat stops me short. Out the open hole, lumpy grey scales twist away, turning through the water to reveal the gaping mouth and jagged grin of Rubem's crocodilian. Baring my own teeth, I wave a farewell to the crocodilian's good eye and slide back into the main cabin.

Fern towers over Thais, her own lips drawn back, jaw open. "It's his fault those bones were crushed! People gave me them, parts of themselves, trusted them to me, trusted me not to be a liar in this—this one thing. And he destroyed them. He defiled them."

Thais scowls, both hands clenched. She peels her fingers apart like they're welded together. "Killing him will not make it right."

Neither of them points out that it was Xera who dropped the tree, or my life they dropped it for, that Rubem is a pathetic bystander in this mess. Neither do I. Maybe Thais isn't the only hypocrite here.

As I approach them, my heart pulls me toward the ignits. *"You don't really believe we'll make it to the hoard?"* I have a new answer for her: *We'd fucking well better.*

I grab Fern by the arm, yanking her up the stairs. She goes limp in my grip, and as though forgetting to pull away, she lets me drag her, her shock thick as a midnight mist. A bug net blocks the top. I stutter, my tail slipping back down the steps without the forward momentum. Fern comes back to life. She shoves the net aside and bursts onto the main deck, hauling me with her, Thais so close behind that she nearly skids on my tail.

Boxes and empty seats populate the main deck, the canvas top wrapped up and laid across one rail. More stairs ascend on either side of the cabin entrance, wrapping around to the upper deck where the bearded human sits near the wheel. They startle at the sight of us.

Rubem's crocodilian rams the hull, but the high railing rises too far out of the water for it to easily climb over. The small boat of three cartel members veers toward us, abandoned dice rolling across their little center table. One last human stands on the other vessel to our right, taking up position behind a massive mounted slingshot. A fist-sized purple ignit nestles in it, wrapped in a thin netting but activated and fully alight.

The ignit launches at us, propelled from the gun, fast enough to blur. It hits Fern square in the hips, immediately recoiling as the gunner drags it back with its netting by a rope. A tremor runs through Fern so violently I can feel it along my ridges. She goes limp, splaying across the wood, still breathing but very paralyzed, like the effects of the purple ignit stick Rubem used at the treehouse but amplified excruciatingly. Prickles spark across my scales in response.

I look at Thais, and Thais looks at that damn gun—that damn gun which reloads at lightning speed. I see the direction of her feet before she moves: the way she'll swing herself in front of me and take the next shot. But I won't let her drop for me, especially if it brings about another spasm. I'm a hurricane and a thief, but I won't be an idiot, not today.

I grab her by the shoulders, flinging both of us into the water. The ignit flies over our heads. The river engulfs us. From beneath Rubem's big boat, his half-blind crocodilian twists its massive jaws our way. I *am* an idiot after all.

Grabbing Thais around the thighs, I shove her nicely padded rump into the small boat. As she sprawls onto its deck, I reach madly for something to pull myself up with. My hands close on the ankles of the human manning the gun, but the crocodilian's jaws clamp around my tail before I can climb. Pain shoots up my spine, and I dig my fingers deep into the human's skin. When the crocodilian yanks me back into the river, the gunner comes, too, their chest vibrating in a piercing scream that dies the moment the water covers their head.

They kick me in the shoulder. I let them go and turn my attention to the crocodilian chomping on my flesh. I wrap the rest of my tail around its neck. It shoots forward and slams me into the side of Rubem's boat. The blinding pain makes my brain stutter.

My head breaks the surface. Just before the crocodilian drags me back under, my vision clears. I find Thais perched behind the cannon and loosing slingshots like she was born for it. Her ignit eyes flash with mine. Silt streams, I hope she's thinking the same thing I am. Otherwise my tail might get a lot shorter today.

The crocodilian yanks me down and rolls us toward the riverbed, fish fleeing from our path like flickering silver and gold sparks. We hit the dirt so hard it knocks the air from my lungs in streaming bubbles. I don't let us linger. Tightening my tail around the crocodilian's thick neck, I yank its head back toward the surface. We come up near the front of Rubem's big boat. I grab the railing. The crocodilian tries to drag me back down, and my tail screams in a flare of black agony. But I hold on.

Splinters wrack my arm muscles. My fingers slip. As I plunge toward the water, the netted purple ignit knocks into the crocodilian's side. It trembles through the massive beast. The excess flows into my tail, jarring it, then numbing.

The crocodilian's limp body sinks, the weight of its bulky muscles dragging it down. My numb tail pulls me with it. I thrash, pawing at the boat as we go under. The hull slips away beneath my fingers. The crocodilian's scales press against me, lumpy squares, too much like fishnets or rotting bark or—

I rub my thumb over my ignit, feeling the dull pulse of it like a second heartbeat, a soothing rhythm that flows through me. Using my hands, I unwrap my tail from the crocodilian's body. A cloud of blood seeps from the fresh gashes twisting through my scales. I bare my teeth at the few brave fish edging closer. They scram.

Now for the boat.

I pump my arms, wiggling the less numb portions of my tail. Little by little, I force myself closer to the boat. My hands barely reach the railing. My arms cramp as I flop onto the main deck near the front peak.

I heave my tail up after me, like Thais has tried to do so many times. It takes far more effort than she made it look, along with some tugging, straining, and teeth gritting. By the time I finish, the cartel humans lie stunned or moaning from her work with the purple ignit shooter. All but one.

He steps onto the deck, a hand held above his eyes and squinting despite the Murk's natural gloom. The smoke stench and the reek of sticky bile linger on him, but now he smells of the sun, too, awake and determined, his fear gone or maybe just hidden. He surveys the scene. His jaw pulses.

The moment he looks away from Fern's collapsed form, she curls, quiet and subtle. She lunges at Rubem. Her mouth opens and her muscles bulge, but Rubem ducks out of the way, fluid as the fog, and her teeth clamp on air. His elbow crashes into Fern's head, and he steps back in one smooth motion. His emerald-encrusted pistol seems almost to fly into his grasp. The silky contained vibration of it firing rattles my ridges.

Oh, muck. We should have killed him. This was a mistake.

Fern's torso buckles, and with a thud, she hits the stairs leading to the top deck, blood welling along her side. It slips in scarlet rivers through the cracks in her green scales, pooling as more and more seeps out. It drips to the wooden deck. I can't feel the constant plunk from the other end of the boat, and somehow, that makes everything worse, as though it's only half happening, as though closing my eyes could reverse the whole thing.

I writhe an arm's length toward Fern, but my numb tail clunks along, smearing red in its wake. Thais slams the boat with the purple ignit cannon into the side of Rubem's, and I tumble behind a collection of crates in the center of the deck. She leaps to Fern's side.

Rubem aims the pistol at them both, and they freeze. From the other small boat, a dazed human rolls over. The bug net from the cabin entrance curls up in a phantom breeze. Rubem's chest heaves in and out. Fern bleeds.

A bolt shafted in green and brown feathers whizzes out of the canopy above me, streaking toward Rubem's arms. He yanks his hands down just in time. The bolt embeds harmlessly into the wood, and Rubem's aim shifts to Xera. They go still, crouched on a drooping branch over the front of the boat.

"Drop it." He signs the words with one hand, his lips moving in time.

Slowly, Xera lets the crossbow go. It clatters across the deck, the vibrations odd compared to the stillness that exists around its owner. Behind Rubem's shoulder, Thais eases Fern a few steps up the stairs. A few steps toward safety. They stop moving when Rubem turns back toward them.

Xera beats their branch. "Wait!"

Rubem eyes them. "Yes, Murkling?"

He hasn't seen Xera with us yet, not since the early morning, and I don't know if he can remember them with enough certainty to identify them as the human whose house caught fire.

Xera's fingers flicker to one of the feathers on their clothes, touching it gently. They swallow.

I should help. I *want* to help. But I'm too close to Fern and Thais. If Rubem's attention turns to me, he might see them move out of the corner of his eye. So I curl myself smaller instead, rubbing my ignit as though somehow that will make the words come for Xera.

"You are, uh . . ." Xera's hands tremble, wobbling through a series of motions clearly not meant to be words at all, and finally land on, "very red."

Rubem blinks, the wrinkles around his narrowed eyes multiplying. "Yes, as well as very busy with an excruciating headache and a mess you'd do best not to involve yourself with."

Xera glances at Fern and Thais who are now halfway up the stairs, but they immediately switch their gaze to the small boat drifting farther down the rivulet. "You—you shouldn't be here. No river people in the Murk. Not right."

The base of Rubem's throat vibrates, and he pushes his hand against his brow, pulling it away finally to sign. "You're right. But we will be leaving soon, and this young person—" he waves toward Thais, who freezes. His attention must not have shifted enough to see the progress she's made up the stairs. "She's no Murkling, and neither is the boiuna hiding behind those crates."

I squeeze my ignit a little tighter and give Rubem a tiny smirk.

His lips twitch in return, but he shudders the smile away, looking back to Xera. "I apologize over the one I shot, but it was in my own defense. The three of them attacked my crew and invaded my boat to kill me in my sleep."

A clumpy knot forms in my still partially senseless gut, as though a wallop of mud slinks through it. Rubem is wrong, of course. But only barely.

Thais pulls Fern up the final step. The bearded cartel human struggles to rise from their slumped position across the seats on the top deck, but Thais grabs the purple ignit stick lying at their side—that same one that Rubem used on us in the treehouse—and pokes them with it. They go limp again.

Xera's fingers flutter over their feather, and they bunch their lips. "I think, you should know, that in the, um, the case of all of you, the surface is, is rougher."

"The surface?" Rubem asks.

"Um, the surface, yes. It's rough and hard, but inside are more things, things you did not see before: beautiful things and good intentions. Just *more*."

"Like a geode?" I sign to Xera.

"Geode, uh, yes," they agree, returning immediately to play with their feather.

As they do, Thais helps Fern climb into the driving console. Fern stretches toward the canopy. Her face contorts, fresh blood draining from her side. She grabs a branch and pulls onto it, twisting her tail around the wood to reach down for Thais.

But Thais clings to the purple ignit stick, looking back at me to sign a muddled, "When I throw, run."

Motherfucking—she doesn't know my tail is still numb. And judging by Fern's fast recovery as a larger boiuna, I know somewhere in the water must lurk a mostly functioning crocodilian waiting to swallow me whole.

I try to give Thais the slightest shake of my head, but I can't tell her no without lifting my hands into clear view of Rubem. *Don't do it, Thais. Let Xera help me once you and Fern are gone.*

Like a fucking hero, she ignores me, readying her aim.

"People act like geodes," Xera concludes.

Confusion and suspicion flood Rubem's scent name. Ironic, really, because for the first time in their short conversation, I think Xera isn't actually trying to distract him at all, but rather explaining something they consider important. I agree: rocks *are* important. Rubem seems to think otherwise.

He turns back toward the stairs, just as Thais lets the ignit stick fly. It twists end over end. The moment Rubem spots it echoes through his body in the fluid drawing of muscles and shifting of balance. But his notice comes an instant too late. The stick hits him, the holder smacking into his shoulder. It falls to the deck without the ignit ever making contact.

His pistol comes up. It trains on Fern and Thais as they try to pull themselves properly into the canopy, Thais, still hanging from Fern's arms, stares down the barrel of Rubem's gun. Just staring.

I move without thinking, a mad half lunge, half roll, all scramble. I shove into the back of Rubem's knees. My momentum carries us both forward, landing me directly on top of the ignit. It digs between my head ridges, and the mix of paralyzing energy and vibration against my skull shatters me inside, casting me into the dark.

FOURTEEN

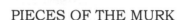

PIECES OF THE MURK

I don't miss the Murk.
I don't miss the Murk.
I ~~don't~~ miss the Murk.

I WAKE TO THE throb of my own blood pounding in my head, a rush and slide like the waves along the coast. My scales tingle, half of them numb and the rest aching. Water caresses my tail and tickles at my waist, but thick glass presses against my side, and the Murk's muggy air fills my lungs.

Rubem's fish tank?

The understanding seeps in like fog, taking so much energy that none remains for my panic. My head ridges brush the tank's mostly closed lid, sending a streak of painful shudders along my skull, and my tail curls awkwardly in the long container, filling most of the water space. Only a few fish remain, small harmless brown things that dart around in a group below my chin.

As I try to orient myself, the whole boat seems to tremble. My heart lifts into my throat, giddy dragonflies tumbling through my stomach. It has to be Thais. What the fuck is she doing? Rubem's scent wafts down from the open stairs to the deck, though, followed by the rap of one of his cartel humans' boots, and I realize the quavering came not from an attack but from the activation of the huge ignit that powers the vessel.

No one is here for me.

That makes me ache all the more. I twist my torso and shove my shoulder against the tank lid. Despite my heaving and lurching, the resilient material pushes back. My muscles burn, and fresh blood seeps from the gash Rubem's crocodile left in my tail, tinging the water pink. I collapse back into it.

Am I going to die here or be carted around eternally like a part of Rubem's collection because I risked everyone else's lives for my greed? Because I refused to ditch a couple pretty stones? The words come from my own mind, but they look like my forebearer's, like the council's and the elders', like apprehensive neighbors and traitorous friends: sharp and accusatory. I can't lose like this. After everything I've been through. If I give in now, then why didn't I give in when it meant I could still have a home?

Home.

It drifts past the window, the late afternoon cast in the deep gloom of the rising fog. The same mist spills through my mind, and muck, muck, I missed the Murk. I'd rather die than be kept as Rubem's eternal prisoner, trapped in his riverboat, never to see this beautiful swamp again. If I do die, at least it'll be here. At least I'm home.

Another breeze twists sluggishly down the stairs, and I pick out Rubem's scent once more, muddled by a metallic buzz in my nose and the grubby smell of his many pets. He makes no vibrations as he descends, only breaking the stillness with a heavy exhale when he sees me. His fresh shirt creates a shock of white beneath the ruby accents of his vest.

"Finally awake?" He approaches the tank slowly, drawing out a key.

I flinch from his new fishnet gloves. The sight of them continues to haunt me as he pops open the lock and lifts the lid. Muck, I need my ignit. I feel the brush of every rock on my necklace and the hidden tracking compass tangled beneath the largest of them, but the wiring that should be holding my ignit lies empty against my scales.

Time to go.

Keeping my eyes on the stairs, I launch toward them. My weak tail thrashes against the glass, and my hip catches on the lip of the lid. I fall halfway to the ground, smacking my elbow, half of my tail still coiled inside the tank.

Rubem's paralyzing stick appears in his hands. Just the sight of the purple glow at its end calls me to it, but its active state pulses through my worn skull, flaring pain along my head ridges. My bones all feel as though they're being corroded away, and I can do nothing but recoil.

I curl into the corner, between the tank lid and the back wall, trying to still my breath, and sign in jagged shaking motions, "Don't you wave that thing at me, silt-breather."

Slowly, Rubem tucks his stick under his arm. His gaze moves along me, his brow tight. "If you don't make another mad break for the stairs, I won't point any weapons at you. Is that acceptable?"

Just being here isn't acceptable. But my head throbs like an open wound, and the route to the stairs seems longer than the entire span of the Murk. Rubem has his pistol tucked back into his belt too. Hurricane or not, I don't think I could kill him with the way my tail feels now, and I don't want to bet on him not shooting me if I fail. So I nod. I regret the motion when a wave of pain splinters my head. "What are you going to do with me?"

Rubem lowers himself into a rocking chair beside a wire cage with a skunk bird in it. The creature picks at its wing claws, spinning its red eyes toward me, feathers fluffing. It reminds me of a hoatzi.

Rubem pours himself a glass of wine dark enough to be the night sky, tendrils of a musty sweetness mixing with the bite of the alcohol's smell. He takes a sip of it and sets the glass down, leaning back in his chair. It rocks ever so slightly, and he stops it with his foot. "I'm still reevaluating. Next question, please."

In my wildest rankings of weird conversations, this one tops all the charts. I sink back into the tank enough to rest my shoulders on the lip and face Rubem properly. "What happened to the others?"

"They left," Rubem replies. "My scouts did notice a large group of Murklings moving in on us—we're sailing away from them now, toward the coast—but I haven't seen the three you traveled with since they abandoned you. Which is unfortunate for us both. I was hoping you might lure Thais in. It's half the reason I kept you."

He could be lying; I don't know what signals to look for to tell. But Thais does have new Murklings to help her reach her hoard now. They could leave me here for good.

The thought doesn't match the Thais and Xera I know, but it sinks in anyway, twisting like a poison in my stomach. Xera could guide Thais through the Murk with fewer problems than I. Thais could reach her mother's hoard without ever needing to give away a single ignit. She would be better off. Maybe she would leave me. The memory of her bile burns my nose, and I touch the twist of her lost hair encircling my wrist.

Desperation makes people do crazy things.

I prop my shoulders a little better against the back wall. "What's the other half?"

Rubem's brow comes up. "Of what?"

"The reason I'm here."

"If I'd dumped you into the water, you'd have drowned."

I've little time to dwell on that because my blue ignit appears between his fingers. He twists it absentmindedly. My hands ache to reach for it, as though my very soul pools inside them, yearning to be closer. I bare my teeth. "Give it back."

Rubem glances at the stone, then drops it into his shirt pocket. "No. You've stolen from me: ignits, a prisoner, a boat, one of my pet's eyes, my only green ignit tracker, the lives of many of my crew and whatever teetering respect I had from them, and a much-needed morning of rest. I think I'm justified in relieving you of this *one* ignit."

The words dig into me like barbs because they're true. They're true and I hate it. I hate that, while I want that ignit more than he ever will, I took things from him that he seems to have needed and loved more than I ever could, and that somehow, in some bizarre way, that makes the ignit's subtle blue glow through the ruby-embroidered lip of Rubem's pocket justified.

I glare. A few fish mosey a little closer to my still-seeping wounds, and I flick my fingers at them. They streak away.

Rubem stands, his attention caught on me as he walks toward the tank. He moves with such soft fluid motions, so similar to Xera's, that I feel nothing from him above the throbbing of my head ridges. But he doesn't scare me. If anything, he reminds me oddly of the way the young hoatzis would creep closer to my sleeping forebearer, their curiosity pushing them forward until the old boiuna awoke and snapped at them, jaws always not quite clipping their tail feathers even when she could have easily gobbled them all down whole. Rubem's not a Murkling child, though. He's a dangerous cartel leader, and he can fuck off.

I bare my teeth again. "That poison that's polluting Thais now—why'd you make it? If those damn green ignits are so rare, why go to all the trouble of splitting one down so far that it could only be used once?"

My question makes Rubem pause. He traces his fingers along the rim of the tank. I rub the stones on my necklace to keep from focusing too much on the fishnet gloves that turn his hands into something wrong and broken and painful.

Finally, he lifts them and signs, "They're dangerous ignits, those green ones. It's better to have them used up than to risk them slipping into the wrong hands." His eyes lock with mine, and even after I look away, I still feel them boring into me. "Imagine the destruction the fishers would cause if they could kill anything with just a stone."

Not just a stone. My brain skips to nets with the green ignits bound into the weights, slowly killing my body as the ropes pierce my soul, to bullets of green, sinking into Fern's flesh and choking her from the inside out, to the stones dropped like poison into nests and pools and beds. The Murk survives because it stands as one, but none of us could fight something like that. My certainty trembles through me. I aggressively rub my necklace with one thumb, but my free hand feels empty, useless, like it might shake clean off.

"I destroyed most of the ones the cartel had when I became its leader," Rubem finishes, his words turning into disconnected fragments in my head as his hand moves toward my arm. His fishnetted fingers brush against my scales, agonizing.

I tear away from him, instinct and pain driving me backward. My head thuds against the back wall. Dark fire pulses through me, and my scales slip apart. I can feel them crisping up, flaking off, falling away. I breathe in water.

I cough, breaking the surface and sucking at the air, but my lungs remain too tight, too heavy, too damaged. Through the pain, a soft thrum soothes my head ridges the slightest bit, drawing me toward it. I catch the ignit as it sinks into the water, finding the familiar smooth side where I've been rubbing my thumb. Clutching it to my chest, I wait to feel alive again.

As my body fits itself back together, I sense a second, third, and fourth stone drop into the tank. I scoop them up, creating a dazzle of red and blue and yellow and purple. Their nearness soothes me like a cold balm spreading over a burn.

My vision focuses, finding Rubem. He's pulled his chair close and perches on the edge of it, two fingers tapping furiously. They slow with the same beat as my heart. His fishnet gloves are gone.

He *gave* me the ignits. His ignits. Four of them. It must be some kind of trick. Thais offered me the blue ignit back at the mechanic shop because she's some crazy hero, and it was never hers, and she didn't want it. But Rubem has none of those reasons.

"If you're all right coming out of there, we can get your tail wrapped up," Rubem says.

With my bones back into place, I feel the subtle ache of my oozing gashes again. And Rubem—Rubem who gave me ignits—is offering to fix that, and to let me out of this confinement in the process. My mind flickers back to my earlier assumption that he's trying to trick me somehow, but if this is a ploy, I can't figure out what he means to accomplish. I also can't find a good reason to say no.

With great care, I pull myself free of the tank, holding my new ignits in my mouth until my entire tail lies properly across the ground. I soak the floor with water and a little blood. Rubem watches, never attempting to touch me no matter how many times his fingers twitch my way.

I curl the wounded part of my tail in front of me. My body seems to have come back together smaller and weaker than before, more child than adult. "Have at it, I guess."

"Yes. Right." He shakes his head and takes a sip of his wine, then pulls out a container with medical supplies.

For all the confusion I smell from him, his now fishnet-free hands never waver as he cleans and bandages the fresh gashes, surveying the old ones while he does. I think, maybe, his bewilderment has nothing to do with the cuts, and everything to do with me.

"Why give me these?" I sign, one hand still clutching the ignits to my chest as he finishes tying off the last bandage.

"You needed them." Rubem scoots backward to rest against his seat. "I didn't know if there was a certain color or number, so I improvised." His hand moves to his wineglass, and his fingertips touch the rim before he yanks them away. "I have something I need as well. I don't suppose it's quite the same, because I wasn't always like this, and the pain its lack causes is more emotional than physical. But still, I understand." His fingers twitch, and he lifts the glass properly this time, taking a long sip before he sets it down. "Besides, these few ignits are nothing to me."

Of course. Nothing compared to the number Thais's hoard will supply him. "You're not getting Thais's ignits."

Rubem's chest vibrates in something like a huff or a laugh. "What does she even need that multitude for?"

My hands stay up, but no response comes because I've asked the same thing since I first learned of her hoard. I curl a little tighter around the ignits Rubem gave me and ask instead, "How many is a multitude?"

Rubem's lips curve in an expression that could be everything or nothing at all. "More than there's ever been in one place before, on the rivers, or in the mountains, or throughout the swamps, or even around the rest of the world, I'd wager."

The mere idea of it overwhelms me, desire bursting like a dam, too torrential to catch it all, to do anything but be swept downstream. The more I think, the more I wonder if it's too good to be true. "How do you know?"

"Speculation, mostly," Rubem admits. "Thais's mother spent fifteen years scouring this side of the continent for every ignit she could get her hands on, stealing, trading, murdering. Outside the Murk, we were just beginning to harness the ignits' powers, but we never would have had enough of a supply vacuum for the cartels to take control if that woman had not siphoned off so many of the stones." He takes another sip of his wine. "Maybe she destroyed some of them, maybe she threw them into the sea, maybe she had them shipped to some distant continent to sell there, but I don't think so. I think they're all at her old trove, thousands of inactive ignits. And I need to be the first one to reach them."

Thousands of inactive ignits. My chest flutters. Then it clenches with guilt because my focus still sweeps right over Thais's need for a green ignit and straight to my desire for her hoard.

Rubem interrupts my musing with a rumble deep in his throat. "You know, I could use someone like you—someone who could get into the deepest cracks beneath the mangroves."

Suspicion rears its head within me. I flick out my tongue, but he smells weakly of interest and nothing more. "Why? Do you want me to collect the Murk's ignits for you?"

"No, no. And I'd prefer not to rob the Murk of anything, but I may be able to solve most of our problems if I can get ahold of one of the ancients."

His other signs were all present in the boat human's dialect, but this one—the specific word he uses to say *ancient*—is a Murk sign. *Only* a Murk sign. The boat humans called them nothing but *Big Trees* and *Dangerous*, because they never figured out what lay within the hulking rock-hard trunks, the glimmering life that wasn't plant or animal. Yet Rubem, like Lily, signs it as though it's a usual part of his vocabulary. But I still have to ask, "You know what an ancient is?"

"I know." Rubem leans forward. "I'm well aware that the ancients are a life-form all of their own, a fungal-like creature, but not a fungus at all. They take over the mangrove from the inside, latching to its energy source, which they've used to produce ignits with fresh enthusiasm in recent generations."

I shake my head. "There were ancients along the river systems once, but they've all died out since you fucking boaties moved in. If you could get one now, what makes you think you can keep it alive?"

Rubem takes a sip of his wine, but his gaze never leaves me. "They died out because my father's *fucking* people were destructive fools who wouldn't nourish the land if their very existence depended on it. If I had to keep an ancient alive, I believe I could do it. I know better than them."

"You're not really one of them, are you?"

"I'm not anything." He downs the rest of his glass in one go and stands to refill it, his fluid motions like a silent breeze. Like a piece of the Murk. But just a piece, not a whole. More questions jump to my hands—what if the boat humans learn about the stolen ancient and come for the rest—but he doesn't turn back, just stares into the wine, swirling it around, then around again. "So, would you do it? Would you join with me? For the moment. Or perhaps longer. You'd be an apprentice of sorts, I suppose."

Join Rubem? A burning flash of bile rises in my throat, but as it fades, I realize the distaste comes from a flimsy instinct, meant to protect me from someone who was never my enemy to begin with. The longer I dwell on the idea, the more I find I like it. And I like Rubem. He's blunt about the edges, but not unkind, just rational and a little messy. I could enjoy working with him, under the right conditions. I could enjoy molding myself after him too.

I brush my fingers over the ignits in my lap, watching their slow glow shimmer under my touch. I wanted a solitary ignit-hoarding life. But what if I could have more? An ever-growing hoard of ignits *and* people to belong with. A family.

But that thought drags my mind to someone other than Rubem. "And you'll leave Thais alone if I do?"

"I'd want to." Rubem frowns. He sips from his glass. "If we get an ancient, I won't need her hoard. Whatever the case, I was never the one who wished any harm on her—or you. If you help in this, you will be granted as many ignits as I can spare."

As many as he can spare. I trace the four he's given already, and a part of me wants to settle forever in their thrum, to be happy with just this. But the other part thinks of multitudes. If I work with Rubem, I would be settling for merely many ignits instead of a whole host. If I work with Rubem, Thais will still need someone to help her reach the hoard and dampen her poison.

But she has Fern and Xera now, and I have an opportunity for a life with enough ignits, free of cartels and fishers hunting me. A life that wouldn't include Thais. Thais, who would leave me after we reach her hoard anyway. Thais, who hasn't come for me.

I cringe. "I don't know. I have to think."

Rubem's chest contracts, and he rubs his fingers against his forehead. He takes another sip. A deep stillness settles in, broken only by his drinking as he stares out the window. Through it, the swamp turns to grey, fog curling in between the roots of the mangroves.

I think of Thais, of her gleaming eyes and her hero's heart. Nothing stirs. Not that I'm waiting for the soft plodding of her bare feet or the crash of Fern's great tail or the tiny ping of Xera's crossbow bolt. But I tap out Thais's rhythm anyway, embedding it into the colorful stones in my lap.

The gentle vibrations of my fingers against the ignits almost drown out the thrum of an arriving boat. Someone calls from the deck. Rubem's eyes widen. He sets down his glass so hurriedly the wine nearly sloshes, and his hands clench and unclench as he calls up in response.

He turns to me with widened eyes. "The fishers are here."

FIFTEEN

———⌇———

THE PATH OF THE HURRICANE

Maybe all people find friends
in the most mysterious of places.
Or maybe it's just us
who can't find them any other way.

THE SIGN POURS THROUGH me, a chill first, then a flood of boiling oil. "But I saw . . ."

My words hang, because I'm such an idiot. What I saw was Lily and Wolf becoming penajuar lunch, not the whole fisher's guild annihilated. Maybe those two fishers I feared most were Rubem's primary contacts, but more horrors like them pollute the same river.

"You can't let them in here, they're fishers! They kill everything that isn't human." I wave to the assorted creatures around us, as though Rubem's love for animals will slap him out of this nonsense.

"I can't keep her out." Rubem's throat bobs; his signs mirror the movement. "But I doubt Lily will harm you now, as long as she thinks you're under my control."

My brain sticks to the fisher's name, digging in with rows of teeth. And I am still such an idiot, because she's not dead at all. She's smarter or faster or just plain luckier than I anticipated. I shove my blue ignit into my necklace. Lifting my torso into the air, I pull back my lips. "I don't care. She's killed my kind. I would eat her for less." It comes with a dual threat: I will eat her, and I can eat you all if you try to control me. Not that any of these humans are small enough to fit nicely in my stomach.

But Rubem shakes his head with such vehemence his braids jerk back and forth. "That's not a risk I'm willing to take, not yet. Not when she might have the North prepared to storm our jungles at her brother's word."

Over the course of our conversation, his hardness has gone soft, his sharp edges receding, turning a violent cartel leader into a tired lonely man with Murk skin. His red undertones remain, but as his whole being draws itself together, they only serve to make him all the more terrifying. He is not from the rivers or the Murk. He is something deadlier than either. His hands flash like bullets.

"Get into the bathroom." The thud of a new pair of boots hits our deck, and the light from above shifts and flickers as people pass in front of it. I pick up no scent but Rubem's, his sun-kissed smell turned night dark with dread, scorched in the fires of a terrible resolve. His gaze burns me down to mere cinders. "You are on my boat, and you will listen to me like your life depends on it."

"You..." My sign droops because through his fear-laden determination, I catch a whiff of salt and metal. Despite all my anger and desire, my blood goes cold. I make the sign for Lily, dragged through the chest-pounding motions for evil.

Rubem nods. He ushers me into the bathroom, shutting the door so forcefully that it clunks against my coiled tail. A little silver lock with a keyhole holds the window closed now. Not that I care. I may be hiding from Lily, but I won't flee from her too.

As Rubem charges up the stairs, I crack the bathroom door back open, just enough to peek through. Near the top step, he all but throws his body in the path of a human with familiar black boots and billowing blue pants, blood staining the fabric in splotches.

I can barely make out Rubem's hands as they shift angrily through a series of signs. "If you touch my animals, I swear by the stones I'll gut you and your brother, consequences be damned."

The human takes another step downward, forcing Rubem back. Her hands come into view, oddly pale skin almost glowing in the dim light. "—yet more demands." Her salt and metal scent follows, like gunpowder blasted on a cold wet coast, a hint of something floral barely rising through the sewage.

Rubem stiffens. His fingers flinch toward his pistol. "These are promises."

"If you say so," Lily replies. She shoves past him, marching down the stairs like she's half metal herself—resolute and nearly indestructible.

This close, with no fight or flight to distract me, it's like I'm seeing her anew. Her nose sits tiny on her face, her jawline stiff and her eyes round. Little brown spots cover all her exposed skin, and beneath her dingy bloodstained clothes, the top of a brooch peeks out, its golden design gleaming with lines that glow a faint silver, like an ignit turned to liquid.

"That's not a risk I'm willing to take, not yet," Rubem said. Maybe he's right. If Lily could survive the penajuar and still reach us here, then my measly attack would be futile.

I cannot see the creatures her gaze flickers over as she wrinkles her nose, but I smell her disgust turn her already harsh scent even more bitter. "Your crew tells me the girl was here."

From the base of the stairs, Rubem remains silent, his hands going still in a way that overflows with unused energy. His fury and pain rake across my senses. I close my nose tight to keep from coughing it out.

"And you let her escape. Again." Lily pauses to trace the edge of the birdcage. "What is this now, the third time?

Fourth? We put you in charge of this cartel because you claimed you could do a job for us." She turns on Rubem. Her fists seal around the front of his shirt, and she slams him into the wall, knocking aside the skunk bird cage in the process. Angry vibrations bellow from the bird as it struggles to right itself, and I nearly miss the tremor in Lily's throat. With one hand, she signs, "Next time, you keep her. Whatever it takes."

"The poor child is already suffering." Rubem's jaw pulses. "I don't want to hurt her more."

Lily releases him with a shove. A little knife flips into her hand. She presses it to his pulse, the tip digging into skin just red enough that I almost miss the drop of blood it draws. "And I don't want to hurt you—I have actual villains to dispose of. Sullying my hands with your barbarian blood is wildly inconvenient for me. But I will do it. I will raze your precious Murk for every ignit it's worth if I must."

Between the odd angle of my viewing and the impeding lines of the doorway, I doubt myself. His precious Murk. But it's my precious Murk too. I must have seen right, because even if I don't belong here, the fire to fight for it burns through me, just as I smell it burn through Rubem, turning him back into a sun so bright it hurts to watch.

He moves like a vengeful wind, knocking Lily's arm away and slamming her backward. She slashes at him. He ducks from her reach, so fast my eyes nearly fail to track, and blocks the attack, once, twice, three times before they come apart, sliding into their original stances.

"I said I would get you that hoard, and I will," Rubem snaps.

"Sooner than later, Veneno." A rough vibration comes from Lily's chest. "Is that really your surname? Veneno. *Venom.*" She gives him one more look, then turns back toward the stairs. "I can't wait to leave this pathetic jungle behind."

It seems like something she should be muttering to herself alone, but the reaction it inflicts in Rubem—relief flooding his scent name—makes it obvious why she signed it. She wants him to know he has only this last act to get rid of her. Only to find and torture a dying hero.

She pauses at the first step. With her lips sealed closed, she continues, "There's always the other way to fulfill your end of the bargain. If you tell me where the ancients are latched, then I'm happy to take one of those instead."

With that, she leaves.

Rubem rushes to his fallen birdcage. His throat vibrates gently as he puts it back into place. I wait for the clatter of Lily's boots to leap from the boat before I burst out of the bathroom.

The open stairs form a perfect route back to Thais or to my old life or to anywhere but here, in this mess, with this dark northern omen hanging over it. But my irritation billows up, too hot and heavy to run from. "You silt-breather, you don't want the ancient for yourself, you want it for *Lily*."

Rubem slumps to the ground, grabbing his wine bottle on the way. He takes a long drag directly from it. His chest vibrates, and the alcohol overwhelms his smell, all but the dosing of sunshine. Laughter. He's laughing, but with something dark and senseless mixed in, as though bitterness drenches his hilarity. It makes no sense. Not when he shakes so hard he looks like he'll come apart at the seams, or when he launches up, waggling his bottle and taking another swig.

"That's it, that's a truth," he replies, his dismal humor infiltrating the fluidity in his signs, turning them stiff and abrupt. "I want to steal the Murk's most sacred creature to make a crazy foreigner leave without ripping apart either it or the young woman I put in her path. Because somehow, some gods-forsaken-how, I'm accidentally the emissary for a place that won't even recognize my existence."

I stare at him. "This is fucked up."

He lifts his glass and signs with the other hand. "I'll drink to that."

"So, you made a deal with Lily and Wolf to save the Murk?"

"Not entirely." His hands fall.

"You going to tell me about it, or like, not?"

"How about *not*?"

My bubble of frustration pops, urging me toward the stairs. Prodding an out-of-sorts cartel leader for information that may do me no good sits very low on the list of things I want to be doing right now. Things like finding Thais and demanding to know why she abandoned me. I pluck the ignits up and slide toward the exit, signing a very muffled, "Then I'm out. Thanks for the shiny rocks."

Rubem leans to catch my attention. His braid beads gleam in the cabin's low lantern light. "Wait, wait. That was sarcasm. Sit down." He points to the floor across from him. "Or curl. Whatever boiuna do."

I flip the ignits between my fingers, looking from Rubem to the sliver of dark canopy visible through the stairs. It begs for me to slip up and out and forget all of this. But I might as well learn whatever Rubem knows before I leave. I flick my tongue, soaking in the dark hilarity and subtle determination oozing off him, and sink back down, leaning against his bed and setting the ignits into my lap. "Talk, then."

He holds up a finger. Lifting his bottle to his lips, he downs the rest of it in a series of expert swallows. His teeth come away purple. He fishes more wine from beneath a table and pops it open. "I have a place up on the river, right outside the northern edge of the Murk. I caught Lily and Wolf snooping around when they first arrived to the region—came from one of the northern isles beyond the siren seas, where, from what I've gathered, they have ancients, too, only Lily and Wolf can't get to them, at least not without one of their own first." He sips from his new bottle. "They liked the number of ignits and ancients the Murk holds, and they were so close to calling in their northern friends to launch an attack."

My muscles feel raw, my stomach turned inside out, as though the knives of these new colonizers already joined the fishers in their conquest. The boat humans alone were bad enough, but a force with more technology, one which doesn't keep to the river, which doesn't fear the Murk? Banishment means nothing if the place that evicted you no longer exists. "And that's why you made the deal."

Rubem nods. "They wanted an ancient, and if not that, then ignits, and I knew how to get those, or thought I did, anyway. There are legends of Thais's mother across the continent—in some, she's a dashing thief, in others, a powerful hag, and in a few, she's the incarnation of evil, a darkness that steals away light and power. But I met her, once."

"What happened?" I lift my brows in question.

"I was fifteen or so when she came past my territory to get to the Murk—the only year she ever went through it instead of around, I think. For all that she craved the Murk's ignits, she had a proper fear of the people who used them. I tried to stop her from going in, with a machete and a lot of growled threats. She would have killed me, I'm certain of it, except that I was still just young enough to look a bit like a child. The last time she knocked me down, she said, 'I have a little girl, you know, four months old today. She's keeping me too close to home.' And then she laughed, 'She's made me soft.' She put the safety back on her gun and left me there."

"So, you knew she had a child," I conclude, "somewhere nearby, probably across Murk territory if she was willing to go into it to get back to her infant."

Rubem nods again. "I promised that if Lily put me into a position of power, I would find this mysterious daughter, and if she were anything like her mother, I would threaten or bribe her into handing over the hoard. I know the people of the river, and even of the Murk, more than she ever will. Having me find her an easy trove that wouldn't require bringing in ships and crews and waging a small war against a swamp that might never reveal its ancients' locations was appealing to her."

"Except you can't get Thais to give up the hoard."

He tips his drink at me. "Precisely."

His skunk bird flaps its wings as a creature roars

somewhere out in the darkness of the night.

Rubem's gaze follows the sound, but for the moment that I watch his eyes, they don't find a focus. The full width of his wine-touched lips catches the light, affronted by the heavy droop of his black brow. A few silver hairs mix between his braids. For all his jewelry and poise, something about him refuses to fit the position Lily placed him in.

"Why a cartel leader?" I ask.

"It was easiest for Lily and Wolf. They were in good with the fishers after they caught a boiuna nearly large enough to be an elder on the Murk's outskirts, and the Fang Cartel's second-in-command—my second-in-command now—didn't much like the current leader anyway. And I admit, I was hoping . . ." He runs a fingertip over the top of his wine bottle before raising his hands again. "The cartel are scoundrels, but they're not picky on who they take in, so long as you can do your job. Since the Murk wouldn't have me, maybe this was my chance."

I could ask him about it: ask him why the Murk won't take him, or when and how he tried. I could commiserate with him. I could make him less alone.

But my heart catches on this: *they caught a boiuna nearly large enough to be an elder.*

"The Warmth of Summer Twilight. That was who they killed." The words spill out of me, unbidden and unstoppable. "I'd smelt her—she'd always been nice to me, nicer than the others, and I had to be sure."

I can almost taste her soft scent name sticking dark and hot in my mouth, along with something bitter, fouler: death. But I hadn't quite believed it, not until I saw her body stretched across the deck of the fishers' dark-wood ship, her severed head propped beside the wheel. Lily and Wolf, with their blazing hair, stood over her, their chests rattling. Laughter, I think.

A shudder drives through my spine, tearing into my skull and growing thorns along the back of my neck at the recollection of their eyes on me, their nets and guns raised, Summer's blood sprinkled across their faces. My body had frozen, as if my fear had grown hooks and latched me in place, until a gunshot on the other side of the boat had startled us all, drawing the fishers' attention long enough for me to flee.

Rubem's hands yank me out of the memory. "I thought it was you I saw that day, in the water." The statement barely makes sense. "I shot into the air. Told them I was scaring you off. For a moment, I was pretty sure they would kill me for it."

It feels all levels of wrong and all kinds of right that it was Rubem there, Rubem who might have saved me. I could thank him, but the words would be useless. They change nothing now. The past is the past, both the good and the bad. My thoughts spring forward to what matters: the future. Thais's future. A future I may or may not be a part of anymore, even for the short half-day's boat ride between us and the coast. A future that Rubem's conjoins with, whether we like it or not.

"Lily and Wolf can't have Thais's hoard." I toss one of my ignits into the air, catching it and plopping it back down with a grin. "So, we'll just have to get them an ancient."

"You'll help?" Rubem's eyes flash to mine so fast I barely have time to look away.

"Yeah." I bounce my shoulders. "Lily will go north if we get them one, right? She won't just try to take the Murk anyway?"

"I believe so. This is what she's wanted from the start. Besides, her brother is hanging on, but his wounds could turn infectious any day. She's already antsy to leave."

"And if they go north, then the fishers will back down too? Leave the Murk alone and return to their whole riverside murdering?"

"They won't have the courage or the tech to invade the Murk if the northerners don't provide it."

"Then, how I see it, Lily will either take Thais's ignits— which I can't allow, not just because they're mine now too—or she'll rip apart the Murk for whatever she can get a hold of, probably churning up some ancients in the process. If throwing one at her will really make her and her brother run back home, then that's the best way to get rid of her." Run back home and leave the route to the hoard open for Thais, and the route to Thais open for me. So I can reach the hoard too. And just a little, so I can reach Thais.

Rubem's scent name turns into a chaos of emotions so heavy I can't pick one from another, bright and acidic, sweet and dark all at once. "We'd still be giving up an ancient, a part of the Murk, something the people respect and rely upon."

"You were the one who suggested this," I remind him.

He points his bottle at me, nearly sloshing some of the wine out. "Yes, and that doesn't mean I don't hate the idea."

"The Murk sucks. They kicked us out, didn't they?" Despite my best efforts, I flinch at my own signs, and from the gloomy smell that clouds Rubem's former turmoil, I think they must hurt him too. "Besides, we're only taking one ancient. The Murk will still have eight more. They'll survive."

After another swig, Rubem drops his forehead onto the lip of his bottle. With one hand he signs. "All right." His chest rises and falls, the motion heavy, as though he's breathing in an entire fog bank and letting it out as a condensed sea. He plops the bottle between his folded legs and claps his hands together once. "Which ancient do we give Lily? Preferably one along our current trajectory and nearby, since that band of Murklings is still somewhere behind us. And it must be guarded by something we can handle alone—you, me, and my *Sheila*." He signs a variation of an affectionate feminine term for that final name, and I assume he must mean his crocodilian because that's the only fight-worthy creature—feminine or otherwise—who seems particularly fond of him around here. "And, it shouldn't be an ancient known for producing anything too dangerous. Nothing that's ever spit out a green ignit, at least."

I feel another cringe coming. The darkness of the night seems to twist itself through the window and smother me. Is Thais out there somewhere, wrapped in the fog, thinking of me? Is she nearer to her hoard than I, whisked through secret rivulets by Fern and Xera, or is she struggling somewhere behind Rubem's ship, hiding from the encroaching Murklings and heaving, Xera there to hold her hair instead of me?

The weight of the poison-finding compass I stole from Rubem sits heavy against my collarbone, like a well-worn promise. One I fully intend to fulfill. "Most of them are clustered farther inland, but there's a notoriously basic ancient—creates blues and reds, mostly—pretty near to the coast. How's that sound?"

"Like a plan." Rubem raises his bottle and drinks to our decision. "After this, you can stay with me or leave, or I can take you anywhere you want, the hoard or another village or—or the moon, if you'd prefer. I'll owe you that much."

"The moon?" I sign it without emotion, staring at the center of his chest, until the little crisscross of strings near his collar begin to rattle the back of my skull, and I have to strum my ignits to make the feeling fade.

Rubem shrugs, his lips turning up. "I'm not certain how we'd get you there, I admit. But, if I could, I might form a moon rock cartel." He winks at me, his scent relaxed in a brittle sort of way, like an ember waiting to flake apart. "Do you think people would go for that?"

I roll my eyes. "I think not even those damn fancy ships your people sail on the sea can fly high enough to get to the moon, so it's a dumb question."

His chest vibrates in something far more recognizable as a laugh than what I felt from him earlier, and he stands.

After consulting and reconsulting me on the best way to reach this ancient, he saunters to the deck to signal our new directions. I settle across his floor, playing with the ignits as I doze in and out of a dreamless sleep. Every time I wake, I look first for Thais. The lack of her presence sprouts an ache in my chest that grows with every hour, just as Rubem's wine bottle empties.

Dawn stalks the horizon by the time one of the crew calls

down. Rubem swirls the final residue of the wine bottle around. He lifts it like he plans to chug the rest. I snatch it out of his hands and down the contents in one go. It burns along the back of my nose, a shudder running through me when I take the final swallow, but as the worst of the alcohol fades, it leaves a subtle fruity smell. "Fuck it all, let's get on with this."

Rubem grabs limply for the empty bottle, his brow somehow both raised and scrunched at the same time. I drop the thing on his bed. Finding a fresh glass tucked against the leg of his rocking chair, I fill it with the clean water from a jug he keeps near the door and shove that into his hands instead.

He stares at me pathetically.

"Last time you caught us both on fire," I add.

"I did, didn't I? That was never my intention, you know."

Now it's my turn to stare at him.

With a sigh, he downs the water and discards the glass. We ascend to the deck.

I catch only glimpses of the crew through the night fog: a blur of the bearded human near the helm and a shadow passing in front of the smaller boat's light. What did they say about me to the fishers? Did they know I was here and held some last bit of loyalty to Rubem after all, or was Rubem right, and Lily only cares about me because of my connection to Thais? She was never a fisher by trade anyway, just a murderer taking advantage of a guild who wanted the things of the Murk just as much as she wanted its ancients?

Even through the mist, I clearly make out the massive mangrove this ancient lives within. It looms over us, a shadow of gnarled bark and twisting branches rising high into the canopy. The trunk itself stretches farther around than Rubem's entire boat, three times over. A few of its leaves twinkle on the surface of the water, silver and black. One of them floats through the twisted caverns formed by the ancient's elaborate root system, vanishing into the shadows.

Somewhere in there lies the creature who turned this mangrove from a simple old tree into a great energy-producing amalgamation.

I slip off the boat, tailfirst. The moment I touch the water, Rubem's crocodilian charges me. I tense, but Rubem puts his hand out, signing a simple word for *friend.* The beast slows. She comes up beside me, cautiously.

Rubem signs the word again. To me, he adds, "You can pet her."

I don't exactly want to, but I stretch out a clumsy hand anyway, rubbing her nose. Her thick boxy scales make my own crawl, and I pull my fingers back quickly, clutching the ignit on my necklace instead. She snorts at me.

"Yeah, okay, I'm sorry I ruined your eye. You were trying to eat me." I don't think she understands most signs, especially my one-handed ones, but I make the motions anyway.

She must accept my apology, because she bumps her head against my side and slips below the surface. One less enemy I have to worry about, and one more ally. Potential ally, anyway.

"I can trust you, right?" The lingering tang of wine accompanies Rubem's question.

Trust. Trust is the thing I have with Thais. The thing I have, at least, when I'm near her, when ignits and ancients aren't stealing my attention. Is it still trust if it's not consistent? And do I have even a little bit of that with Rubem? I don't know, so I tell him the part of the truth he needs to hear. "I've got this. We'll send those damn northerners frolicking back home in no time."

I start to sink into the water when a thick green blur launches at Rubem from the canopy. Fern's musty scent tickles my nose just as she barrels into him. Her tail wraps around him, pinning his arms to his body before he can reach for his pistol. She works her way toward his neck.

My heart stumbles over itself. I scramble back onto the boat, awkwardly wiggling to keep my bandaged gashes from rubbing against the railing, and lunge at Fern. She balks and loosens enough for Rubem to spring free of her. I hold her back, stopping her from leaping at him again as he shouts something consoling to his crewmates through the fog.

She whacks her hip into me. "Let me save you, dammit!"

I elbow her in the shoulder. "You're a little too late for that."

The scent of fresh blood hits me in full force, and I find Fern's bullet wound leaking through a half-fallen wrap of what looks like part of Thais's clothing. I grab Fern's arm and lift it, trying to get a better look. She shies away, but some of the fight leaves her.

As if on cue, a ruffled Rubem appears at her side, somehow lugging along his medical kit despite never seeming to have dipped back into his cabin. He props it open. "May I?"

Fern bares her teeth at him. "You shot me! You destroyed my house and you shot me."

I wrap my tail around her waist once, holding her back as she flings forth the words.

Rubem doesn't even flinch. "I shot you after you tried to eat me. The treehouse was an accident, for which I'm very sorry. Now, you're bleeding."

Fern replies with nothing but silence and the stiff smell of mistrust. Her fingers bunch, but as Rubem leans in to tend to her wound, she merely looks away, her jaw stiff. She lets him work.

"Why are you here—did Thais come?" I pay close attention to my head ridges, searching for any sign of a boat human trudging through the trees. A monkey hollers in the distance, and some small predator pounces on a bird a little ways above me. No Thais. "And what took you so long? Were you guys planning to come rescue me someday, or were you just waiting around to see how Rubem would dispose of my corpse?"

I don't know what makes me say it, but I know the pain in my words comes straight from the center of my chest. It hurt being left behind, no matter how civilized Rubem turned out to be. It hurt that Thais had apparently given up on me. Thais, the fucking hero.

Thais, my friend.

"Thais had a bad spasm." Fern's expression remains unreadable and her scent name empty, but her hands shake just the slightest bit. "Someone had to watch her and steer the canoe and someone else track Rubem's boats. Now that he's stopped, it's the first time Xera or I could be spared."

"Oh." Guilt tangles in my gut like thorny vines. I stroke my necklace ignit, trying not to think about Thais's pain or the fisher's ability to distract me from it so thoroughly, or my own stupid desire for them to have dropped everything to come after me. And they did. They came. For me. "Hey, you did what you could." I smile at Fern, but I don't feel the grin beyond the forced tug of my lips.

She cringes. Though, that may be from Rubem tightening a bandage around her torso. "Yeah, but see, there's more." She glances over her shoulder, out into the fog, back the way Rubem and I had just come. Her signs speed up. "We can't stay here. Thais and Xera and I, we've been behind you, but that group of Murklings from the village, they've grown larger, and they've got three elders with them, one huge enough to take down Rubem's boat in a single swoop."

The world dissolves around me, spinning itself into a deadly point. I shake. "Is it . . .?"

"It's her," Fern confirms. "Brine's coming for you."

SIXTEEN

---❧---

THE LIMIT TO GOODNESS

An idea which seems like a million ignits in one moment
may twist into an unattainable fog the next.
Not all that shines is precious stone.
(Some of it's actually just sparkly muck.)

ONLY THE PULSE OF my ignit against my collarbones holds me together, its gentle heartbeat seizing each of my shattered pieces and sealing them back into place bit by bit. I pull air into my lungs and push it out again. Brine is coming. Brine is coming, and we can't be here when she arrives.

"Right. Well, Rubem has to continue driving the boats to keep them as far from Brine's reach as possible. But this rivulet turns for a ways before veering back toward the coast. I'm small enough to swim through the groves, so I can get to the ancient and still catch back up with the boats where the rivulet swoops toward the ocean again."

Fern startles. "Get to what now? Why do you—"

"You're sure you'll be all right?" Rubem signs in front of her.

"No." I reply with one hand, rubbing my ignit with the other as though it might fix this the same way it fixes the exploding pain in my bones. "But I'm doing it." I give him and Fern no time to object, slipping neatly back over the boat's railing.

Fern follows, confusion wafting off her in waves. As her body plunks into the water, Rubem shouts something up the deck. His boat's engine reverberates to life, its massive blue ignit sending a tremor through my skull.

Fern vanishes below the water, sinking out of sight. I nearly follow, but Rubem waves at me.

"Wait!" he signs. Reaching into his vest, he seems to fish through a couple inner pockets and finally draws forth a handful of ignits, smaller than those I left in his cabin. Knowing I won't be back on this boat immediately, I have a sudden urge to grab them. But as I hold back, Rubem tosses me a few: a purple, a yellow, and a red. I catch them, plucking them straight into my mouth for safe keeping.

He opens his vest to put the remaining ignits back, revealing a pocket made of fishnet fabric. A familiar poisonous glow peeks through it, larger than the other stones and far more deadly.

A green ignit.

"Come back in one piece," Rubem signs, but his words hurdle through my head in a blur.

I want to reach for him, for his green ignit, for Thais's life, but a thought stops me: If I get this ignit now, if I hand it over and it cures Thais, then this ends, all of it. No hoard, no journey. No more us. We both immediately go back to our old fucking poisons, the slow ones eating us up over the course of a lifetime. Alone. Her off in the world without me.

Rubem's boat bursts into motion, carrying him and his green ignit away, carrying my choice with it. My chest tightens, sparks like lightning tingling their way down my limbs, taunting me to throw off this paralysis. Fern shoves into me, reaching past, but her fingers barely brush the hull before the boat pulls out of her reach, vibrating off into the gloom.

"You—he—he had one," her hands sputter. "Cacao! He had a poison ignit, I saw it."

"I know." What else do I say? "I panicked." Such a harmless

truth, so many meanings, so many lies. If Fern knew, she'd probably appreciate it.

But in her current state of horrified bewilderment, she only continues to point. "We have to follow him. We have to take it from him!"

"There's no time." I shake my head, even as my heart throws fits of guilt, yanking me all directions at once. "We have an ancient to steal."

We have an ancient to steal. I repeat it to myself, sinking into the water. I already shoved Thais to the side for this long. I set myself on this path. I have to carry it out.

Not bothering to look back at Fern's floating form, I head for the ancient. Away from my aching heart. Ignoring it is both way too hard and far too easy.

I pause in the shadows of the mangrove's arching roots and retrieve the ignits from my mouth to hold them out like little lanterns. There's no law that the ancients must be guarded by some kind of dangerous beast. It just happens that way, like the creatures are drawn to the presence of the being within.

I can't decide whether attempting this at night is madness or brilliance. Drunkenness, maybe. But beneath the slight buzz of the alcohol I took from Rubem, a high of terror and determination courses through me, complete with the anxious intoxication that comes from having one glorious terrible option that might fall apart at a moment's notice.

A glimmer of blue scales shifts between the mangrove's roots. The gentle pulse of the ignits growing in the tree's center calls me like a siren song, a tiny heartbeat that makes my body move to its rhythm. Using the vibrations as a beacon, I slip through the nearest root tunnel.

Another glimpse of blue gleams in my ignit's rainbow light. I feel the creature's movement along my ridges, starting with the beating of its massive gills three tunnels to my right and twitching down its long body, a body that keeps going, and going, and going. Panic swells in me.

I shoot through the roots, careening the opposite direction

of its head, but the sudden motion draws its attention. It slithers through the tunnels behind me. The roots split, new passageways leading off constantly, before winding back together, veering up, then down, then up again. I dive through them, narrowly avoiding the creature's winding tail, trying not to thrash too much, not to draw its attention any more than I already have.

This is where Rubem's Sheila would have come in real handy.

My heart beats like a drum, but even it can't block out the shuddering vibrations of the beast moving around me. It seems everywhere at once, eternally coming closer and closer.

At a brush against my tail, panic constricts bubbles from my mouth. I shove my extra ignits into my mouth and twist, coiling myself around the creature. I'm met with a body far smaller and leaner than the monster's. Strong arms grab me. I give Fern's shoulders a shove. She lets go.

"What—" I start, but the beast's head appears behind us, eyes sightless and a hundred needle-thin teeth bared. I shove Fern forward and burst after her. As we flee, I sign a simple question, making the grabbing motion of *caught*, aimed from her and yanking back toward the boat: "You caught Rubem?"

She shakes her head, replying with *you—here—be eaten*.

I motion with exasperation to the monster now chasing *both* of us.

With a roll of her eyes, Fern grabs me, shoving me through a bundle of roots and into a higher tunnel. She wiggles in afterward. The beast knocks its head against our entrance, but the roots hold. It pulls back. Probably seeking out a new route to its favorite meal of idiot boiuna.

"Are you really taking an ancient? That's fucked up." She gazes off to one side. Maybe she doesn't like the idea. Maybe she's not sure whether she should help me or stop me. Maybe she's just tracking the monster's movement.

"I'm not taking it for myself." I strum my thumb over my necklace ignit once, ignoring the subtle twinge of my lungs telling me I need another breath soon. "I don't have time to explain, but this is what's best for the Murk. For once."

Her gaze bores into me so hard I feel the urge to cover my eyes, as though that will remove her scrutiny. "Xera trusts you, so take the ancient. I'll distract the guardian near the rim of the mangrove. But I want all the details on this later. And there better be some skeletons involved."

"Just don't let any of those skeletons be yours, thanks," I grumble.

"Hey, I think that's the nicest thing you've ever said to me." Her lips twist. A smile maybe, or a smirk. "But I make no promises."

With that, she peels back the way we came, bashing against the roots as she goes. Her vibrations resonate with such enthusiasm that they nearly drown out all else, and it takes me a moment to track the movement of the endless monster's head. It slithers after Fern.

I spit my little ignits back into my hands and swim toward the gentle pulse in the mangrove's center.

The root maze opens to a small chamber glowing with the blue light of two ignits nestled on the ground, surrounded by curls of black glass that I know from experience will take an hour of tedious knife work to break through. But, oh, muck, it's lovely. My fingers twitch, and I find myself moving toward it. Swallowing my greed, I focus on the far side of the room.

I don't have time to waste. The elders will be here any moment. My life or the stones, my life or the stones. This should not be a hard choice. I can't enjoy the ignits if the elders strangle me. My life. My life is more important. My life, my life, my life. I chant the words as I approach.

A peaked ceiling of black crystal stretches above the ignits, weaving into the wood of the trunk. At its highest point swirls a spot of darkness that gleams in a million different colors. The ancient.

I float beneath it. How the fuck does Rubem think I can detach the ancient from the rest of the tree? Maybe I should have asked.

I shift my ignits into one hand and poke the creature with the tip of my finger. Nothing happens. Carefully, I press my palm against its side. Its surface greets me, smooth and soft, like a velvet-covered rock. A tremble runs down my shoulders.

As though it might hear my thoughts, I think at it, *Hey, so, would you mind moving out of this mangrove? There's some silt-breathers who want to mow it all down, and you might be the only way to stop that.* The only way that doesn't involve me giving up a multitude of ignits. *So, if you could come with me, that'd be really fucking useful.*

The monologue is only a portrait of my worries, not meant to be anything more than a halfhearted release, but as the words form in my mind, the ancient's velvet exterior moves beneath my touch. It releases a single wave of vibrations which settles every itching and splintered fragment of my body, as if it floods my veins with Rubem's crushed ignits, filling me with a pulse far stronger than my own heartbeat can muster.

Light glimmers off the creature, dancing rainbows around the room. Under the gentle pressure of my touch, it twists away from the trunk. It slips from the niche and curls around my finger, suddenly far smaller than it first appeared. The dark crystalline streaks in the wood it once clung to turn from hard obsidian to fragile embers.

I drop my hand from the trunk ceiling. It holds fast to my scales. My chest goes light. What if I can never get it off, what if—

A vibration grinds through the tree, cutting off my panic with a loftier fear. Above me, the mangrove crumbles. The fragments of wood fall into the ancient's old hollows, gaining speed and ferocity with every passing moment.

This tree is coming down, not in the tottering way that Xera's did, but the shattering of a glass sculpture. I hold the hand with the ancient to my chest and dart out the farthest exit. An ashy substance billows through the crumbling root tunnels. The great guardian beast's long body writhes as it flees. The world thunders. I knock into a root, and the ignits in my hands spill into the darkness, gone before I even know which direction they fell. My tail continues slamming me onward through the water even as my heart yearns to go back. I smell Fern, and fear, and death mixing into something like charred wood in my nose.

Ahead, a shift from black to grey gives me hope. I lunge for the open swamp water. The roots collapse around me. Chunks of wood tumble down, grating against my bandaged gashes, and pain shoots up my spine. Fern slams into me, yanking me forward.

She pulls, but the moment we gain momentum, a fresh slew of debris buries me. The rush of it flings Fern away, rolling her into the billowing silt. Slowly, painfully, blurrily, the world lightens and contracts, falling back into place in hazy shapes and disconnected lines. The final pieces of the ancient's host-tree fall like stars through the foggy water, the first touch of dawn lighting the world. The thick scent of a team of Murklings pollutes the area.

My heart tells me to flee, but I pull back instead, retreating into the settling wreckage of the mangrove and letting the smell of its blistering raw wood and ash cover me. I go perfectly still, hiding my necklace ignit with my palm.

Through the silt, a familiar silhouette rises. Fern.

Acai's massive form bursts from the gloom and tackles her. She thrashes. The two of them twist through the water. Acai pins her down, an otter perched on their shoulder. The stirred silt blurs their conversation, but the elder's huge hands make it easy to interpret despite the haze.

"Who did this?" they sign. The force of their anger comes out in each blunt fierce motion. "Where are they? The truth, child!"

Fern only shakes.

Another boiuna dips down from the surface at their side, not nearly large enough to be an elder but still twice Fern's size. "Acai, the boats have kept moving downriver."

"Then we follow," Acai responds. "Leave three volunteers to investigate what's become of the ancient." They release Fern's body, but their looming makes it clear she's one wrong move away from confinement. "Come. Brine will make you talk—"

They swim into the rivulet proper, down its arcing path toward the boat. As their outlines fade, I split in two, or maybe three different versions of me that argue and scream and tremble. Fear for Fern hits first, quickly pushed out by fear for myself when I remember that this is her first real infraction, one they might not even be able to pin on her, and the elders won't harm her for that. But they will eat me whole.

With the ancient still tucked to my chest, I squirm slowly free of the rubble, relying more on precision than strength. Slipping from beneath the final sliver of wood, I burst through the silt and into the roots of the surrounding mangroves. I breach the surface between them, risking one glance back.

In the space where the glorious mangrove once stood, a grave of broken wood floats beneath a solemn fog. It makes my heart twist inside out. To the rest of the Murk, it must look even worse, as though the ancient itself died.

The rainbows have retracted from the creature around my hand, leaving it black and dull and lifeless as an ordinary rock. Maybe the ancient did die. And I killed it. In the back of my mind, I knew it was possible and had made this choice anyway, but it still blisters inside me.

It shouldn't. The Murk doesn't want me, and these creatures aren't a part of my life, and the pain of taking my home's most prized treasure shouldn't be mine to bear. But it hurts all the same.

One of Acai's otters scurries through the wreckage of the ancient's mangrove, and I swear its beady gaze locks on me through the mist. I flee, setting a straight course for the ocean. The rivulet vanishes behind me, but my heartbeat takes a while to realize it, lurching through my chest at every little vibration from the canopy.

My bones react to the slightest change in texture,

grimacing beneath my muscles as I slither over a tough root and sending shudders through my scales when a gooey water plant brushes my tail. I cling to my ignit's faint rhythm, trying not to think too hard about any of the things that have already fallen apart today and the million others that could still go wrong. Instead, I focus on what a multitude of ignits all lying beneath me might feel like, and take in the sea breeze gusting through the mangroves with the coming dawn.

I sense the main rivulet before I reach it, not just from the churning water, but by the other vibrations: pounding feet, shouting humans. A gun fires. My chest aches like a well-worn rock beneath an ever-plummeting waterfall. But I smell no elders, no boiuna or hoatzis or even the woody leather scent of Murkling humans.

I stay hidden in the roots, pushing out just enough to see. The lanterns on Rubem's boats swing violently, lighting up the morning mist in chaotic yellow halos. Lily's hair shines in them, the edges a flaming orange while the shadows stay deep auburn. She holds Rubem's emerald-studded gun, and at her feet lies the bloody body of a caiman.

I don't see Rubem on the deck, but the way Lily talks with the bearded crewmate and the subtle kick she gives Rubem's pet as though checking that it's truly dead, I get the feeling he isn't welcome there. My stomach jerks. Rubem might need rescuing, if he's still alive. And if he still has that poison ignit . . .

Maybe I should help him.

The thought feels wrong, foreign, haunting: feels like Thais. I force it away, running my thumb over the seemingly dormant ancient still swathing my fingers, but another selfless thought crashes into me then: the desire to wrap Lily in my tail and drive the life from her, just like she took it from that caiman and from so many other innocent creatures. She may not have come south as a fisher, but she proved herself to be one all the same.

In an odd burst of instinct, I wrap my hand all the way over the ancient. I can't give it to Lily. Whatever I told Rubem, whatever I told *myself*, this creature belongs in the Murk. And Lily is the very opposite of everything the Murk stands for.

She spins Rubem's pistol, jolting me out of my right-eousness. Whatever she is, she's not someone I can fight on my own. Rubem's life or poison ignites or not, I'm one boiuna, and she seems to have Rubem's old crew under her thumb. My only advantage—the mist—recoils in the dawn light as I watch.

If I hurry to Thais and finish the trek to her mother's hoard, everything we originally wanted will still work out. That's my best bet right now. My only bet. I conveniently ignore the fact that it's the only bet that lets me see Thais the longest and still gets me all the ignits I want, just as I ignore some other facts, facts revolving around the Murk and a fisher's threat. Maybe the group of elders will find Lily before she can get to the coast. This is their home—they can deal with her.

I draw back into the mangroves and slip far beneath the surface. With my belly brushing the silt, I swim across the rivulet and dive back into the trees. Something large and crocodilian moves along the edges of my senses, but when I pause to consider my heading, I lose track of it.

I pull Rubem's little compass free of the wire caging. I can't wish for Thais's suffering, but the needle steadily pointing me toward her current spasm douses me in relief. Judging by the way it shifts as I swim, she's a slight curve to the north and a little closer to the sea.

I nearly miss her and Xera curled in the hollow of an old split mangrove, a dead branch half covering the opening, their canoe wedged into the roots a few trees away. The fog lingers in the shadows outside, and the gentle morning light turns everything silver and grey. Thais sleeps with her head in Xera's lap. I climb in with them, my ancient-wrapped hand tucked beneath my necklace. Only the distant clamber of monkeys through the trees breaks the stillness.

Xera smiles at me. The reek of rotting wood blocks out their smell, but from the way they duck their head afterward, their expression must not be entirely happy. Their gaze moves out the hollow's entrance. Slowly, that half-sad smile falls. I don't have to smell their worry to know what it means.

"The elders got Fern," I tell them.

Xera's hands flutter in a soundless *oh*. They close their eyes. "She'll be all right," they finally sign, their motions stabilizing with each word.

"Yeah," I repeat, "she'll be all right."

I fiddle with Rubem's compass for a moment. With a great heave, I throw the whole mess out of the tree. A watery plop vibrates over my ridges, then it sinks.

Thais shifts in her sleep. Her face pinches, and her arms wrap tightly around her chest, dirty curls rubbing into the tree's brittle wood and dusty floor. My heart does a terrible painful thing at the sight of her, as though it alone shatters the way my bones do.

As slowly as I can, I wrap my tail beneath her, lifting her into the coils. Chunks of her hair stay behind. Bile rises in my throat, and I look to Xera, who swallows.

Thais's long lashes flutter. A rumble vibrates through her chest as her eyes creep open. Crust rims her swollen lids, and red veins turn her haunting ignit irises into a terror.

"Cacao?" she signs with small shaking motions.

Her rain-cleaned scent floods me, calming and exhilarating all at once, but a tinge of sickness coats it, sticking to the inside of my nostrils like a mold, growing fuzz and digging through flesh toward my brain. I glance at the locks she left behind. She follows my gaze. Her whole body trembles, and she presses her face against my scales.

I scoot closer and run my hand along her back, trying not to catch my fingers in her hair. What can I say to make this better? *Nothing.*

I caused this. I didn't get that poison ignit from Rubem, I took too long at the ancient to save him from the fishers, I thought of myself when I should have been thinking of Thais.

Worthless greedy me caused this.

Xera tucks their lip in their mouth and touches a steadying hand to Thais's shoulder. "I will shave it off for you, make it look nice. When you're better, it will grow back, and look, look nice long again then too."

Thais sniffles a few more times and weakly sits up. She pats her hair, cringing as it comes out in her hands. Closing her eyes, she flicks the strands away. "Do it."

Xera draws out the little blade they keep in their belt and sets to work. They move like the mist. Thais's hair falls in long coiling strands until it coats my scales. A short patchy fuzz remains. Thais tries to pull away, water—tears—brimming in her eyes, but Xera wordlessly holds her in place. They draw their blade smoothly around the thinner patches. As they shave, a pattern appears, spiraling out like the tendrils of a vine or the fluttering end of Thais's scarf when she dances.

Thais touches the designs tenderly. When she looks at Xera, her lips turn up just a little, but the smile immediately falls away. Her legs shake as she stands. She grabs the side of the hollow for support. "I'm going to sit in the trees."

"If we're not leaving, you should sleep," I protest.

"I've slept enough."

Somehow, I doubt she can sleep enough until she has a green ignit in her necklace to dampen the poison flooding her veins. "I'm coming with you, then."

"Fine." She stares straight ahead as though I no longer exist, despite my announcement.

When I offer her help, she hesitates. She reaches past me for the next branch. Her foot slips. I catch her, and she shrugs me off like I'm part of the scenery. If that's what it takes for her to accept my aid—if she needs to pretend she's not being helped in the first place—then so be it.

An era passes between each of her clumsy steps, and she holds herself with the weight of the world. My heart refuses to piece back together, like her weakness torrents the broken bits farther and farther apart. I grip the backside of my necklace with my ancient-wrapped hand.

The ancient's soothing pulse returns. Its velvet body wiggles free of my skin, twisting itself around my blue ignit, a soft rainbow sparkle flickering off its surface. Then it goes dark again, looking like nothing more than a big black rock in my collection. I poke at the ancient, a little worried for my ignit's sake, but I still feel the gentle pulse of it through the layers of its otherworldly creator.

Above me, Thais finally settles into a crook in the strong branches of a young mangrove beside our hollow. I wind loosely around her. She leans her head against my shoulder. Watching her suffocates me, but looking away is impossible. She's beautiful—her bravery and her determination and the lovely patterns wrapping around her skull, her blue eyes still alight despite all she suffers. But the poison taints every part of her body now, her skin ghostly and glossy, her lips chapped from stomach acid.

I could have stopped this. If I had been fast enough, certain enough, selfless enough. The knowledge settles like a weight between my collarbones, my rock-holding necklace three times too heavy.

Thais's hands move, slow and shaky. "I wanted to rescue you." A shudder runs through her, and she wipes the edges of her eyes.

I slip my fingers under hers, brushing back the tears. Whatever earlier annoyances I had at being left with Rubem vanish entirely when she leans into my touch. I wish I didn't need to pull away to sign. "You were too sick—there's nothing to feel guilty for. And it all turned out fine, more or less."

Maybe the sickness wears on her too much to object, because she only asks, "What happened with Rubem?"

The words wall up inside me, coated in a heavy film of shame. How can I tell her the truth? How can I explain that I chose to stay with Rubem, to steal an ancient for him, even after I had agreed to help Thais get to her mother's hoard? How can I convey the way the shock overtook me when I saw

Rubem's poison ignit, or my decision not to dash after him?

I can't. I won't. Fern isn't here to prove me a selfish silt-breather.

"Nothing happened," I reply. "Rubem's not such a bad guy, really. It turns out he wants your hoard to give to those light-skinned fishers so they don't bring their friends from the north and try to tear down the Murk."

"They want to *what*? Why didn't you lead with that?" She tries to swat me in the arm, her attacks bouncing off. She could lose a fight with a mosquito right now. "Wait, but those two died?"

"Apparently, they're harder to kill then they look."

"Damn fishers." Thais mumbles, her hand motions sloppy and her brow lowered. "I might not be a Murkling, but the mere idea of tearing down the Murk makes me shudder. Those northerners must be despicable."

"Despicable? That's the best you can do?"

"Despicable as foulmouthed sons of corpses oozing fungal slime."

"There's my ignit eyes." The words slip out, and I regret them the moment my hands finish moving, because Thais's whole being changes. For better or for worse, I can't tell. I search for something—anything—to distract her, to help her relax. "Lily took over the cartel boats while I was on my way here. I don't know what happened to Rubem."

The admission hurts like a spear to the gut, despite the fact that when I ran, I ran to Thais's aid. When I'm away from her, it hurts, and when I leave behind people whom she would've wanted me to save, it hurts as well. This is a fucking mess.

Thais's chest shudders. "Then we have to help him." She leans forward, another tremble wracking her body.

My lungs catch, and I grab her shoulders. "What's wrong?"

"I saved one of them, remember?" Her signs form so small. "If those two fishers are here, killing people—if they come destroy the Murk . . ." Tears slip down her cheeks, making a new kind of rain now that the smell of sickness pollutes her scent name. "I couldn't just let him die, but . . ."

"You did what you felt was right, ignit eyes." I pause to wipe her clammy cheeks again. "And, maybe I still think that thing was a little bit dumb, but it doesn't make all the bad things Wolf's done since then your fault. He's his own person. He gets his own blame."

"You make it all sound so simple." Thais reaches up as though to tuck a curly lock behind her ear. Her fingers meet only air. They shake. "My hair . . ."

"I'm sorry. It was so long and silky. You know, before you decided to fall in the swamp a few dozen times and spend the night in a log." I smell nothing except her failing body, but I catch an upward twitch in her expression. "If it means anything, though, I think you look beautiful with the haircut. I'm a boiuna after all, I'm attracted to bald heads."

"You're attracted to me?"

"I didn't say that." But even the implication stings like a lie on my fingers, my scales aching with the memory of Thais's hands when we danced. "I also didn't not say that."

She smiles, a real smile, I think, and melts against my side, tucking her head into the crook of my neck. Her breath seems to sink straight through my scales, warming my chest until it must glow with heat. I ache to touch her in new ways, but I scold the instinct. Thais needs to rest more than anything right now. I wrap my arm around her in support as she trails her fingers in weak circles over my stomach, a slow rhythm to them, harmonizing with my heartbeat.

Her necklace lies against my side, poking through her thin shirt. Its empty edges dig between my scales, and my guilty conscience puts words to her song: *You did this, your fault, you did this, selfish silt-breather.*

That poison ignit probably still sits in Rubem's secret pocket, pressed against his chest. Or his corpse. If we do go back, if we fight Lily and win, then there's a chance to retrieve the ignit. It's not our best option, but Thais deserves to know. My hands tremble as I lift them. Muck, I hope she doesn't hate me.

I poke her. "Hey, Thais?"

Her chest rumbles in response, but her eyes barely open, her fingers still mindlessly moving.

This is so hard; too hard, maybe. As I force my hands to start on the next sign, Xera's soft leather shoes leap through the leaves above us. They drop down at our side.

"We have to, to go. They're here. I don't know how, but they, they found us."

My insides knot together. "The fishers?"

"Worse."

The whole canopy trembles, and ripples appear along the water. A host of Murkling warriors arise from all corners, a dozen humans and hoatzis perching in the trees, outfitted in scales and feathers and crossbows. Four boiuna, each a little bigger than Fern, slide up the nearby trunks. But the fear building so thick in my lungs that it clouds me with its stench comes from the three great ridges growing in the swamp, nearing us at a speed I could never match.

The massive boiuna breach the surface in unison, water streaming off scales. One of Acai's otters lies across their green shoulders, and the sharp-smelling Cayenne bares fangs so big he could bite my head clean off, the rows of his teeth nearly the same banana hue as the splotches along his deep-grey body. Between them swims a boiuna larger than either and twice as angry.

Her deep-brown scales warp around the edges, as though age is turning her into a crocodilian, and her ridges jut like horns from her skull, a twisting mess that resembles living roots. Chains of beads and sharp carnivorous teeth hang off them in such a painful number it seems the ancient ridges no longer feel a thing, but I know she can sense the very beat of my heart in my chest and the thrum of every ignit for a mile. A harsh briny scent like the entire wind-whipped sea compressed into a single breeze flows from her, nearly demolishing the names of everyone in her vicinity.

I force a grin, wrapping myself around Thais like she's my ignit. The stone buried beneath the ancient on my necklace barely keeps my bones from jittering out of my body as I sign, "Hey, Mom."

SEVENTEEN

---∽---

DAMN SALTY IN HERE

Ugh.

Mothers.

BRINE REMAINS HAUNTINGLY STILL, but her disappointment sloughs off her. I tuck myself instinctively behind Thais's
shoulder. My heartbeat bursts like a fan boat skidding precar-
iously to its doom.

"You, little bittersweet earthen one, are in direct violation
of the council's appointed ruling." My first forebearer's hands
move like the rage of the waves upon the shore, elegant yet
terrifyingly powerful. "If entering the Murk was your only
transgression, then perhaps this slight could've been over-
looked. But you have brought boat humans with you, both the
one you cling to now and known enemies of the Murk,
including a fleet of fishers and members of the notorious Fang
Cartel."

"That's not fair! I didn't bring them here. They were chasing
me," I protest, but my weak signs won't save me. Nothing ever
has before.

"All the same, they are here because of you," Brine replies.

A shudder runs through Cayenne. "Because of you, an
ancient lies in ruins!"

I swear the creature wrapped around my necklace grows

heavier. "I did that, yeah, but, see, I had a reason." *A reason I couldn't follow through on. A reason Brine's unlikely to believe.*

"A reason? Ha!" Cayenne's hands fly, humorless and terrifying, and he bares his rows of dagger-like teeth.

My fingers trace over the ancient as though it's another stone in my collection. Like this, it might as well be one. I drop my hand. "That doesn't matter now. What *matters* is my friend. She's dying. Please, she has to get to the shore to retrieve a cure. That's why I'm here. I never meant to hurt the Murk." There's no lie in my words, but they feel dishonest all the same, a far better portrait of me than I could ever live up to.

"What kind of cure is there at the coast?" Acai asks, the thick mass of darker green scales along their brow drawing together.

I wish for Fern's ability to lie. In the Murklings' mess of scents, I catch a whiff of her wet fern smell. She's nearby, at least.

Thais nudges my waist. "Tell them. It's fine."

I hate that she's probably right. And I hope that right means something good in this case. "My friend is dying from a powdered green ignit infecting her bloodstream. A mechanic made her something that will reverse the effects, but it needs another of the same stone to power it. The only one we know of is hidden near the coast." *But it's not the only one,* my shame objects. I add hastily, "She's a good person, even if I'm not. She deserves to live."

Acai and Cayenne focus on Thais, clearly taking in her colorless complexion, the languid way she lies against my chest, the red veins of her shadowed eyes. But my first forebearer never looks away from me, her gaze boring through my soul. I clutch my necklace and wish to vanish like the morning mist.

Thais stirs in my arms. Her breathing feels too heavy, but when she signs, her motions come out strong. "Whatever this boiuna has done in the past may have warranted his banishment, but he's not the same person as he was then. I care about him, and he cares about me."

Despite the fear and guilt and dread, a blossom of warmth springs in my chest. Tenderly, I set my chin on her shoulder, pressing my forehead to the side of her shaved hair's spirals. "I do, ignit eyes."

"The only green ignit, you say?" Brine's chest vibrates, not with sound but with sheer fury. "Would your friend feel the same if she knew you were so near one just this morning, that you could have brought it to her, but you didn't?"

My chest seizes. Motherfucking—how, how does Brine know? She saw me, she or another boiuna or—or—

Fern. Fern, with all her lies and fibs and half-truths, must have slipped up in this, accidentally or on purpose, I don't know.

"That's not—"

But Brine continues her assault, not pausing for the mess of thoughts in my head and the tangle of my hands to settle. "What are you gaining from this, little earth? Ignits?" she guesses, her salty scent turning bitter. "Or have you progressed to taking life for the fun of it?"

No. No, no, no, this can't—*oh muck.* "It's not—I don't—I wanted the ignits, yeah, but I—" Muck. Motherfucking—

Thais slips out of my coils, her whole body shaking, shaking. She looks at me, but then she doesn't, flashing her eyes elsewhere, red and wet. The smell of her shock and pain fills the air like a downpour. "Cacao, you really . . ." But her hands fall. She wobbles, and Xera catches her.

"Yeah?" A million explanations rumble through my head, so many my hands seem bound by them. I fight for an apology, a promise, something. Something to make it right. But I don't know if there is any way to make this right, just like there's no way to make the Murk take me back or make my body not revolt at the sight of a net. "I was going to tell you."

"You were going to *tell* me?"

"It's not like there's anything we can do about it now!

Rubem's been abducted by the fishers—I would've gone back for that ignit if I thought we could get to it easily."

"So, you didn't take the green ignit when you had the chance, *and* you were going to make us continue to my mother's hoard when we could save me by saving Rubem?" Her signs snap, and the impact of each settles in my skull like a physical ache. "You're just here for the ignits, aren't you? It doesn't matter how much I've grown on you." She chokes, wrapping her hands around her waist, and Xera holds her steady while she heaves bile. When she finally wipes her mouth, fingers brushing bleeding lips, they tremble harsher than ever. "You're still just as greed-poisoned as my mother."

"That's not . . ." *Not true.* But maybe it is. Maybe every time I was a little bit selfish, every time I thought a little bit more of my ignits and not of Thais or Rubem, every time I acted to preserve something because of how it made me feel and not what was good for us all, maybe all those instances have compiled into this. Into a poison. I can't say it's not so.

Thais watches me with those terrible beautiful ignit eyes. Slowly, a drop of liquid slips free. She cries.

Her tears slice into me more than any foul name ever could. I was already going to lose her, I knew that. But I never wanted her to be hurt when it happened. I never meant to hurt her.

Brine rears closer, her monstrous head looming over us. "Little earth, you have proven you will change only for the worse. You have ignored every chance your elders and the two-legged council have given you, twice over. You have condemned yourself in the eyes of the Murk, and you are the only one to blame." The aggression fades from her scent like the retreating tide, replaced by the grainy damp sadness of the exposed shore. "You were my final offspring, and I am sorry."

She's sorry. *Sorry.* As though she knows me enough to *be* sorry. I'm not sure whether to laugh or scream. Boiuna often shared the work of raising their young, but it always seemed my forebearer retracted from me like I was a plague, not a child. Everyone did. And now they'll execute me and feel *sorry* about it.

As Brine turns away, sinking into the water and retreating out of view, the elders at her sides rise up, all teeth and scales. Part of me knew this was coming, the moment I chose to enter the Murk. I knew this would be my end. No ignits can save me from the elders. No ignits can save me from my past.

Before Acai and Cayenne can inflict their justice, though, Thais wobbles across the branch, half tripping over my tail, and plants herself in front of me. "If you intend to hurt him, you'll have to do the same to me."

The air fills with the scent of confusion. Hands shift, the watching Murklings talking in tiny motions. Cayenne tries to lunge at Thais, but Acai grabs his arm.

"She's a boat human!" Cayenne protests. He yanks away from Acai, forming waves that crash against the nearby roots.

Acai bares their teeth, the otter on their shoulder mimicking the expression. "We are no better than them if we judge based on where they come from and not who they are. Can you prove she has done anything to us?"

Cayenne snaps back with fiery hands, but my focus moves to a wobbling Thais, sweat slipping down her already grimy glistening face.

"Thais!" I sign.

She gives me no time to add an objection or a request, her lips pulling into a staunch line. "I'm not doing this for you. I'm doing it because it's the right thing."

"This isn't the time, you damn—" I adjust my words at the last moment, trying to find some new argument. "This is my fault, Thais. I made my choice. It shouldn't bring you down too. You have a chance still, to get to the ignits, to save yourself." I can't watch Thais's face as I sign, and by the time I glance at her, I find her gaze on the canopy, where a thick white cloud rises from one of Xera's little pots.

The ghastly smelling steam rushes out, creating an impenetrable veil around us. Xera darts through the branches, and I feel the impact of a blunt-tipped crossbow bolt hitting

Cayenne in the forehead. The elder boiuna's huge body wavers. A second bolt follows.

I scoop Thais up and flee in the direction of the coast. A human warrior appears through the cloud, but I shove them off our branch, and one of the hoatzis catches them. We burst free of the artificial mist, leaving a stunned group of Murklings behind us. They give chase. The soft rhythm of their feet on the wood is drowned by the giant crash of the elders diving into the water. I glance behind us just in time to see the wave they make slosh over a row of warriors.

Someone leaps to our side, and my scales jump, my grip on Thais tightening until that someone comes into focus as Xera.

"Get her to the hoard," they sign.

Thais's chest rumbles in reply, but they peel away again, crossbow already in their grasp. They fire it at the nearing Murklings. No shot strikes our pursuers, but they slow all the same, Xera's uncanny aim hitting just before the tips of their toes.

Far behind us, the trees shudder, roots and branches cracking. The elders are coming. I can smell my forebearer already.

When I draw in another breath, though, it's not Brine that suffocates me, but the true salt tang of the ocean gusting through the trees. *We're so close.* I press myself to move faster, my muscles burning, bark digging into my scales. If we can just get to the sea . . .

The canopy lightens, and I drop to a lower branch. A host of colorful birds take to the air, zipping around us with a hundred vibrations, squawking and flapping. Xera turns back from firing another bolt. They crash into the flock straight on and shy away with a flinch so violent it sends them off the edge of their branch. One of the pursuing boiuna catches them as they fall, wrapping them in a restraining hold. I falter. Thais struggles in my arms, trying desperately to go back for them, but Xera waves us away. Three Murklings keep to my trail, giving me no other choice.

The rush of fire that pushed me this far starts to fade, leaving only pain in my muscles and tight burning in my lungs. Thais's paper-light weight grows heavier by the moment. The Murklings gain.

I have nothing left to throw them off, no ignits or arrows or smelly mist, no weapons but my tail and teeth. Maybe if I leave Thais and attack these three outright, she can get to the ocean on her own. Maybe.

She clutches tighter to my shoulders, crushing the weak hope as her whole body wracks and heaves, not even bile coming up. I guess if I'm going to die, it might as well be from exhaustion. I push onward, straining my muscles, seeking the smoothest path through the trees. A hoatzi behind us swipes at my tail, but I yank it out of their reach and crash through a cluster of leaves. The branches give way.

Oh, muck. Thais and I hit the water. I burst forward, doing my best to keep her head above the surface as we swim between the mangrove roots. Sunlight peppers my back. Gentle waves hit us; then the heat of the late morning pours down in full force, the world so bright it makes my eyes roll. The ocean fills my senses, blue sky above and even bluer waters stretching beneath. I swim through the deeper lagoon to a sandbar a little ways off from the trees, preparing to fight whoever follows us out, but the three Murklings only watch from the branches. Apparently, I'm not worth leaving the Murk for.

I collapse, letting Thais go. My arms shake, my tail twitching as if it hasn't yet realized we've finally stopped. I feel like death. But Thais looks far worse, curled up, weak and shuddering. Golden sand sticks to the side of her shaved head.

I force myself to sit up. At our back, the Murk stretches into a crescent peninsula of trees and dark rocks. The tip of the curve points toward a small island as though reaching for it. Unlike the landless mangroves of the Murk, the island is all deep grey rock and weathered sea brush, a few palm trees hanging off the edges. A waterfall tumbles over the near side. In my beaten state, it takes me a moment to wonder where that much water comes from on such a tiny piece of land, but another question immediately overwhelms it.

I nudge Thais's shoulder. "Is that your mother's hoard?"

Thais opens her eyes slowly, and it takes her hollow blue irises a moment to focus. Her lips twitch. "First lucky thing that's happened to us so far." She barely lifts her hands to sign it. A wave brushes her leg—the tide coming in to cover the sandbar. Thais seems not to notice. "You muck-face. Why didn't you bring me that poison ignit of Rubem's?"

The rest of my strength drains out of me. "It's not like that! He was driving away, and I panicked too much. I knew you would stop your trek to the hoard if you had what you wanted already." I stumble over the words. "I *was* about to tell you. I never—"

She looks purposefully away. Slowly, she sits up, her breath heavy, dark circles beneath her eyes. She smells of determination and sickness, the rain-cleaned air gone from her. "You'll get your hoard, like I promised. Just finish your job first."

You'll get your hoard. After everything, she still plans to make good on her promise. I should be happy. But even the thought of a thousand ignits can't seem to lighten my soul when Thais's eyes are so dull and hollow.

Another wave curls around her legs, tugging at a tear in her pant fabric. Her shirt clings to her chest, outlining the hard oval edges of her necklace where it rests against her sternum. "Will Xera be hurt? And Fern, where did Fern go?"

"The elders have them both. They won't be harmed, though. They didn't hurt anyone, at least not badly. They'll get a warning this time, probably be released in a few days, after the Murk has been scoured for any remaining boat humans."

Thais barely looks my way. "Still, we have to . . . shouldn't we . . ."

"Xera told us to leave. It's done."

"But we should have stayed. We could've turned back for them."

"No, we shouldn't have! This was their choice, Thais. You can't take that away from them. Let them be the fucking hero for once." Like I wasn't for Rubem. Like I'll never be.

Thais flinches.

With one last glance at the Murk, I offer her an arm. "Let's go."

Her poison accepts for her, all but collapsing her into my grasp. I pull her onto my back and slide into the water. As I swim Thais to the island, the tide skates in over our sandbank. My muscles should ache or burn or something, but part of my mind has gone numb, and the detachment stretches like a thick fog into the crevasses of my physical body. I barely feel the warm rocks of the island as I yank us onto its bank.

Thais stands and wobbles. I slip my arm under her shoulders, pooling my tail around her in case she falls. A tremble runs through her, from her shaved head to her bare toes, but she scarcely resists. Maybe she doesn't have the strength.

Slowly, we work around the side of the island, picking between rough brush and over jagged rocks, until only the sea greets us, endless and blue. Thais directs me into a deep crack between two great outcroppings. A little rowboat bobs below, with a steam motor and a pair of oars, and a system of giant scoops runs up one side of the fissure, carrying the wave water to the top of the island. It must form the waterfall.

A large metal door fits neatly beneath the machine, hidden in the shadows. Thais digs through the smaller rocks around it. Her hands shake. I catch her arms and force her to sit. Her face pinches, and she refuses to meet my gaze even when I slide my fingers down to grip her own tenderly.

"What were you looking for?"

"A key, made of black stone." She closes her hollow eyes, but her hands keep moving after a moment. "There's an entrance for ships beneath the waterfall—well, boats now; my mom closed the opening enough that proper sea vessels can't fit in or out—but the only place I can disable the shield is from this side, with the key."

I strategically set each small rock out of the way and find the key shoved into a crack. Thais doesn't try to take it from me, her raggedly rising chest the only sign she still lives. I push the key into the lock. For a moment it sticks, then clicks, the vibration of an ignit deep within suddenly turning from an active buzz to an inactive pulse. I help Thais inside and close the door behind us, sealing us off from the brilliant midday sun.

A thousand new lights replace it, glowing along the walls and ceiling of the hallway like living rainbows. A clasp embeds each ignit to the wall as though Thais's mom replicated my necklace into an infinite strand, filling every space with a different-colored stone. The common ones appear most often, reds and blues and yellows creating patterns around little teal and purple flowers, a few orange and pink dispersed through-out, along with a few tiny greens far too small to fit in Thais's necklace.

The glowing walls break for six ignit-draped archways before the corridor ends in stairs. Massive red ignits carved into the shapes of blossoming flowers hang down from the ceiling, casting the steps in scarlet. Every crack between the glowing rocks reveals wardstone shielding the hoard from other greedy thieves.

I start forward sluggishly, yearning to go deeper yet unable to draw away from the gorgeous entry. "Your mom built this place?" I ask, my scales gleaming with a million different hues. "She must have been incredible." I feel Thais snort.

"She was a greedy malicious coward who only cared about herself." The shake in her hands looks different now, and bitterness tinges her sickly scent. "The ship trapped in the cave was originally her older sister's vessel. When she was my age, they were sailing together, taking passengers between the big isles of the siren seas—she with her sister, her sister's husband, and their young son—when they ran off course in a storm. Sirens killed most everyone on board, including my aunt and uncle. Tore into my cousin, too. And my mom just left him to die at the nearest port, left that poor kid all alone when she had a responsibility to be there for him, left him because it wasn't *convenient*."

The way her gaze goes distant, I wonder if there's another child she's really thinking of, one with a heart brighter than an ignit and a mother who never realized that was more important than any trove.

"I won't be like her," she signs. "I won't leave people just because it's inconvenient to save them."

Her pain takes a new shape as I realize it's not just her mom who left her to anguish when it wasn't convenient. It was me as well. My chest fills with gravel, and it aches in all the wrong places, like a baby caiman slowly claws its way free. "You're nothing like your mom, Thais." I make the motions big and firm, forcing her to see them. Her brow creases and her face slackens, but her sad smell pushes me on. "But sometimes the first person who needs saving is yourself, and sometimes you have to let someone else help you with that."

She looks away, tucking her arms around her stomach. I half roll my eyes. Self-righteous fool. I skim the beads covering the nearest archway. My fingers catch on a heavy piece of fabric hanging beyond it, and when I pull that back as well, I find a small ignitless room. A primitive phonogram sits on the dresser, and hand drums of every size and style line the wall, all of them covered in dust.

Thais pulls me feebly toward the stairs. "My mom kept her rarest ignits in her room. All the poison stones big enough to reverse the poison should be there."

"Yeah. Yeah, okay."

I let her guide me, supporting her as much as she'll allow. With our first step, the desire to turn back and snatch a few ignits off the walls hits me so strongly I have to preoccupy my fingers by stretching them. There will be time for that later, after Thais recovers.

A change comes over her as we climb, as though her dying body is giving her its last seed of energy to fight this emotional battle. She straightens her shoulders and lets go of me to step through the ignit curtain shielding her mother's room.

Compared to the glory of the ignits below, this sweeping chamber seems almost muted at first glance. But what it lacks in rows of the stones, it makes up for in looping patterns of them that flow across the ceiling and delicately carved bundles of ignit flowers that spring from pots and bedposts and balcony railings. Glass cases throughout the room display a few dozen ignits, many in unique shades so rare or foreign that I've never seen their like.

"They'll be in a case somewhere." Thais takes off toward the back of the room, so I head the opposite way, peeking into each container as I move along the wall toward the balcony.

I pause by a workbench. Mechanical gears and tools litter it, and a tiny box with a slot for a few small rocks sits half-finished, a mere grain of eruptstone embedded in its spring mechanism. Thais's mom must have intended it to be some kind of tiny precise bomb.

"How did your mom die?" Maybe I shouldn't ask something like that, but I sign it before I can stop myself. The words come out just in time for Thais's drifting gaze to catch them.

Her shoulders bounce once. "She collapsed while checking the waterfall last summer and dropped over the side onto the rocks she'd moved there to hide the back of her stolen ship. I don't know if it was the fall that killed her or whatever caused the collapse in the first place. She had passed out a few times before that, but she'd never stopped collecting and tending her ignits long enough to find a doctor."

Thais's demeanor never changes, but when she finishes, she sets her hands on the case in front of her, and her eyes wander the room, aimlessly tracking the perfectly made bed with its deep-purple pillows and grey rugs, an old blue coat hanging over an open chest of folded pants. A dead room in a dead home.

"You boat humans often live with both parents, don't you?"

She blinks at me as though trying to make sense of my question, then nods. "My mom got pregnant with me on an ignit collection trip to the other side of the continent, a few years after she built this place. I don't think she even knew his name. But I—I'm fine. I'm fine being alone."

I don't need to interpret her expression to see the lie for what it is. I know her. I'm fine being alone, at least for a little while, but she's not. I don't think she ever has been. My soul alights with the desire to never let her feel so again, before that yearning crashes into the knowledge that she doesn't want to be with *me* anymore.

Sliding past the workbench, I run my fingers over the ignit flowers in the balcony railing. For once, the soothing pulse does nothing for me, nothing but turn my stomach upside down. I let go, glancing at the cave beyond.

The only light in the oddly ignit-free cavern streams through the tumbling waterfall over the entrance. The incoming tide rocks a floating dock, its short ladder leading up to a tunnel beneath the balcony. A small steam-powered ship with three decks of deep-brown wood sits beside the dock, aimed toward the rocks Thais's mom died on. Two steam stacks of blue metal run along either side of the ship. The faintest tingle brushes my head ridges: the brush of waves against something that bobs beyond the ship, likely a medium-sized vessel like Rubem's.

I wave for Thais's attention as she moves toward the cases beside her mom's bed—the only ones we haven't checked yet. "Hey, ignit eyes, does the boat behind your mother's ship still work? Is it small enough for us to take out of here?"

Thais's brow tightens. "I sold our smaller boat as soon as I arrived in the first port."

I glance back into the cavern. The tip of the vessel drifts just far enough into view for me to make out the scarlet fang at the front. Oh, muck.

Footsteps from the stairs vibrate along my head ridges. I spin back toward Thais. Rubem stands in the doorway, the bead curtain drawn to one side. It falls back into place behind him.

His scent name hits me like the first time we met, leather and sun and wine in equal proportions. I clutch my necklace, fingers wrapped tight around the dull clinging ancient. Thais leans against the bed, her brow drawn tight.

"You're alive—" I start.

He cuts me off. "You'd better take what you need and be quick about it if you want to leave here alive."

Something about his graceful hand motions seems off— wrong. Rubem's boat drifts forward a bit farther, revealing the deck, where a light-skinned human with a blaze of orange hair sits. Wolf, alive, his head leaning against the back of his seat and a pistol in his lap. He doesn't need to lift it to shoot a bolt of fear straight through me.

As Rubem moves farther into the room on his Murkling light feet, my horror knots itself into my gut. Rubem did not make the footsteps I felt coming up the stairs.

Those were the fishers.

EIGHTEEN

THE COST OF EVERYTHING

The most important price

isn't the one we put on our pasts,

but the one we pay for a better future.

"YOU'RE HERE WITH LILY?" The motions hurt to sign.

Rubem's lips curl, his fear slipping into his scent in pungent waves. "You know it wasn't my first choice." But the *first* wobbles so much that it barely exists. The empty air in Rubem's gun holster and the caiman-high smear of blood on his boots speak stronger than his words. This wasn't his first choice. It wasn't his choice at all.

Behind him, Lily pushes through the beads, her pistol aimed at the center of his back. The green ignit-finding compass sits in her other hand, a Sheila-sized tooth gash in its side. *The crocodilian must be even smarter than I thought.*

Two more humans follow Lily, one I recognize as Rubem's bearded second-in-command and another with a half-folded fisher's net tucked into their belt. The fisher crunches the compass beneath their boot, and they both turn their guns on me.

I squeeze my ancient-covered ignit. If I attack in such a small space, I'll end up with a bullet in my chest. The cavern behind me sings of freedom, but I can't just leave Thais and my ignits with these silt-breathers. Both of Lily's lackeys cock their pistols.

They give Thais a single glance and fix their guns for me instead. The fisher says something to Rubem's old lackey, and I can figure what they must have said by the way their aims lift from my chest to my head: *the pelt will sell better intact.*

"Hey now," Rubem's lips move in time with his hands, each motion soothing and smooth, the vibrations from his throat like a gentle tingle along my head ridges. "We had a deal, Lily. You said you and yours would leave the Murk be, and this boiuna is of the Murk."

The pinches and pulls in every expression around the room overwhelm my comprehension, but I know the thoughts behind them: Lily and her lackeys hold the power here, deal or no deal. Three guns against six open palms. Whatever honorable intentions Rubem had, the fishers aren't bound to anything right now but the steadiness of their aims.

They don't lower their guns.

An awkward vibration rises in Rubem's chest. "With all these ignits, you will have weapons and wealth beyond every cartel combined. What is one more boiuna pelt? You claimed to have better people to kill. Villains, you said."

Whatever Lily's reasons, I don't care. I can't think past the first series of words, a taunt that repeats behind my eyes. *All these ignits.* My irritation bubbles. "Muck no, these aren't your ignits." I sign so fast that I catch the attention of everyone in the room. "You're not getting a single one of them, not any of you silt-breathers."

Lily's lips draw into a hard line, and her light skin turns bright red.

At the same time, the last flecks of color drain from Thais's face. She slips onto the bed, her plea tiny. "Cacao."

Don't fucking pull that. I came all this way for the ignits, and I won't let the fishers leave with them. The words leap through my mind, but they cling to my fingers as I watch Thais, her greyed skin glistening and her hollow eyes digging into me. I can't look away from those eyes, not when my lungs catch and pull and not when my heart shatters. What the fuck am I doing, destroying whatever small mercies Rubem's plea might have bought us? If we all die because of my stubborn selfishness . . .

Thais is more important than some glowing rocks. Even Rubem is more important. And so am I. Not as a greedy banished thief, but as me. A hurricane. A cacao bean.

"You know, whatever, have the ignits. It's fine."

But Lily's stare bores straight through my hands to my wire necklace. The ancient seems almost to tremble beneath her gaze, and it shrinks back, a blister of colored light twisting over it.

"Give me that." Lily's signs turn messy, and she steps toward me, her gun wobbling.

I clutch the ancient. The soft fungal-like creature melds to my fingers as though grabbing me in return. "Why?" I ask with my free hand.

A smile tugs over her lips, teeth revealed as if ready to snap. "You must have seen hints of its power, even if your people are too foolish to probe further. It does make ignits, after all."

I run my thumb over the ancient, soothing the fear and confusion that strangle my chest. "What I know is that it's a living thing, not a possession to be stolen or traded."

Lily steps toward me once more, her flaming hair a rage.

I glance at Thais. She sinks deeper into the pillows, now closer to where Rubem's traitorous bearded crewmate stands beside the final ignit case. I swallow and turn my gaze back down the barrel of Lily's gun. "But, um, what *would* you give in return for it?"

I know I can't hand the ancient over, even if she offers me the world. After all I did to the Murk—the deaths and destruction I caused—I can't betray my home again. The damn murderous hateful fishers don't deserve any part of the beauty or the power that the Murk offers. This ancient belongs, not to me or to them or to Rubem, but to the Murk. To my home.

"Give it to me, and you and your little friend can go run back to your disgusting swamp." Lily's nose wrinkles. "If she lives that long."

Thais lies limply across the edge of the bed. Her chest surges up before going still for far too long, heaving again only when I think the ache in my heart might kill me. She reaches with slow creeping fingers for the last glass case in the room, her steady hands a stark contrast to her breath. Relief sinks through me, but my gaze catches on a little box on the inside corner of the case. A little box like the one on the workbench, equipped with an eruptstone and an active ignit. A booby trap.

A series of impulses slam into my fear and spark along my muscles, taking control. I leap at Thais as she yanks the case open, but I reach her too late. The lid clanks against the back wall, and a tiny ominous vibration stirs in the little box. The tremor of it rattles along my head ridges, so terrible that I barely feel the fishers' pistols firing. Pain burns across my tail. I can just make out the soft glow of the poison ignits in the open case as I grab Thais, pulling her into my arms.

Then the little booby-trapped box explodes. A sphere of light forms out of it, expanding in all directions. Thais reaches for the poison ignits, but the light moves far faster than her weak desperate arms can manage. It hits the poison ignits, and those, too, detonate. They transform into their own larger explosion spheres, green power crackling through them like bolts of toxic lightning.

Putting all my strength into my tail, I thrust us backward, toward the balcony. Rubem's bearded crewmate is not so lucky. The light consumes them, engulfing them like a thick oozing swamp mud surrounding its prey. Their scream survives longer than they do, tickling my head ridges as Thais and I fly through the air. The light sphere caresses the ceiling, and the ignit swirls that glide through its center burst in a series of small explosions, tearing a rift from one end of the room to the other.

Thais and I hit the ground rolling. I wrap myself around

her, cradling her fragile body to my chest. As the explosions fade, the light vanishes. It leaves nothing behind but empty air where stone and glass and flesh once were. Cracks shoot through the remaining sections of the rock ceiling. Chunks of it crash down, taking out the balcony's banister and pieces of the floor. Rubem and Lily slip over the edge where the railing had been. The fisher with the net tumbles after them, but they grab my tail to keep from falling into the cavern. Their fingers dig into the deep graze the bullet left. Fresh pain spears up my tail.

Letting go of Thais, I launch at the nuisance lackey. I knock them off me with a fist across their jaw and catch myself on the lip of the balcony as they drop into the cavern. They hit the deck with a thud and careen to a stop beside Rubem and Lily.

An onslaught of ceiling rocks assaults me. I hold tight, but a stone hits my head ridges. The world turns to a mess of vibrations and darkness. I fall. Away from Thais.

The smooth side of the balcony defies my grasp, but I search for a handhold anyway, anything to keep me from falling from Thais and the ignits and into the fishers' grasp. Thais catches one of my wrists. I jerk to a dangling stop, my arm in half shock and half agony. Below me, I feel Rubem sit up, the fishers already scrambling for their pistols.

Thais braces herself against the small stone offshoots left in the balcony railing, rock from the ceiling still falling behind her. Her whole body trembles. She can hold me up, but not for long.

My mind feeds me the future: Thais losing her hold on the balcony, falling after me, her weak body shattering on the layer of fallen stones that now coat the deck. Not moving. Every hurt feels insignificant compared to that image.

Thais's eyes nearly roll back, and her brow scrunches. Her necklace presses against the fabric of her shirt. She needs a poison ignit. But the only large enough green stones we found were in that case, and they're gone, turned to energy and rubble. Everything we sought after, destroyed in an instant.

Almost everything.

My hand jerks to the little eruptstone bead in my necklace.

A voice in my head tries to talk me out of it. Maybe if I detonate an ignit into the cavern, it will kill the fishers, and maybe Thais and I can squish enough small poison ignits into her necklace to make it work. Maybe I can have everything: her and the ignits and my life. Maybe.

Or maybe I can give up everything to assure Thais's life goes on, and to give her what she wants. What she deserves.

A cry vibrates from her throat as she pulls me closer. The knobby bone of my elbow catches on the edge of the balcony. Pushing through the pain, I swing up, reaching for her. I shove the eruptstone between her grasping fingers.

She stares at me. Her hands cling, motionless, to my wrist, the little rock pressing between my scales and her skin, but for once I can read her perfectly, her whole being asking a single question.

I answer. "We can't let Lily and the fishers or anyone else take these ignits. No matter who they are, what they want from them—one person with this much of anything only brings pain." My one-armed motions quake, small and concealed. "I'll get Rubem out and leave the fishers here, in the cavern. You run to the front entrance. Take the rowboat and toss the eruptstone behind you. Let this place be those motherfuckers' poison." I force a grin. "Just save me an ignit before you blow the place, won't you? I might need to replace mine."

Tears brim in Thais's eyes, and she tightens her fingers around the eruptstone. She lets go of my wrist. Her final signs to me hang in the air like a promise. "Go, be my fucking hero."

I launch away from the balcony and twist into a ball, hitting the wooden dock beyond the mess of fallen stone. My ridges tingle with the scuffle of Thais's bare feet hobbling out the door of her mom's decimated room. The moment I right myself, I vault at the fisher with the net.

Lily fires a shot that zings past my shoulder, making my

head pound like a war drum, but the other fisher only fumbles with their gun. I twist my tail around their neck and grab at their belt for the emerald-studded pistol they took from Rubem. My hand brushes their net. I bite down a shudder, snatch the firearm, and toss it to Rubem.

As the human in my coils slumps to the ground, Rubem cocks his pistol. He levels it on Lily's chest in the same instant she turns her gun on him. They stare down each other's barrels.

Rubbing my ancient-covered ignit, I unfurl from the dead human. The movement makes Lily glance at me. She swallows, but her aim stays firm.

How quickly could I cut off the blood supply to her head? Every instinct urges me to try, to take advantage of the distraction Rubem's making and rid the world of her a little sooner. But the way she watches Rubem stops me, her gaze so level with the center of his head that I'm certain she would kill him first.

She'll die when Thais detonates the island anyway. And Rubem and I need to get out of here before that happens.

I glance at the tip of his boat, its scarlet fang symbol poking out from behind the old steamship. "Leave her. Let's go."

Rubem nods once. He moves down the dock with me, each step so fluid he seems to drift like fog, his pistol ever tracking the fisher. She continues aiming at us in return, as still as a penajuar preparing to pounce.

Footsteps ping oddly along my ridges. Fighting through the pounding in my skull and the constant buzz of the waterfall, I focus on searching for their location, but my head aches too fiercely, and the feet seem to arise from every direction at once.

As we round the side of the steamship, Rubem's boat comes into view—Rubem's boat with no Wolf sitting half-conscious on the deck. The trudging finally solidifies in my mind just before its source stumbles out of the cavern's entry tunnel. Wolf steps from it onto the dock, a pistol in one hand and a leather sack brimming with small blue, purple, and green ignits in the other. He appears little healthier than Thais, sweat matting his orange hair and his cheeks so white that the dots on his face look like holes. The skin around his bandages is swollen and red. It stinks of infection.

But he holds his gun steady as he points it at us. Two guns against Rubem's one.

"Run?" Rubem asks.

I roll my eyes. "Silt-breather."

Somehow, my body finds a new rush of fire. I scoop him up and vault us onto his boat, bullets whizzing by. We tumble into the stairs. While I untangle myself, Rubem charges to the top deck, flipping switches in the console by the steering wheel. The thunder ignit beneath us roars. It bursts us backward just as Lily and Wolf round the steamship. Rubem ducks, and the northerner's bullets take out chips in the wheel, narrowly missing the top of Rubem's many braids.

The waterfall pours over us, salt and foam filling my senses. Then we're out. We're free. But Thais isn't, and she's the only thing I care about right now.

"Drive around the island!" I sign to Rubem. "We have to pick up Thais there."

The brute force of my determination flutters out of me as my eyes adjust to the midday light. Gently cresting waves sputter white foam. The sun gleams off Sheila's bulky scales as she comes up beside the boat, and along the coast on the far side of the peninsula, the one that points its mangrove-laden rocks toward the island, the same brilliant rays flash off the pistols and nets of a host of fisher vessels. Much nearer, too secluded by the rocky crescent of trees to notice the approaching horde of humans, the light hits the scales and feathers and weapons of dozens of Murkling warriors swimming to the island, Brine leading the way.

NINETEEN

———— ∽ ————

FUCKING HEROES

If the good die young,

maybe it's because we never bothered to save them.

SUCH A CHILL RUNS through my blood that it turns the air cold.

Rubem drives us around the side of the island, his mess of little braids swirling in the wind as the ignit-powered boat whips along the waves. I wait for the Murklings to notice the approaching fishers, somehow, some way. But their course remains an arrow's path to the island. At this rate, the fisher boats will slip in behind them, cutting them off from the Murk in a surprise attack.

I shouldn't care. The Murk never bothered to understand me. They banished me and sentenced me to death. They don't deserve my help just as much as I don't deserve theirs. I can bring Rubem's poison ignit to Thais, and together we can make a break for it, shoot along the coast, and let the Murklings and the fishers fight among themselves in the wake of a decimated ignit hoard.

But the Murk is still my home.

My fingers find the ancient in my necklace, brushing the velvety surface, feeling the life pulsing within. The Murk is my home, and the home of two Murklings who gave up everything for Thais and me, and the home of the strange creature pressed between my collarbones. I've taken so much from the Murk. Now it's time to give back.

Hold on Thais, we'll be there soon. Just hold on.

I ignore the stairs, twisting up the railing and dropping in front of Rubem. "We have to warn the Murklings."

The light wrinkles around his shadowed eyes deepen. His knuckles tighten against the wheel before he finally lets go with one hand. "I already failed them, and they've failed me." His gaze jumps to the ancient still wrapped firmly around the ignit in my necklace. He knows. He knows I abandoned him. But he only releases a heavy breath. "After we pick up Thais, I'm going back to my little house on the north edge of the Murk with Sheila. Everyone else can be damned." He keeps his course, turning along the side of the island until the Murk sits firmly at our back.

I twist the tip of my tail through the wheel, grabbing it from him. "I'm sorry Lily got to you." It's the best apology I can muster, but it's a true one. I am sorry that Lily killed his caiman. I'm sorry she forced him into this. But I'm not sorry I left him to save Thais.

He exhales again. "It's no worse a hand than life has ever dealt me before."

"Maybe that's true. But I promise that next time, it'll be better. I'll do the hero thing for you, if you do it now for the Murk." I wonder vaguely if this is what Thais feels like: the fire, the hope, the dedication. "You've tried so hard to keep the Murk safe from Lily and the fishers. Aren't the people who dwell in it the most important part of the swamp? We're both Murklings, too, even if they rejected us."

Rubem's gaze lingers on my hands as though he expects me to say more, or maybe he's still trying to make sense of what I did say. A vibration starts in his chest, rising up his throat. Laughter, that same dark heavy sound he made back in the Murk.

He shoves a hand into his pocket, yanking out a flask, and

takes a long swig. A harsh stinging alcohol replaces the deep fruity wine scent of his name. He props his elbows against the wheel, his signs turning a little sloppy. "How about a deal, little cacao bean?"

My view of the Murk beyond Rubem's shoulder slips slowly behind the rocks. "What do you want?"

"What I wanted before." He takes another swig. "If I help those Murklings, you work for me—not the cartel, they wouldn't let me back in if I begged—but for me, for one month, collecting and selling ignits, saving animals, scaring the cartels away from the Murk. That sound like a good trade?"

Sheila's thick scales gleam as she breaks the surface to our right. She's still here. Not one of the cartel humans in Rubem's crew stayed loyal when the fishers offered a better return. He can count on no one but her, no one but a beast who can't even talk back.

I roll my eyes and grab Rubem's flask, letting it slide through my fingers and plunk to the lower deck. "I would've probably done that already, you idiot silt-breather. Now turn the damn boat around."

Rubem gives me an unknowable look, wide and open and endless. He shrugs. "What's one more impossible feat today?" With that, he snatches back the wheel and sets it awhirl.

A grin takes over my face, but it vanishes along with the front of the island and the entrance Thais will leave through. She'll just have to get by in her rowboat for a little while. "I need that poison ignit in your vest, too, for Thais."

"Why would you—" But my expression must say enough, because he amends, "It's in my cabin, under the mattress. Hid it there when Lily reappeared too soon."

I drop onto the lower deck and slide down the stairs to the cabin, my tail thudding unhappily from step to step. Rubem's tanks and jars and cages all sit empty, and I wonder whether he had time to release the creatures back into the Murk, or if Lily let her fishers take them away to be sold or slaughtered. A smear of blood sullies the floor, too dry for me to tell what it came from.

Avoiding the stain, I drop beside the bed and shove my arm under the mattress. The gentle pulse of the ignit greets me. I pull it out: green. My heart leaps, and I pop it into my necklace, its tiny heartbeat so subtle and soothing for something that would kill me if a single spark of electricity hit it.

I snatch a portable transitioner from Rubem's shelves and wave it at him as I climb back onto the deck. "I'm taking this. You owe me anyway."

Rubem shakes his head, but he says nothing.

As we round the side of the island, I glimpse the horde of fishers zipping along the coastline before the tip of the peninsula blocks them out. The full host of Murklings swims slowly toward the island, barely halfway between the mangroves and the waterfall. A few simple ignit-propelled canoes float between the boiuna, weighed down by an overcrowding of warriors. oatzis glide above on their feathered arms, dipp-ing onto the elder boiuna's backs and vaulting off their shoulders to catch fresh gusts of the sea breeze. Brine still leads them.

Rubem slows the boat as we approach, cutting the ignit power just before we reach their ranks. The boat drifts, and the Murklings surround us in a wide V. Brine motions for them to wait. She turns her gaze on me, unyielding.

I try to meet it, if only to convince her to listen, but shudders run along the back of my neck, forcing me to stare at her hands instead. I grip Thais's green ignit like it might save me. I have to get through this and back to Thais.

"Are you surrendering yourself, little earth?" Brine asks.

"Fuck no—I mean not *preferably*—"

As I form the denial, Brine's own fingers flick. Three Murkling warriors leap from the nearest canoe, two hoatzis and a boiuna joining them to grab Rubem. They hold him in place and prepare to lunge for me next. Fear bites my throat.

"Wait, wait!" My wrists tremble. "We're here to help you, to warn you!"

They tackle me anyway, holding my tail down. Slamming

into my shoulder, they force my chest to the desk. A hoatzi's claws dig between my scales. Muck, muck, this was a bad choice, I never should have—

"What warning?" my forebearer asks, her irises tight, and the two pinning my torso let up enough for me to move my hands.

But my panic remains, tight and jittery. "There's fishers, boats of them, coming up the other side of the peninsula. If you don't return to the Murk, they'll cut you off."

Cayenne releases such a skeptical huff that his huge chest vibrates like a drum. But Brine looks to Acai, who dives beneath the water, streaking toward the peninsula. The canoes bob in their wake. Acai surfaces a little ways out.

They go still, and their giant otter poses on their shoulder. "I can feel something. The trees and waves cloud it, but there does seem to be movement."

A weight drifts off me, or maybe that's just the Murklings slowly letting go of my tail. "They're fishers, Mom, you have to believe me. You can do whatever you want with me after this— as long as Thais gets her ignit—but I won't let those murderous silt-breathers hurt my home. Or anyone who belongs to it." My motions come firm and strong, and I stare at Brine's shoulder with such force that maybe it'll make up for the fact that I can't glare directly into her eyes.

Brine looms a bit closer, blocking out the sun with the entwined ridges on her head.

My gaze weakens. "Please, Mom."

One of her rough hands cups my head, so huge she could crush me with it. But she only pulls away, mumbling, "So, you are a Murkling after all." When she rises up to address the group, her signs grow huge and precise. "Back to the coastline! Send the runners to Salt Root for every warrior they can spare." She looks down at me, and for the first time in ages, I don't feel singed by her attention, only warmed. "We will not allow these fishers to harm the Murk either, little earth."

The Murklings take to their canoes, Cayenne and Acai

catching some of the warriors on their backs to speed the way. Brine lingers. She watches as Rubem leans over the side of his boat and motions to his waiting crocodilian, signs which seem to mean he wants her to return to the swamp with them. She bumps her nose against the hull, but she turns and follows the Murklings, leaving Rubem alone once more.

Cautiously, he steps down the stairs, "Hello, I—"

Brine rises farther out of the water. The boat tips as she inclines against the side, looming over Rubem. He sinks down, like ice melting into a puddle. I never see his feet move, but somehow, he drifts back a few steps.

Brine continues to loom. "You are familiar."

Rubem swallows. "My first forebearer was the One Who Leaves No Trace When Stepping on Water, a woman of more. She came from the village of Gilded Flower."

Brine's hands hover in an exclamation of understanding. "We will speak of this later." She draws back, returning to her place in front of the boat. "For now, you will both wait in the Murk."

I rub the poison ignit and shake my head fiercely. "Not yet." Before Brine can respond, I add, "Thais is dying out there, on that island, and I have the only thing that will save her. I'll face your judgment, I swear on the mists, but I have to get this to Thais first."

Her hands remain still so long that my lungs hurt. Finally, she signs, "I will grant you this final chance. Go help your boat friend. Both of you."

I look Brine in the eyes now, just for an instant, but it's enough. She smiles at me. My chest grows a little warmer beneath the pulse of Thais's poison ignit, but a tremor destroys the feeling, blurring my senses into a mess of pounding dread.

I wheel. Through the blotches of my vision, dark spots fall from the side of the island, like a grey waterfall. Rocks.

Thais. She did it, she—

But as the avalanche of stones plunges into the sea, the

ignit-laced side of the island stays calm. The old steamship bursts through the drifting dust. The waterfall pounds along one of its edges, smoke streaming in clouds behind it like a poisonous mist. I clutch Thais's ignit tightly. That can't be her aboard the multideck vessel, which leaves one option: Lily and Wolf. Thais's explosion won't kill them now. Despite the potentially deadly problem they pose, a thunderous rhythm starts in my soul. Now I get to strangle Lily myself.

Xera taps my shoulder.

I nearly launch out of my scales. "The fuck—"

They lift their brow.

Fern coils around them, grinning. "I think Cacao is even deafer than you."

"That is less funny than you think," Xera points out, but their lips curl.

The Murklings vanish into the trees, all but Acai, who lingers by the side of the boat. "These two requested to fight with you instead of the warriors," the elder explains.

"I guess I can stand that," I reply, before tackling them both, winding them in a momentary embrace. They smell good. Like friends, my first in a very long time.

A cannonball bursts from the stolen ship, disrupting our reunion. It falls far short of our boat, but it seems to hit the base of my spine all the same, rattle its way through me. What the fuck are we going to do against it? Even Rubem's decent-sized vessel looks like a stick compared to the solid log the northerners sail toward us.

Acai and Brine submerge an instant before the first of the fishers slip through a gap in the rocks near the end of the peninsula. Their boats veer our direction, still a little ways away, but approaching fast. We have a minute at best.

Their threat is momentarily muffled, though, by Thais's entire island vanishing beneath an orb of light. The sphere crackles, rainbows of electricity shooting through it. Then it disappears. In its wake, it leaves only a hollow in the sea.

Water rushes in to fill the gap the ignit explosion left,

dragging everything with it, quickly at first and slower once the sea collides with itself in the hollow's center, sending swells back out in all directions, like a pebble thrown into a still swamp where we are mere bugs flitting across the surface. Rubem's boat sways and dips.

My heart shudders for the ignits destroyed, thousands of precious gorgeous stones lost forever. But they should never have been gathered together in the first place, and if they had remained, the fishers would have found a way to collect them. I've no doubts about that. Just like I've no doubts that the hoard would have kept calling to me, no matter how long I managed to deny it.

The Murk said this desire would latch inside me, claws through flesh. And now that it has, it might never go away. But I don't care about that. Thais though—Thais, and her hopes, and her life—Thais I will care about.

I push through my mourning. Its ache seems unimportant compared to the fresh destruction that arises in my chest after, because in the vanished island's wake, I see nothing. No Thais.

No. No, she—she would've gotten off, she's too smart to stay. She has to be safe, she has to be—

Then I spot her, a dot bobbing in a little wooden rowboat. Rubem's vessel rises over another swell, and I fling myself up to the top deck to keep Thais in my line of sight, ignoring the flare of pain when I crash against the railing. I cling there, like Thais clings to her oars as the waves pummel her. Already a few fisher boats veer her way.

My quickening pulse tingles along my head ridges, agonizing. I'm so useless over here. I have to get to her.

Fern must smell my longing, because she shakes my shoulder. "The fishers will reach her before we can, and we won't be able fight them all alone."

She's right. They pour from the cracks in the end of the peninsula like bees from a hive. I bare my teeth. "If we can lure them toward the swamp, we won't have to."

Fern's fangs show through her grin. She grabs the wheel as I flick the buttons on the console. Through the din in my senses, I think Rubem yells at me, but I must've done something right, because the boat lurches forward. Fern brings us around, aiming for the lead boat in the line of fishers. The steam-powered ship fires another cannon. It lands near enough to splash our railing.

My gaze jumps back to Thais's distant figure. Hold on, ignit eyes. I'm coming for you.

Rubem appears beside me, gripping the railing with one hand. "This is a bad idea."

I can make out the expressions of the humans in the lead vessels, their pistols and nets and hooks prepared. "Probably."

As we come upon them, I wrap myself around Rubem and Xera, pinning us all to the deck. Fern turns the boat, her circle so sharp and close to the lead fisher that the spray of our hull crashes into them. She speeds us off, leading the fishers along the tree line. The main pack swerve after us like predators, nipping at our heels.

On the stolen steamship, Lily and Wolf veer back toward Thais.

My thumb cramps from the pressure I put on her ignit, but without its soothing pulse, I think I might fall apart. Diverting our course won't help anyone now. I have to believe she'll be safe a few minutes longer.

We race down the coastline, the farthest reaches of the canopy shading half the boat. As the last of our pursuers take their place behind us, Brine bursts up from beneath them. She arcs through the air and dives into the water on the vessel's other side, her body forming a dark shadow across her target. The fishers' bullets create little more than light gouges in her thick scaled flesh. Her seemingly endless tail slams into the deck. The wood cracks. She tightens herself, and the boat splinters in half.

At that shuddering vibration, the Murk comes to life. Cayenne and Acai crash down on the smaller vessels, tipping them over, while hoatzis dart to the farther one, crossbows firing rhythmically. Boiuna drop from the branches, slinging their human companions into dive rolls that end with their knives embedded into fisher spines and slashed across necks.

But I can't focus on the fighting for long, can't focus on anything but Thais in the distance, being dragged onto Lily's steam-powered ship. A fleet of fishers waft in the waves between us. I sign her name to Fern.

"On it."

"You know that this is in fact *my* boat," Rubem objects, squeezing himself between us.

Fern flicks her tongue at him, but she slides to the side, letting him take the wheel.

He surveys the console, and his nose wrinkles. "We had better make this quick, or we'll cease to be a moving target."

Around us, the fisher boats flee into the deeper water, trying in vain to escape the Murk's onslaught. Rubem steers expertly through them, narrowly dodging debris, boiuna, and the bodies of boat humans. As Lily's ship moves along the edge of the battle, though, the smaller boats flock toward it. A few waterlogged fishers climb aboard, returning to their own vessels to distribute something small and glowing. Glowing *green*.

The rhythm in my chest skips a beat.

Acai swims toward them, an ominous crest of water forming above their back. I can do nothing, nothing but cling to the railing of Rubem's boat as we drive closer and closer, close enough for me to see the gleam of the tiny active poison ignits flying through the air, hitting Acai in the chest when they rear up. Close enough to make out the sickly bubbles forming between Acai's scales and the wrongness of their eyes and the blood that streams from their nose and the corners of their lips. Close enough to feel the spray of their massive body plunging, lifeless, into the sea, dozens of ignits dropping with them.

Those even near—Murklings and boat humans alike—fling

from vessels and swim with a lethargic desperation. Some get far enough that they can pull themselves up on distant driftwood and heave the content of their stomach, like Thais has done so many times. Some only flail, then sink. Cayenne swims around the outskirts of the desolation, sweeping up a few of the smaller limp figures and dragging them to safety. I don't spot Brine anywhere.

The sight of it all raises bile into my throat. *Acai.*

Acai couldn't be dead. The elders, especially those as old as Acai, are ancient, untouchable. They've survived famines and wars and tragedies and migrations, the toppling of tribes and empires. A few dozen boat humans can't be the thing that finally takes Acai down. But their corpse drifts along the surface of the water all the same. And I know it's not just a few dozen boat humans. It's a few dozen gathered green ignits as well.

I rub Thais's single one like it's my life source.

Xera leans against Fern, and their hands wobble so much that I barely make out their words through their stammer. "T-too, uh, many f-fishers." Yet they smell not of fear, but of misery and anger.

I follow their gaze to find Thais lying in the center of Lily's ship, one shoulder propped against a metal case of spare cannonballs. What if she's dead already? I can't swallow the thought, but I can't spit it out either. It rests like cotton against the back of my mouth, suffocating me.

"Please," I sign, to myself and the Murk and to no one at all, because it's the only thing I can do.

As my hands fall, the water parts to our right. Brine surges forth. For the first time, her old face looks truly ancient, red veins gleaming in her dark eyes. Her teeth bare in a smile. My heart clutches. She leaps over Acai's corpse and plunges through the hulls of the nearest fisher boats. They flip, dumping screaming humans into the water. A few fishers manage to throw tiny ignits, thunder blue and paralyzing purple and poison green, but Brine slams her tail through their vessels, the wood cracking beneath each blow. Blisters flare between her scales, forming a distressing tapestry among the gashes torn by blue ignits, and she wipes blood from her nose, but still she chases after the fleeing boats.

Be safe, Mom.

Rubem swings our small vessel close enough to the steamship for Fern, Xera, and I to leap from our top deck to their lower one. A dozen fishers swarm the vessel, pistols and nets and machetes at the ready. I spot neither of the northerners' fiery storms of hair among the dark heads, but Thais still lies beside the cannonball case, a chain around her waist. She reeks of sickness even from here. A fisher hovers over her, like they can't decide whether she's alive enough to use as a hostage anymore.

Her chest doesn't move.

My own heart stops with hers. Movement blurs around me, Xera and Fern deftly taking out the nearest fishers. A gunshot bangs in the distance, followed by cannon fire, the vibrations warbling against my head ridges as though they come through water. My body moves, numbly vaulting me across the deck, hurtling through a boat human and slamming Thais's uncertain guard out of the way.

Her ignit sticks in my necklace, the wires tangling. I yank. My fingers slip. Another desperate pull, and the wires come undone, spilling the poison ignit out. I struggle to catch it with shaking hands while ripping out the necklace from beneath Thais's shirt. The metal feels as warm and clammy as her skin. I slam the ignit into its protective coils and spark it with Rubem's portable transitioner. The green glow alights, brilliant and blazing. Such a deadly thing turned into a cure by mechanics and genius. But there's no cure for death.

Thais doesn't move. *Oh, muck.*

Oh, muck.

Oh, muck.

No other words come. I wait, like waiting will help, because it has to. Because there's nothing left for me if it doesn't.

Oh, muck.

Pain screams through my tail, a fisher machete embedded there, slicing between my scales just below Rubem's bandage job. I jerk forward, and some instinct drives me to wrap myself around Thais, to protect her even now. Even after I've lost her.

My blood pools along the deck, flecked by the fisher's as Xera's knife comes through their neck. An ignit beats weakly against my chest, and a second gentle pulse joins it. Not a second ignit, but a heart. Hope assaults me, the sort of ragged teetering optimism that's balanced on the edge of a knife prepared to cut straight through my chest the instant it falls.

Thais coughs in my arms, and instead of falling, I fly. She takes in shallow lungfuls of air. Her long lashes flutter. By the time her eyes open, their red veins withdraw, and her ignit eyes gleam again. She smiles, a small half-alive smile. "You took your damn time, didn't you?"

"This hero business is hard," I protest, grinning as though my heart isn't skipping beats and my veins aren't on fire and my stomach doesn't have fifty butterflies all crashing and exploding in puffs of color.

She laughs. "You going to let me up, fucking hero?"

Uncoiling, I offer her one of my hands. "Can you stand?"

Thais answers by doing so. One of her knees buckles, but she catches herself on my arm. As she steadies her full weight on both feet, the chaos of the ship hits us in the form of Fern's tail. The boiuna dodges a machete before leaping at her attacker.

I'm suddenly aware that she and Xera have been circling us this whole time, keeping the fishers off us as best they can. Blood streams from a gash in Xera's arm, and a palm-sized space of Fern's tail caves in as though the ribs there have been crushed. Still, they've killed or tossed off nearly every fisher in sight. From below deck, the cannon fires again, its shot splashing into the sea just behind Rubem's speeding boat.

As Xera finishes off the final fisher, a flame of orange hair appears in the entrance to the deck below. I grab Xera's waist with my tail, yanking them behind the cannonball case with Thais and me. Lily fires into the air where Xera's back had been a moment before.

They flinch straight out of my grasp, knife raised, but their breathing settles, and they sign a quick, "Thank you."

Fern joins us, flattening herself to the deck. With a stolen pistol, she fires back at Lily. Rubem's boat makes another pass toward us, but it sputters to a stop, ignit finally giving out. He slams his palms into the wheel, his shoulders drooping. A cannonball blasts through the cabin beneath him. The boat tips, and sea water pours in, black smoke billowing up in its wake. I swear a blur clears the space between Rubem's boat and the ship, but I can't be sure of anything through the sooty haze.

Lily fires another bullet, and Fern returns it with one of her own. Thais's chain rattles as she tries fruitlessly to free herself.

To our right, a few surviving fishers drag Brine's netted body onto one of the last intact fisher boats. Blood drips from her nose, and blisters boil between her scales. She struggles weakly, crushing one of the fishers' feet. They pin her massive torso down, and two of them prepare machetes.

Xera's hand tightens around their knife.

"Save her," I sign. "Thais and I can handle this."

Xera nods and grabs Fern, who fires off one last shot before swinging them both toward the fisher boat.

Thais holds out the rusty lock on her chain. I reach for the thunder ignit in my necklace, but my fingers brush only the ancient's velvety exterior. Is there even a stone in there anymore? I rub the ancient's smooth surface, glancing across the deck. One of the fishers' tiny deactivated thunder ignits nestles in a crack in the wood.

The stillness from Lily's side of the boat taunts me, free of bullets and footsteps alike. I slide out and grab the little ignit. Nothing shoots me. Nothing even moves. I shove the ignit into Thais's lock and activate it with the portable transitioner.

The lock rattles and jerks open, but I leave the device

pressed against the ignit a moment too long, and it vibrates against my scales. I yank my hand away before its bruise turns to anything worse, and it clatters across the deck.

As I peek out to watch it, I spot both northerners. Wolf grips the lower deck's entrance. Lily seems to be scolding him, but the more she waves him below, the harder he struggles to join her. The smell of death clings to him, as putrid and sour as it had Thais. Its brand shines in his sweaty inflamed skin and his blood-drenched bandages.

Thais yanks off her chains. She rolls out from our cover, snatching up a pistol from a fallen fisher.

"Fucking hero," I sign at her.

She smiles, aims for the northerners, and pulls the trigger. Nothing happens. Her lips move in a silent curse. I launch myself at her. Curling my body around hers, we roll across the deck, a bullet zipping by us, and hit the railing.

My necklace stones dangle from the tight wire cord as we come to a stop. Lily's gaze locks on the ancient hanging in the center casing. I can smell her desire from here. She wants it with the same terrible lust that drove me toward Thais's hoard. And she refuses to let it go.

There's only one way this ends.

I lunge at her. As I burst forward, though, my straining muscles pull at the gash the machete left in me. Fresh blood spurts, and my tail whips the wrong way, careening me over a clump of dropped fishnets. I crumple to a stop in front of Lily, and my bones so blistered that I don't know how to move my fingers, don't know how to stop moving my shoulders. Everything but the ache of the net's touch filters away as I writhe. Lily looms over me. Her fingers wrap around my necklace. Wolf pins me down, and Lily yanks, weeding the ancient and its ignit free of the casing. She leaps back, aiming her pistol for the space between my eyes.

My head pounds anew and my lungs seize up. Between the gaps in my vision, Thais barrels into Lily. The ancient flies from her grip, rolling across the deck. Thais shoves the northerner's arm to the side as her pistol fires. Hot blood slides across my shoulder in such a sudden ruthless rush that it propels me out of the netting. But I feel no pain. It isn't my blood at all. The red stream surges from Wolf's stomach, a slow waterfall he tries fruitlessly to catch. He falls to both knees.

As he does, the ancient comes to rest against the heel of Rubem's sea-soaked boots. Despite the heaving of his chest and the wobble in his legs, he brushes back his braids and picks the ancient up with one perfectly smooth motion. All around him, the world stills. A slight smile tugs at his lips.

Beneath his grasp, a rainbow glow spreads across the ancient's black form. It peels off my ignit, pieces of its dark glittering body stretching and contracting. It drags itself up Rubem's fingers and across the back of his hand. The once blue ignit slips from his grip, clattering on the deck, now nothing more than a grey stone. He shakes his wrist. The ancient moves faster, vanishing beneath his shirt. He pulls at the fabric, tugging and twisting, first around his hips, then his waist, and up his chest. The creature slips across his collarbones and comes to rest in the crook of his neck. His hands tremble as he touches it. He digs his fingers into it, but it melts away from his touch, holding on to him like it's a part of his skin.

Shock takes me. I carried that thing on my necklace—it bore the accumulation of my shame and renewed my desire to help the Murk—and now it clings to Rubem as though it might slide into his pores and populate him like a new mangrove.

Lily lurches toward him, toward the ancient, but I burst after her. I grab her arms. She slams her hands against my head ridges and stomps her heel into the gash in my tail. My senses mix in a wave of pain. So much pain. Too much pain.

Thais appears at our sides again. This time, though, Lily expects her, launching an elbow at her face. Thais hits the railing of the deck, and the old wood cracks, two of the panels falling out of their slots.

A wave of sickness hits my nose, curling my still blurred

vision. Through the lingering pain, I make out the strained wrinkles and sunken shadows of Wolf's face, scarlet sloshing out of his stomach. He launches at Thais, hands outstretched. She fights, but his dying fingers wrap around her necklace. He tears the ignit out.

The world slows to a single heartbeat. Death takes Wolf in blisters and blood, dropping him like a rag doll. As he hits the deck, the poison ignit bounces once, then rolls. I try to follow its movement, but my gaze sticks to Thais.

Without the ignit masking her poison, her hollow strength crumples, revealing every crevasse of the weakness still plaguing her body. A single line of blood slips out of her nose. It pools above her top lip. She falls through the broken railing, and the red tear drops into her open mouth.

In a blur of bounces and rolls, the poison ignit shoots past me, just near enough that it infects me with the first hints of its sickness as it passes: a wave of fatigue and a twist of nausea. It notches itself between deck planks, waiting for the ship to tip and throw it out.

The vibration of Thais's body hitting the water echoes through my skull, vanquished only by the stillness that follows. No splashing. The tiny poison ignits scattered across the sandy sea floor cannot be emitting at the moment, too small to give off energy for the hours upon hours Thais's large ignit can. But she'll die anyway. Without the ignit in her necklace, she doesn't have the strength to swim to the surface.

I grab for the clingstone in my necklace, but it slips from my numb fingers, the small rock tumbling through a crack in the wood and disappearing into the lower deck. My gaze sticks to the gap where it vanished, yet I swear I feel every heartbeat around me: Rubem's pounding with fear as Lily slams him into the deck for the gentle thrum of the ancient in his neck; the ignit's pulse, a song of death and life; Thais's weak rhythm, slowing, slowing; and me.

I have to choose. Rubem or Thais. Thais or my life.

The ship wobbles, throwing Thais's ignit back into motion,

rolling it away from me. I lunge. With a single finger and thumb, I grab it and launch over the broken railing, barely feeling Rubem's limp body collapse to the deck a ways behind me.

As I hit the water, the poison ignit leaches into me. My stomach curdles, and pain spears through my insides. My flesh burns between my scales. My muscles go numb. I can smell the weight of my own mortality.

Fuck off a moment, death.

With everything left in me, I propel myself to Thais's body where it floats just beneath the surface. I wrap my fingers around the ignit to push it against the rim of her necklace. Blisters tear me apart, and pink tints my wavering vision as I shove the stone in.

Live. Live. Her heartbeat awakens, and mine fades to a distant hum. *Buh-bum. Buh-bum. Buh-bum.*

Something—someone—grabs me, yanking me onto a wooden deck. Through black stars, I can just make out the shape of Lily's retreating ship charging into the open sea. Fingers lace through mine, and a cord brushes the side of my neck as my soul slips away.

TWENTY

———∽———

THE RHYTHM OF A DUET

You and I,

the king and queen of nothing,

the homeless heroes,

the full of heart,

two idiots in love.

And I'm loving it.

LEAVES SHIFT ABOVE ME, a glimmering pattern of greens and golds, late afternoon light peeking through to caress my scales. The wood beneath me bobs to the gentle ebb and flow of rolling water. Up, then down. *Buh-bum, buh-bum, buh-bum.* Fingers tap a melody between the heartbeat, the rise and fall of a chest amidst the waves. A thin cord of metal rests against one side of my neck.

Buh-bum. Buh-bum. Buh-bum.

The deep musk of the Murk and the whip of the sea's salt tug for my attention, but Thais's rain-cleaned scent wins out, her sternum lifting and dropping beneath my cheek, her fingertips tracing the back of my neck. I press my head ridges to her heart and feel the beat of her life through my entire being. Her chest shakes, suddenly. I jerk upright, panic lancing out all other thought. The necklace chain goes taut, looped around both our necks, tying us together. The pendant hangs between us.

But Thais smiles, and her ignit eyes shine.

"You're alive." I must've signed the words, because she nods.

Her laughter trembles through her hands. "My heartbeat didn't clue you in?" She slips her fingers along my scales and draws the chain over my head, settling it properly against her own neck again.

"I thought maybe we were both dead, and our souls were hovering together in the mists?"

"Aw, I didn't think you were that poetic of a person, Cacao."

I bare my teeth at her playfully, pressing my forehead to her temple. "Fuck off." My shoulders shake. The quaver travels down my spine and along my arms, rattling my whole being as though every ounce of fear and relief and joy has hit me all at once. "You're alive."

"We've covered this already." She prods me in the side. "You're alive too." Lines spring up in the corners of her lids. Puffy lids, a little red. "For a while there I thought . . ."

The moisture filming her ignit eyes hurts my heart. I brush my thumb under her lashes. "You saved me. Like a fucking hero."

Her smile returns with a little vibration in her chest. "We saved each other this time." Her tears gather anew, but the rain-cleaned smell of joy and affection never wavers. "You let me destroy all those ignits. You gave up everything."

"Everything? That's a silly word. I never gave up you. Never again." Not even a hint of regret can weed its way into the warmth of my chest. I chose Thais. I will always choose Thais, so long as she lets me. "We both have nothing now, but we've got each other to complain about it to, so it can't be all bad."

She fiddles with her pendant, brushing the protective metal piece that covers the green stone. All the while, she watches my necklace—my ignitless necklace. "But you need an ignit."

I want to say no. I want to say that on top of being my

everything, Thais is also all I need. But while I know now I don't need an ignit hoard or even a jar of the pretty glowing stones, I do need to stop my bones from feeling as though they're shattering out of place. "We'll find one, I'm sure, you and me. I don't have to worry about it on my own anymore." I lean against her. Our foreheads brush. "I think I kind of love you, ignit eyes."

"You'd fucking better, cacao bean."

With my gaze on her hands and her teasing words bouncing joyfully through my head, the soft press of her lips to mine catches me off guard. I stiffen, then melt, sinking blissfully into her kiss. Suddenly it's not her kiss anymore, but ours, perfectly shared, equally ferocious and tender, greedy and selfless. Her fingers trace up my arms and search my back, running along my spine and cupping my neck. I press against her until I feel the perfect beautiful beat of her heart above the pulse of her ignit.

After an era, she nudges me away, taking a deep breath into the crook of my neck. "That was me saying I love you, too, by the way."

"Are you sure?" I flick my tongue at her. "I think you'd better try it again."

She laughs, her face scrunching. "You perfect wonderful hurricane-brained—"

"Shut up already." I snatch her hands, lacing our fingers together, and kiss her again, letting the motion linger and expand, until it becomes our whole world. Until we become each other's world.

At some point I find her arms wrapped around me and her face settled lightly against mine, her eyes closed. I draw my fingers over her swirls of stubbled hair. The salty ocean breeze stirs her worn clothing, and the edge of the Murk's canopy shifts above us as a monkey dashes through the leaves. Fern's and Xera's tangled scents lure my gaze along until I sense the vibration of them cuddled together in a tree to the left of our stolen fisher boat. On our other side sit three warriors who watch Thais and me with too little subtlety to be anything but our wardens.

Before us stretches the little bay, remnants of the battle sullying the otherwise beautiful expanse. Driftwood bobs in the cracks between rocks and roots, the shapes of decimated vessels lying on the sandy floor, obscured by the shifting water. A pair of warriors stand with paddles on a long sturdy board, using an extremely long net to fish out green ignits, then deactivating them. Bodies still bob in the waves, but once enough of the deadly stones are eliminated, a group pulls them up, one by one, signing death proclamations over each before wrapping them in sheets for burial, fishers placed beside warriors. It takes the full team to lift Acai's body from the water.

I watch even though it hurts. This was my doing. And I would not have chosen otherwise, not if it meant more people would have died in the end, but I still can't run from the consequences. I can accept that I made the right choice, and that the choice still hurts. Because, I think, both are true. Our good actions are not always without pain, just as the bad ones sometimes hurt us more than they hurt anyone else.

I jerk upright. "Oh, muck. Rubem. Did anyone save Rubem?"

Thais's smile falls. Her fingers tap an anxious rhythm. "They were too far away, moving too fast. We have nothing that can catch a fully powered steamship." She pulls her legs beneath her and leans against my shoulder. "He seemed to be alive still, and with only one person trying to crew the entire vessel, Lily couldn't have taken him far. If she turned them toward a port though, she did it after they vanished over the horizon."

My stomach sinks for him. I promised Rubem I would save him this time, but I chose Thais again. I chose Thais over an island of ignits, and I chose Thais over Rubem, and I chose Thais over my own life. I regret none of those things, but Rubem's and the ancient's captures still hurt. I owe him more than this.

The canopy rustles as a dozen Murklings filter through it. A set of human warriors climb down to the boat first, then an old couple, a hoatzi and a human, their patchy heads covered in strips of what must have been each other's locks and feathers during their younger years, accented in beads that gleam red and gold when the sun hits them. Cayenne loops himself around the nearest trunk to help support the aging pair.

The water stirs, and everyone, even the eldest of each species, tips their heads respectfully. An instantly recognizable woman with silvering pink fur climbing across her chest draws herself onto the edge of the boat, her dolphin's tail draped over the side. Janaina: the dwindling botos' only leader.

One of each. Whether they've come to condemn me or honor me, they've decided that my actions warrant a representative from each of the Murk's intelligent species. But I don't see my mother among them. My scales crawl as I rise properly onto my tail, my fingers flittering instinctively over my necklace. The wide endless ocean looks like a fantastic escape. But I made my choices. I don't regret them.

The hoatzi councilor's scaled bracelets clank together as they sign, "Little One of the Bittersweet Earth—"

"Cacao," I correct. "I am the Cacao Bean which Grows from the Bittersweet Earth."

They blink, their red eyes dilating.

I look away until their hands move again. "Little Cacao Bean which Grows from the Bittersweet Earth, your actions today cannot reverse the previous deaths you have brought to the Murk."

"I know. And I didn't help the Murk in an attempt to make up for anything." My hands tremble, but I've committed myself to this path, for better or worse. "It was just the right thing to do, so I did it. I did some fucked up things before I was banished, and after I was banished, and also just yesterday. But the people you care about are the most important thing there is, even if they can be silt-breathers on occasion. It was time I started acting on that."

The human elder watches me with such intensity that I can't escape their gaze no matter how far from their eyes I look. I nearly miss their question. "And the ancient? We know of your involvement in its demise."

I grimace. "It's not dead—I would never kill one, not on purpose. Taking it just looked like an easy way out, I guess. I thought I could have everything that way, and no one would get hurt. But it was wrong. I was wrong." And Lily possesses it, along with Rubem.

The human wrinkles their nose and looks to their partner.

The hoatzi shrugs. They whisper, the vocal vibrations shivering along my head ridges.

As they finish, Cayenne adds his own accusation. "Were you the one who detonated the island?"

"Yes," I sign, before Thais can protest, because it was my decision. If anyone takes blame for it, it should be me.

The human's expression bunches farther.

A sharp scent of disgust wafts off Cayenne. "Those ignits could have been used to better the Murk."

Anger blisters beneath my scales, righteous for once. Is this what Thais feels like all the time? "Fuck that. They're just ignits. Like I said, the people are what's important, and I did it to try and save them—Thais and you all, and, and even me. Because I'm important too."

Cayenne blinks, and slowly his lifted hands drop, his scent unreadably muddled.

The human looks about to protest in his place, but Janaina grabs their arm. She nods to the hoatzi and Cayenne. "I believe that's all I need to know. His own kind may make the final judgment."

I cringe as I glance at Cayenne. But he draws back, clearing the end of the boat for a new elder who slides in like the salt of the sea. Blisters still bubble between her scales, so irregular that the inside of my skull crawls. Blood pierces her eyes, and she lays her torso over the edge of the boat with a deep excess of breath, as though simply existing right now exhausts her. The vessel bobs heavily beneath her weight.

Thais scrambles to offer the use of her necklace.

Brine waves her away. "I'll live, child. I suspect I'm too large for that to do me any good anyway." Her hands move slow and sluggish, but her eyes fix on me with all her raging intensity. "My little earthen one, I may have misjudged you."

At her words, the child still curled inside me comes awake again, dying to be seen and understood and accepted. I don't know if I can survive this, not with the way my heart aches to explode and my ribs tremble, pain and anger rising up, along with something else. Something I see a little clearer now that Thais's love saturates me: self-hatred, borne out of a deeper disturbance, a feeling that if no one else could accept me with my needs, then there was no reason to accept myself. For that, I have to try to make Brine see. I need her not to let it happen again.

"The Murk is a conglomerate whole, right?" I ask. "We all work together to help each other. Everyone sacrifices so that no one suffers."

Brine narrows her eyes. "Yes."

"Suffering, though, it isn't... it's not..." I start, but a tremble runs through my hands. I can't meet Brine's graze. I can't look into her eyes and see that same flat nothingness that first banished me from my home.

Thais's fingers press against mine, just long enough to settle their flailing before she signs, "But suffering for one person might not look the same, or be the same, as suffering for someone else. Every person in a community is unique, and what is right for one may not be right for another."

That Thais understands—that I am understood, even if it's not by my mother—gives me a strength unlike any I've felt before. It cracks through the darkness. It lets me suffer where someone can see me. Where someone can hold me through it. I lift my head.

"I needed the pulsing of an ignit to make all my irrational pain go away and help my mind settle back to normal, but you and the council and—and everyone—wouldn't accept that, just because you didn't know what it felt like." My fingers waver toward the spot where my blue ignit should have been, but I force myself to keep talking. "You treated my need like a flaw until it finally became one. And that's half my fault. I shouldn't have let my fear of not having ignits drive me to steal and hurt for them. But I shouldn't have had to fear that in the first place. I deserved better, as a child." I believe that now, believe it because I was a child then, hurting and alone, and now I'm a hero, even if I'm not a perfect one. But I've been much worse in between. "I don't know what I deserve now. I guess that's what we're here to find out."

Brine's hands hang in the air a long time before she signs, her salty scent overwhelmed with everything and nothing all at once, impossible to make sense of and just as impossible to avoid. "I see." Her large fingers seem almost small suddenly, their edges too soft for such an old being. "I see also that you've grown past that flaw of your own accord. I'm ashamed that I did not learn at your side. You are a part of the Murk, my child, and what you deserve is to be with us, and to feel safe here. We are willing to accept your return, and we—I—would like to learn more of this, to do better in the future. Our resource distribution may not be as sound as we once thought."

Warm blossoms in my chest chase my lingering worry away. I grin at Brine, my fingers tracing the edges of my ignit. Only for my mood to fall. "That's great, Mom, but it wasn't all my own accord. I had help." I glance at Thais, then Fern, hanging from the branch above me, and finally Xera, perched in perfect stillness to my right. "I can't come back unless they can come with me. Thais too—Thais especially. I love her, ignits or not."

She wraps her arm around my waist, leaning her head onto my shoulder.

Brine reveals rows of gnarled pointed teeth. She reaches

out and rubs the top of Thais's head with one ancient finger. "I think the Murk could use another hero." Her gaze drifts to Xera and Fern. "And those two were already pardoned. Though the witness of the Way the Dew Slides off the Fern will be better questioned in the future."

Fern smells far too pleased with herself. "Really, you should have picked up on that lie before I involved the skeleton monkeys."

I roll my eyes. "I take it all back, I don't vouch for Fern, at all. Please throw her out of the Murk."

"You still owe me your bones," she retorts, her eyes creepily wide and her smile obnoxiously big.

I turn my back on her, but the scent of her laughter follows me, coated in her aroma of wet foliage.

Janaina's chest vibrates with a great sigh, and she shifts her dolphin tail. "These fishers are gone, but their absence will leave a vacuum easily filled with more hatred and death. Perhaps now is the time to send ambassadors to bridge the gap?" Her gaze moves to us, the rest of the councilors following suit.

"What?" I sign the word a moment after thinking it, as though it sinks out of me in my shock. "You mean us? Be ambassadors?"

"Oh, dear, no. I am asking only for your insight. You've lived far closer to these humans than any of us. Do you see a path to peace between our people? Though, if you are offering to take the first steps, do you believe you are the best suited for the job?"

"No, no, not the best suited, at all. Literally anyone would be better." My hands shake from how funny this is. "Literally anyone. And being an ambassador sounds boring—no offense."

Thais nods, her stomach clenching as though stifling giggles. "We respectfully decline such a prestigious title. But I think having ambassadors would be a good decision, and we'll help wherever we're needed."

"For the humble price of two ignits," I add with a grin.

Thais smacks me in the shoulder.

She wobbles, the green glow of her necklace ignit fading out. Panic shoots through me, and I grab her arm, steadying her. But her lips turn up despite the worry tinging her scent. "I'm fine, for the moment. The necklace already cleared the lingering energy from my body while I shared it with you, so the poison can't hurt me unless it gives me a spasm while its ignit is inactive."

The pieces fit uneasily together, sinking like rocks in my stomach. "They may not be overlapping right now, but at some point, they will. You'll still get sick."

"Occasionally," Thais admits. "But I'll always get better. And during the bad points, you'll just have to take care of me." She nudges me in the side, gentler this time.

"Always." I press my lips to hers.

Her heart beats against mine as she returns the kiss, her ignit pulsing softly. "Or," she adds, "you could find me another large green ignit to replace it with when this one is recharging."

"If it's as easy as getting this one was, it'll be no problem."

In the midst of our teasing, the council grew bored. Their warriors guide them back into the depths of the Murk without as much as a farewell. They probably assume we'll come stay at the nearest village for the evening. Maybe we will.

Brine lingers behind with a few physicians. The canopy rustles, and a hoatzi appears through the leaves, out of breath. They give Brine a small package. She unwraps it carefully, her huge worn hands peeling back the crackly covering with calm deliberateness. A necklace of feathers, hair, scales, and beads lies within, an inactive blue ignit hanging from its center.

She offers it to me. The cord runs between my fingers, soft and intricate, a piece of the Murk all on its own.

"Because you lost yours," Brine says.

I slip it on, tightening it enough that it won't fall off in the water. The glowing stone hangs a little below my old necklace of more ordinary rocks. Just this single ignit shines more beautifully than the halls of hoarded ones, as though it beats with love instead of pain and greed. I grin, tracing my fingers over it. "Thank you, Mom."

She smiles. "Take care of yourself, little cacao." And with a deep inhale, she sinks back into the Murk. The surface goes still, and the physicians slowly make their way through the trees, tracking the massive brown shadow of Brine's body as she meanders into the depths of the Murk.

We watch in stillness, as though we cease to exist until she vanishes from sight, leaving us young and alone and tangible once more. Only the warmth in my chest and the gentle pulse of the ignits tell me it was all real. Fern flops across the deck at my side, giving an overly dramatic sigh.

Xera creeps up to her and prods her in the back with their foot. "We, um, should go home."

"Your home crushed mine, pretty sure."

Xera's lips twitch. "We will build new ones." They hesitate, running their fingers through the feathers on their necklace. "Or, just one. For both of us."

Fern stares at Xera. Then she grabs them in a hug, dragging them down with her. Between her protective snuggling, she signs, "I'd like that." She entwines her tail with mine, winding the tip around Thais's ankle. "You two had better visit."

"But not, uh, too often," Xera teases, slumping across Fern's torso.

"Why would I ever want to see you muck-faced silt-breathers again?"

Xera blinks at me. "You said I could, could choose what I wanted for helping you later? Now, later?"

"Now later works."

They nod. With the head of one of their arrows, they sever a lock of their hair. They grab my wrist, tying it beside the lock I've kept of Thais's. "What I want is for you to keep this."

"Always." I grin and catch Xera's fingers, giving a little squeeze. But when I turn my smile on Thais, I find her distant gaze caught on the shadow of Rubem's giant crocodilian as the beast lies across a mess of roots and logs and stares out to sea. I sigh, shaking my head. "You want to rescue him, too, don't you? Fucking hero," I grumble.

Thais barely glances at my hands before looking out across the water, past the flat stretch where her mother's island once sat and off into the horizon. Toward Rubem. "Of course."

"I love that about you." I slip behind her, wrapping my arms around her waist and perching my chin on her shoulder.

She leans against me. "It'll be tough. We don't know where those fishers will take him, or even if they've left him alive. But I think we have to try."

I grin with every last one of my teeth. "Well, then, Thais like the *t* at the beginning of taunt and the funny ice stuff, we'd better get started."

WANT TO KNOW WHAT HAPPENS
TO CACAO AND THAIS NEXT?

To receive the first in a three-part short story series
documenting the rest of their adventures as they set out
to rescue Rubem, sign up for D.N. Bryn's newsletter at
dnbryn.com! (Those who've read *Our Bloody Pearl* might
just spot Perle and Dejean's kid along the way.)

REVIEWS FEED WRITER'S SOULS
(AND THEIR STOMACHS.)
If you enjoyed this novel, please consider telling other
readers by recommending and reviewing it!

Keep reading for a teaser of the next book in
the *These Treacherous Tides* series!

ACKNOWLEDGEMENTS

I had never planned to write another *These Treacherous Tides* book. I gave it a series title, not because it was meant to be a series, but because I couldn't choose between that and *Our Bloody Pearl*. A series title allowed me to give the book two names. *Our Bloody Pearl: These Treacherous Titles*. Two titles for the price of one. I figured myself a right damn genius for this.

This right damn genius really played themselves.

The moment *Our Bloody Pearl* came out, readers immediately asked where I was with the second book. I wasn't anywhere. (Or, more accurately, I was riding feathery dragons through the snow and escaping spaceports with ghosts.) But bless these poor souls banging on my door, because three months later I sat down and wrote *Once Stolen*.

I had always wanted to write a main character who experienced the world the way it felt to me, with all its soothing tranquilities and skull-shattering irregularities. I wanted this in part because every character I write is a piece of me, but more importantly, because both my mom and I spent half our lives thinking we were alone in this. If we had seen this as a valid part of certain fictional people, maybe we wouldn't have taken so long to realize it was a valid part of ourselves, too.

Cacao would never have come this far, if not for a whole bunch of (if I may) fucking heroes.

Firstly, my family, who has continued to stand by me as I charge onward in this publishing adventure, despite the fact that some days it feels like trying to swim up a waterfall. Secondly, my amazing group of beta readers, who guided this story from the cobbled mess of its beginning to the (still slightly cobbled but much more readable) novel it is now. Thirdly, the gang of *These Treacherous Tides* cheerleaders who have put so much of their time and love into this series.

And, finally, a huge thanks to the God of Abraham. Next

time, can I get a personal manual? My factory settings clearly aren't the default here.

COMING JULY 2022...

ODDER STILL

The ship groans, as though the old steam vessel is purpose-fully taunting Rubem, poking at the headache pounding behind his eyelids. Each roll of the lower deck rubs against the bruises that seem to extend all the way to his bones. The damp, salty air knives its way through the gash Lilias left in the side of his forehead. His face twitches against the cracking blood.

In the darkness, he swears he can feel it festering.

He focuses on the pain, on everything he's felt during bad days in the past, trying to block out the thing in his neck, the dark, silent thing that's turned the skin beneath it numb. If he has skin there anymore. If he's even himself anymore.

What he wouldn't give for a drink.

The ship groans again, light ricocheting from far above as Lilias opens and closes a door on the middle deck. Maybe she'll bring him something to curb the gnawing in his stomach, or maybe she'll come knock him out again. At this point, he has no preference.

That's a lie.

His torn body aches for the void of darkness, but what he wants more than food or peace is to turn this ship around. To go home. To poor little Sheila, whose blinded eye should still be tended and to his caiman triplets—triplets still, even though Lilias killed one of them—and to the deck swing of his house on the river north of the Murk, with a glass of merlot in his hand and his jaguar kitten leaping at the parrots. To put this damned ancient in a tree where it belongs, pray his neck comes out in one piece, and drink himself into oblivion. And never, ever see that bittersweet silt-breather of a boiuna again.

That's what he wants.

And by the gods, he'll get it.

OTHER BOOKS BY D.N. BRYN

OUR BLOODY PEARL
Forty years before Once Stolen...

After a year of voiceless captivity, a blood-thirsty siren fights to return home while avoiding the lure of a suspiciously friendly and eccentric pirate captain.

This adult fantasy novel is a voyage of laughter and danger where friendships and love abound and sirens are sure to steal—or eat—your heart.

CPSIA information can be obtained
at www.ICGtesting.com
Printed in the USA
BVHW031728190721
612325BV00005B/82

9 781736 296608